TILTED
LIVES

By
Naomi Joy Neuwirth, MFA

PublishAmerica
Baltimore

First printing

This is a work of fiction. Names, characters, places and incidents are the product of the author's imagination or are used fictionally, and any resemblance to any actual persons, living or dead, events or locales is entirely coincidental.

ISBN: 1-4137-2772-7
PUBLISHED BY PUBLISHAMERICA, LLLP
www.publishamerica.com
Baltimore

Printed in the United States of America

For my mother, Anna Wunderman,
with great love and respect.

~

~ *Acknowledgments* ~

There are many people who helped me on the road to becoming a writer. I wish to thank my husband, Jerry Neuwirth, who emotionally supported me.

At Sarah Lawrence College, many teachers encouraged me, but Ernesto Mestre-Reed believed in my writing ability the most.

Among my women friends who had confidence in me, I wish to thank Diane Dolin, Marti Blazick, Eva Steen, Kristan Ryan, Ina Cooper, Sharon Magin, Mary Ruddat, Karen Israel, and Maura McCaw.

Before attending Sarah Lawrence, I was encouraged by other teachers. The professor who started me on the path was Professor William Stull (The University of Hartford). He was followed by Michael Friedman (Trinity College), Kate Walbert (Yale University) and Megan MacComber (Southern CT University). I wish to thank all of them for believing in my ability to write.

SECTION ONE

~

Family Vortex

Hannah

~

Hannah sat in the car in the doctor's parking lot. Across the street, she watched women and children going into the Waldbaum Food Store as though nothing was wrong. *She throws a rock through the glass plate of the grocery store. Children scream and their mothers shelter their bodies. They are frightened of her. The police arrive, but she kicks them. They wrestle her to the ground and pin her hands behind her. She wails at them.* During her routine exam, Dr. Glantz felt a lump in her left breast. Today, she received the results of the biopsy. She has breast cancer. When Dr. Glantz recommended a radical mastectomy, she wanted to call Irwin, her husband. Instead, her mouth fell shut. *After they place her in the squad car, she asks, "What the hell did I ever do to deserve this?" She is a good wife, mother and sister.*

She touched her small breasts, but they didn't hurt. The diagnosis must have been a mistake. She was the smallest breasted woman on her side of the family. Her sister, Rachel, and her mother were bigger women. She had always prided herself on being small bosomed, able to wear snug fitting shirts. She planned to call Rachel and her mother after she told Irwin.

At home, Nina was jumping rope in the driveway. Every time Hannah saw Nina, she felt blessed. They adopted six-month old Ethan after she and Irwin tried for five years to have children. Afterwards, she became pregnant with Warren and eighteen months later with Nina. "Mom, look at me!" Nina's brown pigtails flew up and down.

"What a terrific job you are doing," Hannah said.

"Did you buy Oreo cookies?"

"Of course."

Nina helped unload the lighter grocery bags. Hannah smiled at what a good helper her seven-year-old Nina was. Hannah couldn't tell her she would have to go to the hospital. Bedtime would be a problem for Nina when she was away because Hannah always slept next to Nina until she fell asleep. The previous night, in bed, Nina pointed to the wall. "I see a roaring lion and he is going to eat me."

"Sweetheart, there is no lion, just a shadow." Hannah pulled the covers tightly around Nina. Irwin felt Nina was too old for Hannah to lie down with her. Hannah hoped Irwin would be more understanding when she was in the hospital.

Warren, in a T-shirt and shorts, came into the kitchen. He was tall for his age at nine years. He pushed his glasses back up on his nose. He looked at her with big brown eyes. "Any good eats?" he asked.

"Want an Oreo?" Nina held one up.

He poured glasses of milk for himself and Nina. They sat at the table while Hannah put the food away. She stopped for a second and watched. He took out the Adams Family card game to play. She bent over to kiss the tops of their heads. Nina's thick, brown hair smelled like apples. Warren's hair felt sticky from the Vitalis he had borrowed from his father. *She can't afford to be ill. She and the big C are in the boxing ring. He laughs and she punches him in the stomach. She kicks him in both his knees. He grasps his fat belly and staggers. He falls to the ground and she stomps on him. She wins her round.*

Nina put her arms around her mother. "What's the kiss for?"

"For being good kids," said her mother.

"That's us, two terrific kids." Warren puffed out his chest.

After the children went outside to play, Hannah rubbed the rim of her coffee cup. She wanted to call Irwin at work to tell him what the doctor had said but she didn't know how to say it. *Irwin, I have cancer, the big C, the disease that kills you. I may be dead a year from now. They're going to butcher me. The surgeon is going to slice off my breast like he's cutting up a hog. Take a piece of me and stuff it in the garbage like rancid meat.* She was not very good at expressing herself with Irwin, who was more demonstrative. She knew it bothered Irwin, but she still felt shy with him. When the children were young, before he left for work, he liked to smooch. At the garage door, she would feel uncomfortable with the children watching and back away from him. One morning, he whispered "Don't you love me?"

"Of course." She tilted her head.

"I wish you kissed me goodbye like it was the last time," he sighed.

"What a sad idea," she said.

After that conversation, she had tried to be more demonstrative, but he would still try to caress her when she was making lunches, setting the table or washing dishes. At these times, Hannah didn't feel romantic. Irwin couldn't understand her reluctance. Irwin told her she was "cold" and withdrew. For the last year, he had started working longer hours. She decided not to burden him about her surgery until she needed to. In the past Irwin spoke to her about his concerns managing the company, but not in recent months. Hannah wasn't interested in hearing his business problems. By the end of the day, the children had exhausted her.

At that moment, above the record "A Beautiful Morning," she heard banging on the floor from the room above. It was Ethan, jumping up and down. She wished Irwin were here because he had a calming effect on Ethan. The psychiatrist said jumping was the way Ethan coped with stress. She shook her head. When Ethan was three years old and playing in the park, without provocation, he randomly punched a smaller child; Ethan continued hitting the child until she pulled him off. "Stop it, Ethan," she yelled.

"I hate him," said Ethan.

"He wasn't bothering you," said Hannah.

"He gave me a bad look," said Ethan.

She had to stop taking him to the park because he continued to hit other children. Hannah didn't understand why Ethan behaved the way he did.

At the kindergarten teacher's insistence, Ethan started play therapy for uncontrollable temper tantrums. Irwin resigned himself to Ethan's treatment, but told Hannah "It's a waste of time." In middle school, she was regularly called about Ethan's aggressive behavior. Recent testing revealed he had a genius IQ, but he couldn't get along with anyone. Hannah wished Ethan had little less intellect and better social skills. She was tired of Irwin bragging to friends that Ethan was a mathematical genius and excusing Ethan when he lashed out at his siblings or classmates. Hannah understood why Warren and Nina were frightened of him.

The week before, Ethan asked Warren and Nina if he could play catch with them. Hannah looked out the kitchen window to watch them. The three of them were laughing. Relieved they weren't fighting, she went down to the basement to fold laundry. Twenty minutes later, Warren yelled down the basement steps. "Ethan is hurting Rusty." She found Ethan swatting Rusty with a stick. The dog was yelping. "What are you doing?" she asked.

"I'm teaching the dog not to take our ball."

"You're hurting him. He's going to yelp more," she frowned.

"I don't care."

"Give me the stick," she said sternly and broke the stick into small pieces. "Go up to your room." *She grabs the stick and hits him with it. Ethan feels the pain he inflicts on the defenseless dog.* When she told Irwin about the incident, he asked, "Are you sure it wasn't just horseplay?"

"He wasn't playing with Rusty. He was hurting him," she said.

Irwin shook his head as though she was a hopeless case.

Hannah worried who would watch the children while she was in the hospital. She wondered if her mother could stay with them. She might have to ask Irwin but he had never stayed alone with all three children. He didn't have any patience by the time he came home from work. She wasn't concerned until now because she loved being home with Warren and Nina. No one but Irwin or her mother would tolerate Ethan's antics. She tried to remember the last time Irwin and she had gone away together without the children. It was two years after Nina was born. Ethan was nine and Warren was four years old. They returned home early from that vacation because Ethan had tried to drop Warren out of a second-floor bedroom window. Their housekeeper, Margo, red-faced, met them at the door. "Ethan is impossible. He doesn't listen!"

"I'm so sorry," said Hannah.

"Did you antagonize him?" Irwin asked.

"Ethan fought with Warren every minute. He's unmanageable. I quit." Margo left the room to pack her bags.

"Why were you upset with Margo? I'm sure Ethan was a handful," said Hannah.

"She doesn't understand him. He's a prankster," said Irwin.

"He needs to gain control of himself. He's wild," said Hannah.

"You sound like my mother. You want him to be a sissy," said Irwin.

"Trying to throw Warren out of a window is not roughhousing. Ethan needs to be punished!" Hannah said.

"I'm not going to side with Margo against my own son," said Irwin.

Hannah was appalled that Irwin compared her to his mother, a chronically depressed woman who spent most of her time in bed. As far as Hannah was concerned, Irwin's mother had treated him like a lap dog. When Irwin was a child, she had coddled him. Irwin would sometimes get angry when his mother expressed concern about Ethan. But if Hannah said one unkind word about his mother, Irwin defended her.

Hannah didn't understand what came over Ethan. He was calm one minute and explosive the next. His attacks were focused on Warren rather than Nina. Ethan came into the kitchen. At fifteen, he was tall, almost six feet, and lean. He towered over her. He had shiny brown hair, angled cheekbones and dark eyes. His riveting appearance demanded notice. He had managed to put on the one ragged Beatles tee shirt she missed when she cleaned his room. When she said "hello," he grunted and opened the refrigerator. "Isn't there anything good to eat?"

"I just went shopping. What about those pretzels you like?" she asked.

"Sure, good idea," said Ethan.

She handed him the pretzels. He flashed his perfect white teeth at her. For a moment, she felt drawn to him. "These aren't the ones I like. They're too salty." He spit the pretzel into the garbage pail.

"What kind would you like me to get you?" Hannah asked.

"I don't know," he said.

"Maybe you would go with me?" she asked.

"Right, go to a grocery for fun." Ethan slammed the refrigerator door.

"It's just a suggestion. We could do something together," said Hannah.

"Thanks, but no thanks." He shook his head. "You've some weird ideas. I'd rather starve than go into a grocery store." Ethan grabbed an apple from a bowl on the counter and headed out the backdoor. Hannah sighed. She didn't say anything because she had learned from bitter experience that nothing she said was right. He became more incensed. She had tried to reach out to him, make a connection, but had failed. She was angry that he pushed her away, again. *She tells him that he can starve. She dumps all the food in the garbage. She refuses to let him sit at the dinner table. But he is so thin. He needs to eat. What if she dies after surgery and never has a chance to connect with Ethan, to show him she loves him. She wakes from the operation and the doctor says her body is riddled with cancer. He couldn't cut it all out. She has only a few months to live.*

Within twenty minutes, Nina burst into the kitchen. Sweat streamed down from her hairline. Her tee shirt was muddy. "Mom hurry, Warren's hurt."

Hannah ran outside, "Oh my God."

"Help me, help me," screamed Warren. The rope was coiled around his neck, torso and legs.

"I'll have you out in a minute." Hannah fumbled with the rope.

"Hurry, Mom. I can't breath," wailed Warren.

"I'm trying." Her hands were sweating. The knots were too tight for her to undo. She yelled to Nina, "Get the cutting shears from the garage. It's hanging on the wall."

"Is he going to be okay?" asked Nina.

"Hurry," said Hannah.

"It hurts," whispered Warren.

"I'll have you out in a minute." She holds Warren. *She is going to choke Ethan until he stops breathing.*

"Here," Nina, red-faced, hands her the cutting shears.

"Just one moment longer." Hannah cuts off the rope.

"My neck hurts. My wrists hurt." Warren rubs his rope-burned hands.

"You're okay, now. What happened?" Hannah pulls him to her.

"I was showing Nina how to jump faster. Ethan said he wanted to try. When he couldn't jump as well, he pushed me to the ground, grabbed the rope and tied me up."

"Warren attacked me. I was defending myself!" Ethan yelled from his window.

"You were defending yourself against a nine-year-old by tying him up?" Hannah put her hands on her hips.

"He's a big fat liar," yelled Warren. He made his hand into a fist.

"Stay in your room until Dad comes home!" shouted Hannah.

"I don't want to see you, anyway." Ethan slammed his window.

"I'm sorry, Warren." Hannah held his trembling body.

"He hurt Warren," said Nina, tears in her eyes.

"Warren is okay, now. You did the right thing in getting me," said Hannah.

The three of them went back into the house. At the kitchen table, Nina hugged her mother. "Why did Ethan hurt Warren?"

"I hate him," said Warren.

"Don't say you hate your own brother. It's not nice," said Hannah.

"I don't care. I still hate him," said Warren.

Afterwards, Warren and Nina went into the living room to watch "The Lucy Show." Hannah set the table for dinner. *Parenting the three children together is becoming more difficult. She is a policeman, but not a very good one. She ties up Ethan and leaves him. Show Ethan what it is like to be the victim. When she tells Ethan's psychiatrist about his latest antic, he only nods his head. She doesn't know why she continues to send Ethan to him because he doesn't really understand him either. She is afraid that one day she will arrive too late. She can't afford to be sick. The children need her. If she doesn't recover from her illness, she will never forgive herself for being such a terrible mother to Ethan. Irwin will never forgive her. She has to reach Ethan and be the mother he needs.*

Hannah climbed the stairs to knock on Ethan's door. She had to yell above the song, "Spinning Wheel." "Can I speak to you?"

"Why?" He opened the door.

"Do you understand you hurt Warren?"

"I was just playing with him."

"Tying up your brother is not playing."

"He shouldn't have teased me."

"That's no reason to tie him up."

"You don't get it."

"Well, help me to understand."

"I can't. Ask Dad." He closed the door.

"You're in trouble, now," she banged on the door. Whether or not Irwin agreed with her, she would punish Ethan and not allow him to play guitar with his band. Ethan would be furious; he lived to play music with his band, but she didn't care. *If she dies on the operating table, Ethan has Irwin, but what about the two younger children? She sees her casket being lowered to the ground. She blocks out an image of the two children sobbing and Ethan playing "A Beautiful Morning" on his guitar. Who will protect them from Ethan if she dies?*

Hannah took Warren and Nina to the Long Island Railroad Station to pick up Irwin. Even after twenty years of marriage, she never tired of seeing him in his navy Brooks Brother suit as he climbed down the platform. She waved to him. *Newly married, she watches him climb out of bed and walk naked into the bathroom. She admires his taut behind. They are both virgins and shy in bed. She still blushes at the things Irwin asks her to do. She wishes she were a more sexual person. Now, her body will be sexless.* She was proud of how successful Irwin had become. He was no longer the skinny boy she met earlier. He had the athletic build of a tennis player, lithe and sinewy. He reminded her of one of the models in the ads he wrote for Brooks Brothers' suits.

Hannah slid over to the passenger side of the car. When Irwin climbed in the car, he leaned over to kiss her. Then Nina said, "Me too, I want a kiss, too."

"Hi, sweetie, how was your day?" he asked Nina.

"Warren taught me to jump rope faster," said Nina.

"He did. What a good boy." Irwin turned around to smile at Warren.

"I tried to teach her but Ethan wouldn't let me. He tied me up with the jump rope," Warren crossed his arms.

"Are you exaggerating?" Irwin asked.

"He's telling the truth. I could barely free him," said Hannah.

"I'm sick of these problems." Irwin shook his head.

"I feel the same way, but we have to punish Ethan," said Hannah. She reached for Irwin's hand but he squeezed it lightly and dropped it. She frowned. *She grabs his hand back and squeezes it. I have something important to tell you. I have cancer. My breast is tar. My body is going to be butchered. I might die. I need you to hold me, not fight with me. We may not have much time together.*

"If you were firmer with him, he wouldn't misbehave," said Irwin.

"I try to be firm." She hated that Irwin held her responsible for not managing Ethan. Irwin believed Ethan's problems weren't severe; Ethan behaved better with him. After eleven years of taking Ethan to psychiatrists, she knew Ethan had serious problems.

She remembered their first visit to Dr. Carol's with Irwin and Ethan, age four. During the session, Ethan threw the family members out of the dollhouse. Then he stomped on them, afterward, when they met with Dr. Carol, for the results, he said that Ethan had an attachment disorder. Irwin responded by saying, "You don't know what you are talking about. He is very affectionate with me."

"He's fighting with the children in nursery school. The teachers suggested counseling," Hannah said.

"He's sensitive. I was the same way as a child," said Irwin.

"What do you mean?" asked Dr. Carol.

"I didn't have temper tantrums, but I felt things deeply like Ethan," Irwin said.

"How did your parents handle it?" asked Dr. Carol.

"My father died when I was nine. My mother smothered me. I want Ethan to have more freedom than I had," said Irwin.

"Your son has to learn to control his temper," said Dr. Carol.

Hannah had tried to make Irwin see Ethan's rages weren't normal, but he had a blind spot when it came to him. He would have stopped sending Ethan to Dr. Carol, but the school insisted Ethan continue. Irwin said everyone was overreacting to Ethan's behavior. *Hannah screams at Irwin. She lunges at Irwin and knocks him over. Stop it! She is not responsible for Ethan's mental illness. She needs help, not criticism. Ethan's making her crazy. She wants Irwin's support. Her body is in trouble. The cancer is in control. She can't be sympathetic to Ethan, right now. When she tells Irwin, he understands. Irwin hugs her. He whispers to her that everything will be okay, that he will love her after the surgery.* In her mother's house, she learned to keep her feelings to herself and be a "good girl, a "good wife," one who doesn't complain to her husband.

Irwin's negative attitude toward her went beyond Ethan's behavior. The night before they had received a telephone invitation to a dinner party. "Sounds like fun. Get your hair done. Buy a sexy outfit for once," said Irwin.

"Do I really have to buy a new dress?" she asked.

"I want you to be the prize of the party. The pretty girl I remember," he said.

"Okay." But she had felt insulted that Irwin wasn't happy with the way she looked. She didn't like to go to the cocktail parties Irwin enjoyed. He drank too much and flirted with her friends. She knew it was innocent banter but it made her uncomfortable. She wished Irwin admired her the way he did when they were first married. He had never complained about her Peter Pan-collared shirts, dark pants and penny loafers. They were moving in separate directions but she didn't know what to do about it. *She's not going to the party. She refuses to buy fancier clothes. She likes being the plain girl from the Bronx. Clothes are not going to make her a better person. Wearing a sexy dress won't stop the cancer eating away at her. She wants to hide her body. There is nothing to celebrate. Doesn't he see how worried she is?* Since his advertising company had become one of the most successful ones in New York, he bought himself a Porsche convertible. After an argument, she allowed him to buy her a new Oldsmobile station wagon, even though the one she had was only two years old.

Hannah questioned whether Irwin's changes were for the best. She was still President of Women's Strike for Peace. With the generous allowance Irwin gave her, she donated money to the NAACP and the ACLU. She remained a liberal Democrat becoming ever more concerned about the state of the world while Irwin admired Rockefeller and his Republican businessmen. Irwin complained her volunteer jobs interfered with the family. He had become a showoff, starting with the six-bedroom house he insisted they buy wl en Nina was born.

Hannah missed her old neighborhood—the small ranch on Chestnut Street with sidewalks and easy conversations with her neighbors. Ethan had fewer problems when he was small. Hannah had especially enjoyed the block barbecues. During the week, the mothers would gather to drink coffee in the morning and the babies would play. Now the only people she ever saw walking were the housekeepers pushing prams.

She reminisced about the Bronx where she grew up. She could remember the smell of the frankfurters sold by the vendor on the corner of the street where she lived. The butcher, Mr. Lebowitz, had known her name when she picked up their meat order. She had bought lettuce and tomatoes from the back of Mike's truck. Now, once a month, she still picked up her meats from Mr. Lebowitz's tiny shop on the Grand Concourse. Her family's apartment was cozy, overlooking the street below where she liked to jump rope or sit on the stoop, to do her homework. On hot nights, outside, the men had played cards and the women had poured glasses of iced tea. The men had opened the hydrants and the children had run through the water.

She disliked the fancy shops on Middle Neck Road where the shopkeepers barely noticed her. Each store was more pretentious then the next. She hated wearing skirts and silk stockings to go into town. All their money embarrassed her. She liked to blend into a group, not stand out. Most of the time, she kept the three-carat diamond ring in her jewelry box. She wore it when they went out because Irwin insisted. The first time Irwin placed the ring on her finger, he said, "I'm making up for all the years that you didn't have one."

"It's beautiful," she said hesitantly.

"What's the matter?" he asked.

"It's huge," she said.

"I wanted to get you the biggest diamond on the block." Irwin turned her hand to catch the light on the ring.

"It's beautiful. I'm not used to wearing expensive jewelry." The ring sparkled.

"Do you really like it?" Irwin eyes beamed.

"It's gorgeous." She kissed him.

When she was young, her family could have lived for years on the cost of the diamond. *She climbs into the ring with the Big C. She offers him the diamond if he will leave her alone. He grins. He slips the diamond ring on his pinkie. He puts up his fists. He circles her. He wants to fight, again.* She didn't need the ring to feel good about herself. Recently, she had thought about going back to teach English. When they had adopted Ethan, she decided to stay home, but now she missed the classroom. When she had broached the topic, Irwin laughed. "Why work? We have plenty of money."

"I want to teach. I love it," she said.

"Honey, be serious. Why would you want to help other children and not your own?"

She didn't know how to answer him because it was 1967 and Irwin was right. None of her friends worked. They drove their children to piano lessons, helped them with homework or watched their baseball games. In the late afternoon, they went to each to one another's houses for coffee where they gossiped, exchanged recipes and bragged about their husband's accomplishments. *She may not have much time left. Her body is running the show. She is bored and doesn't care what people think. She needs a life, a career of her own. Her brain and body are atrophying.* It was very different from the way she had lived growing up in a one-bedroom apartment in the Bronx with her mother and her sister, Rachel. Her mother worked nights as a cook while she and Rachel took care of themselves. When Rachel was eighteen, she went to work as a seamstress in the lingerie department at Saks Fifth Avenue.

Hannah made a different life for herself by being the brightest one in her class, the only one in her family to go to college. When she first met Irwin, she was teaching. He took her to plays on Broadway that she had read about. He was more sophisticated than anyone she knew. *Where is the gawky boy who says he is going to change the world? He has big ideas about advertising and starting a political magazine with the money that he made from it. They held hands while they walked along the Hudson River and talked for hours about making the world a better place to live. She wanted to be a journalist and work for The New York Times.* She stopped dating a teacher where she worked because he seemed dull in comparison to Irwin.

After Hannah put Warren and Nina to bed, she found Irwin watching *The Ed Sullivan Show* in the den. Staring at the television, he seemed preoccupied. *She looks at his long thin fingers that are delicate like hers. She climbs on his lap and kisses him everywhere, makes him pay attention to her the way he did when they were first married. Hold me. Tell me I'm not going to die.* She stood in front of the television. "I went to see Dr. Glantz today. He had the results of my biopsy," she said.

"A biopsy? Is everything okay?" Irwin furrowed his brow.

"No, it's not. I have breast cancer. I need a radical mastectomy." Hannah slumped down next to Irwin.

"Oh, my God, why didn't you tell me you had an appointment?" Irwin puts his hand in Hannah's lap.

"I didn't want to worry you." She squeezed his warm hand.

"Worry me? I need to know these things." He looked at her with concerned eyes.

"I'm in a nightmare and I can't wake up," Hannah cried. "What am I going to do?" *She can't bear this. She will run out of the hospital.*

She will never let them cut off her breast.

"I still can't believe you didn't tell me!" He shook his head.

"What difference does it make? I'm telling you now." She cried.

"Don't worry. You'll get through this. I know you will." He held her.

"I'll have to, for you and the children." Hannah leaned against his chest.

"Will you stay with the children while I'm in the hospital?"

"Yes, of course," Irwin held Hannah until her eyes began to close. "Go up to bed; I'll be up soon."

"Can't you come to bed with me?" she asked.

"I'm not tired. Don't worry about me. Get some sleep," he said sadly.

She slowly climbed the stairs. In bed, she listened to Irwin making himself a sandwich in the kitchen. How could he be hungry after what she had told him? *Hannah dreams she is a small child sitting on the stoop of her tenement. She and Rachel wait for her mother who is late from work. She is afraid something happened to her mother. She runs onto an unfamiliar street. The people's faces are covered in clown paint. They laugh and point at her. They speak a language she has never heard before. Fire leaps out of the building she passes. Her clothes catch on fire. She screams for her mother.*

Hannah sat up in bed. Her pajamas were soaked from night sweats. Her body was changing hormonally and most nights she woke up in sticky pajamas. *She is a freak. Her body is going haywire. She belongs in the circus. Putting on face paint and adding black tears to her cheeks will highlight how she feels.* In her dream she was lost in a city she didn't recognize. She didn't understand what was happening to her. She looked over at Irwin sleeping peacefully. *She'll wake him. She wants him to hold her. She needs to feel his warm body. She wants Irwin to tell her that her body will not wither when they remove her breast. How can he sleep when her breast is going to be amputated? Can't he hear the sirens going off in her head?* She climbed out of bed to stand outside the children's rooms. Their soft breathing quieted her. Since they were fragile, she wouldn't frighten them by showing how upset she was. She had to be strong.

In the morning, before the children left for school, she started to make a list for Irwin of the children's schedules. He would have to take Warren to tennis, Ethan to guitar and Nina to pottery. She wrote a grocery list for the dishes she would cook and put in the freezer. She couldn't concentrate because she kept replaying in her mind the dream she had the previous night. *The Big C is standing over her and laughing. He tells her not to waste her time making lists. He motions for her to come back in the ring.* She turned to talk to Irwin, but he was engrossed in *The New York Times. She shreds his paper and stomps on it. What is the matter with him? How can he concentrate on the paper when she's dying? Doesn't he care about her?* She touched his hand. "Irwin, I had a terrible dream last night."

"You've quite an imagination!" he answered when she told him the dream.

"I don't feel like myself," she said.

"Don't worry. It was only a dream. You'll be your old self after the surgery." He patted her arm and picked up the paper, again. *She hits him over the head with his newspaper. He is only attentive to her when she discusses Ethan. Didn't Irwin realize that her problem is bigger? What if the cancer traveled to her brain and she became a vegetable? What if she died? Who would care for the children?* She realized lunches had to be made for the younger children since she had forgotten them the night before. Nina walked in without her sneakers and had to be sent to get them. The bus pulled up for Ethan and he flew down the stairs and out the door. When Irwin was ready to leave, she went to the door and touched his cheek. *She loves him and wants to grow old with him.* "What's the matter?" He firmly held her hand.

"I don't know. I want to be close to you," she said.

"Don't worry. We'll get over this lump, I mean hump," he said sheepishly.

"Will we? I'm worried about the children, too."

"I told you, I promise to take good care of them." He caressed her cheek.

For a moment they embraced. Before they could say anything, Warren barreled into the room ready to be taken to school. Irwin said, "See you later, guys." He tousled Warren's thick brown hair and left. *She runs after him. She grabs him and won't let go. She needs him desperately. She can't exist without him. If he really loves her, the cancer won't kill her. He must protect her.* But instead, she takes the younger children to school.

She went to North Shore Hospital for her surgery. The peeling gray walls of her room were depressing. Irwin looked out the window, as she put on a white gown that felt scratchy against her skin. *She throws off the gown. She screams and runs down the hall.* "Irwin, I'm frightened." Her voice quivered.

"It will be okay." He pulled her to him.

Then the attendants came with a gurney. After she climbed onto it, Irwin held her hand and accompanied her as far at the operating room door. She whispered, "Tell the children I love them." She hesitated, "I love you."

"I will. I love you, too." He kissed her cheek.

She turned toward him to be kissed on the mouth. Instead, he pecked her forehead. *Her mother pecks her check before sending her into kindergarten. She stomps her feet. She wants to go to work with her mother. In the bakery's warm kitchen she drops the raisins in the rugalah.*

Her thoughts before being put under anesthesia were how difficult it was for her to tell Irwin she loved him. She couldn't remember her mother ever saying that she loved her. Her sister woke her on school mornings while her mother slept. When they came home from school, her mother left for Sofia's Bakery where she baked all night.

After her surgery, back in her room, her body ached. Her chest felt like a knife had been run through it. She felt groggy. Her mouth was dry. The room was dark except for a lamp on the nightstand. Irwin was sitting on a chair with his head bowed. She looked at the clock. She had been in the hospital for ten hours. Outside, the lights were on in the parking lot. "Irwin," she whispered.

"How are you?" he asked.

"Thirsty," she looked at the empty glass. Irwin poured the water from the pitcher and held the glass for her to drink. Irwin said, "They got it all. You're going to be fine."

"Thank God," she said. *In the ring, the big C lies dead. His fat and sweaty body is wheeled out on a stretcher. As the attendants pass by her, she gives C one last smack to make sure he is never coming back. The crowd gives her a standing ovation.* She dozed off to sleep.

The next day, the children were not allowed to visit because they were too young. Two days later, Irwin brought Warren and Nina to her outside window. Ethan refused to come to the hospital. "Why didn't you make him come? I wanted to see him."

"I guess because we both hate hospitals." He shrugged his shoulders.

At that moment, Nina wailed. "I miss you."

"Come home, Mom," Warren said sadly.

She looked to Irwin to comfort them but he stood with his hands in his pockets. *As they walk away, she yells, wait for me. She grabs the children's hands to run after Irwin who throws his arms around her.* She was upset Irwin didn't know how to soothe them. The only one he had any rapport with was Ethan. She found it ironic that Irwin most identified with the least predictable of their children.

Three days after she came home from the hospital, when Irwin and she were having breakfast, she leaned against the table. Her chest throbbed. *The pain sears through her. She feels faint.*

"The kids are driving me crazy," said Irwin.

"I know, but you've been helpful," she said.

"My secretary called. There are some problems with the Nabisco account."

"Do you have to go?" she asked.

"Yes," he said.

It was difficult for Hannah to return to the routine of daily chores as simple as lifting the laundry into the washer caused her chest to pulse. Nina anxiously followed her around the house while Hannah worked. When she stopped to use the bathroom, Nina stood by the door. "Nothing is going to happen while I'm in the bathroom." Hannah said.

"Are you sure?" Nina implored.

"Positive," she said.

"I didn't like it when you were gone," she said.

"It was only a short time. I'm home. We're going to be fine," Hannah said when she came out of the bathroom.

"Promise?" Nina asked.

"I'm always going to take good care of you." Hannah pulled her close. Her breath smelled of peanut butter.

It was clear to Hannah that Warren was upset, too. He helped her with chores about the house as though he were a grown man. One morning, after he lugged a laundry basket to the basement, she placed her hands on his shoulders. "You can go play. I'm fine. I can do this myself."

"The basket is heavy," he said.

"This is the last day I want help." She cupped his chin.

· It was difficult for Hannah to allow anyone to care for her. She should be able to do everything on her own, especially parent her children, but Ethan made her feel inadequate because she couldn't make him happy.

Since Irwin had gone back to work, Ethan was more out of control then ever. He never asked her how she was feeling and he had several fights with other students. After he was suspended from school for a week, she asked, "Why did you push the boy in the cafeteria?"

"He didn't belong in my chair." Ethan folded his arms.

"It's only a chair. What's the matter with you?" She shook her head.

"Nothing is wrong with me," he sneered.

That night, she asked Irwin to speak to Ethan about his behavior. "What do you expect? He's upset about your operation," Irwin said.

"My operation? He hasn't said a word to me about it." Hannah frowned.

"That's exactly my point. He can't verbalize his pain. He acts it out," said Irwin.

"I disagree. I don't think he is upset about me," she said.

"You just don't understand him." Irwin threw up his arms.

During his suspension, Ethan taunted the dog more than ever. One afternoon, she heard Ethan yelling at Rusty. When she went into the playroom Rusty was in the corner and Ethan was about to strike with a stick. "Stop it, Stop it," she said.

"We are playing," said Ethan.

"No, you're not playing," said Hannah.

"How do you know?" Ethan yelled.

"What is wrong with you? Get out of my sight," she said. Rusty bared his teeth. Drool was coming out of the dog's mouth. Ethan raised his stick to Rusty. Hannah could see by the ugly look in Rusty's eyes that he felt cornered. Hannah was afraid Rusty would hurt Ethan. She moved between the two of them. She wrestled with Ethan for the stick. "He's going to hurt you if you hit him," she said.

Before Ethan could answer her, the stick hit Rusty, who then bit her hand. Hannah screamed. Blood gushed. "Get a towel with ice," she yelled.

"Oh my God," said Ethan. He ran for a towel that she placed around her hand.

She moved forward to comfort Ethan. For a moment, his shoulders slumped and he leaned against her. She embraced him. Then, he gave her cold look. "It's your own fault."

"What are you talking about?" she asked.

"I didn't do anything." He ran out of the room and the door slammed.

Hannah shook her head. She wasn't going to reproach Ethan. His behavior had told her that he felt guilty. She was relieved he had feelings of remorse.

During the next few weeks, she kept hoping their lives would go back to normal. Her bandaged chest was a constant reminder of her missing breast. When the doctor took off the bandages, her chest looked lashed with a whip; it was bumpy and sore to the touch. She imagined sitting in a bath of ice to take away the ache. Her chest was concave, flatter than Nina's. She had become a small child. *Her operation is a mistake. There is no cancer. Her breasts are back. Irwin and she are making out in the back row of the Mid-Manhattan Movie Theater. He reaches under her bra to feel her breasts. She doesn't want him to stop touching her. Her taut breasts make her feel womanly.*

Six weeks later, when her body felt less sore, in bed, she turned to Irwin. He hadn't touched her since before the operation. "Irwin, sweetheart" she whispered.

"What?" He opened his sleepy eyes to look at her.

"I've missed you." She rubbed her hand through the hairs on his chest.

"It takes times for your body to heal." He stroked her arm.

"I want to be close to you." She leaned against his body.

"Does your chest still ache?" he asked.

"Just a little, but I'm okay." She reached between his legs.

"I wouldn't want to bruise you." He stopped her hand.

"I want you," she kissed his fingertips.

"I'm afraid of hurting you," he whispered.

"It's okay," she whispered.

Irwin snapped on the light by the bed. His wary eyes starred at her chest. "I'm not ready." She felt her breast being sliced, again. Her lips tightened as she climbed out of bed and quickly put on her bathrobe. He was not the one who had been gouged.

When Irwin left for work, she stood naked in front of the full-length mirror in her bedroom. She looked at her body and touched her flattened chest where her left breast once was. The scars were healing, but the skin was rough. She was a lopsided monster. One side of her was a woman and the other side was pocked like a boy pistol-whipped for crimes he didn't commit. *Irwin is right not to touch her because she's deformed. She's damaged goods, her skin clawed by a bear. She is grotesque, no longer a woman, but a monster. She is unlovable. She should drown herself in the Sound.*

Later that evening, after the children went to bed, in the den, she tried to speak to Irwin about his reaction to her surgery. "Irwin, I tried to reach out to you this morning."

"I'm sorry. I've been preoccupied." Irwin looked at the floor.

"Preoccupied with what?" Hannah asked.

"Work," he said.

"You could confide in me the way you used to." She sat down next to him.

"I can take care of it," he said quietly.

"I'm having trouble handling my surgery. To make matters worse, your pushing me away isn't helping." She took his hand.

"I can't help it." Irwin sighed.

"What is it? You're so distant," she asked.

"I'm not happy." He removed his hand from hers.

"I haven't been myself for a while, either," said Hannah.

"Your surgery is not the problem. It's our relationship," he said.

"Our marriage?" Her eyes widened.

"The marriage isn't working." He shook his head.

"What are you saying?" Her heart began to race.

"I'm miserable in our marriage." He crossed his arms.

"I know we have problems, but I had no idea you were miserable," she said.

"Well, I am." His eyes glowed.

"We could see a marriage counselor?" she implored.

"No, It won't help," he said.

"What should we do?" She looked at Irwin with bewildered eyes.

"I want a separation." Irwin stood up.

"We've been married twenty years. It's a tough time. Please sit down. You're making me nervous." She reached out her hand.

"I can't live like this anymore. I need to be by myself for a while." He paced.

"What am I supposed to do? How am I going to care for Ethan? He's unmanageable without you. What about Nina and Warren?" She wrung her hands.

"I don't know." He shook his head.

"This is no way to leave a marriage." She stood up.

"I'm suffocating," he said.

"I've barely recuperated from my operation. I need you." She moved toward him.

"I can't help it. It will be best for everyone." He glared at her.

"You're not a child, Irwin. You can help it. You just want to do what is best for you, not the family." Hannah was surprised her voice was so forceful.

"I have to be happy," he said.

"What kind of happiness do you want? Are you seeing someone else?" she asked.

"No, I'm going to move into the city," he said.

"What am I going to tell the children? I can't handle Ethan."

"I have no idea. I'll take Ethan. I can't think. I have to leave," he said.

"Are you out of your mind? I'm his mother," she wailed.

"I thought I was doing you a favor," he said in a surprised voice.

"I don't need any more favors from you," she said.

"I'm done arguing. I'm leaving tonight." He moved toward the door.

"Where are you going?" she asked.

"Into New York," he said.

"It's almost midnight," she said.

"I can't sleep here tonight," he said in a tired voice.

"It's not safe to drive at this hour. You don't sound well," she pleaded.

"I'll be fine. I'll stay at the Plaza." Irwin moved toward the door.

Hannah wanted to scream, but she was afraid of waking the children. Instead, she paced the floor while listening to Irwin in the bedroom as he opened and shut drawers. He was packing. He was carrying away her life in his suitcase. She felt punched in the gut. The room was spinning. "I'll call you tomorrow." Irwin stood at the den door.

She was stunned by Irwin's selfishness. He had no right to talk about unhappiness. She was miserable, too. She was enraged with Irwin. She was tired of playing scenarios over in her head. She was sick of his pathetic eyes staring at her breasts. He was not going to get away that easily. He owed her. She followed Irwin into the kitchen. "If you leave, don't come back!" She raised her fist.

"You're not making any sense. You're acting crazy," he grabbed her hand.

"You're the one leaving." She wrenched her hand away.

"I have to go," he said.

"I need you to stay." She clutched his shirt.

"I can't." He took her hands off him and walked toward the garage door.

"I hate you. You're a bastard!" She stared in disbelief as Irwin slammed the door.

Hannah paced across the living room floor. She wept. She didn't know what had happened to her marriage. Her cancer was a bad omen, but she didn't know what it foretold. Irwin was cutting her out of his life the same way the surgeon had sliced off her breast. At least the surgeon was trying to save her while Irwin was being cruel. She had to accept her surgery to survive, but she was confused about Irwin. He thought that taking Ethan would make his leaving more acceptable, but it wouldn't. As Hannah dragged herself upstairs, she listened to Ethan jumping in his room. He had heard the fight and was upset. Ethan needed her more than ever. Her hands trembling, she knocked on the door and hoped he would open it.

Irwin

~

Irwin looked out of his Madison Avenue office onto the people below. Young men in dark suits and women in short skirts were hustling to their jobs. When he had started out in copyrighting, his advertisements for Book-Of-The-Month Club brought him national acclaim. Now that he was president of his own company, he was relieved he no longer had to prove himself. He couldn't tell if any of the people walking on the street worked for him. If they did, he hoped they were thinking about the ad for his RCA Records account. In thirty minutes, his art department would be gathering in the conference room to present a new layout. He wondered if they enjoyed their work as much as he did. He had built his tiny mail-order advertising company into one of the most successful in New York City. He employed two hundred people. Every morning, when he stepped out of the elevator, seeing his name in gold lettering gave him a thrill. His father, who had died when he was nine years old, would have been proud of him. His mother certainly enjoyed the fruits of his labor, garnered an apartment overlooking the Hudson River. He wished the admiration he felt from his employees, especially Penelope, his secretary, and his mother was more evident at home.

Two nights ago, as he was trying to relax watching The Mets play The Dodgers, Hannah, his wife, had come into the den. He wasn't in the mood to talk, but she stepped in front of the screen and looked at him with tired eyes. "What is it?"

When she told him she had cancer, he sucked in his breath. For a brief moment he wondered if his anger made her ill. When she said she needed a radical mastectomy, he was dumbfounded. "I didn't know you were ill." He turned for a moment to watch the Dodgers score.

"I wasn't sick. They picked it up in a routine examination. I went for a biopsy and today, Dr. Glantz gave me the results," she said in a quiet voice.

"Why didn't you tell me?" He placed his hand on her shoulder.

"I didn't want to worry you," she said.

"You should have confided in me," he said.

"I know how busy you are at work," she said.

"I would have gone with you." He squeezed her shoulder.

"I was trying to handle it by myself." She took his hand.

"Didn't you trust me to help you?" he asked.

"I'm sorry; at the next appointment come with me," she said.

Afterwards, they sat on the couch while he held Hannah, until she said she was tired and went upstairs. Sitting by himself, he remembered in the early part of their marriage when they had snuggled. For a moment, he wished they were still young and naïve before he had started working in the cutthroat business of advertising. In the beginning, he had confided in Hannah, but her worrying had made him feel worse. He decided it was better for both of them if he didn't discuss work.

He was disturbed that Hannah had waited to tell him about her illness. But she rarely confided in him. She kept her feelings to herself. Since she seemed capable of handling anything, he didn't feel important to her. He was angry that he was not essential to her life. He wanted to feel that she couldn't be happy without him. It was difficult for him to believe she was sick because she never complained. She looked the same with her wavy brown hair, dark eyes and matronly body.

Their conversations usually were about the children, especially Ethan. Different from the other children, Ethan required more patience and structure, but he was the most imaginative. He was a talented guitar player. Recently, he began to paint and showed artistic ability. When he was younger and they watched a Yankee game together, Ethan jumped up and down with excitement. While Irwin appreciated his enthusiasm, Hannah was afraid of his emotionalism. Ethan took up much of their time and energy. When Irwin came home from work, the first thing Hannah told him was an "Ethan problem."

Irwin always imagined coming home to a candlelight dinner, Mozart in the background, and a romantic evening with Hannah. After a dinner of filet mignon, they would lie next to each other on the couch. He would tell her about his meeting with RCA where he "wowed" them with his creative copy. She would look admiringly at him. She would unbutton his shirt to run her hand down his chest. They would hurry up the bedroom, slip out of their clothes and Hannah would touch him, everywhere. Then she would climb on top of him, all a pipe dream that would never happen in real life.

The first time Irwin planned a vacation with just Hannah, Nina was three. They had to return home early because the housekeeper reported that Ethan had tried to push Warren out of the second story bathroom window. After that experience, Hannah didn't want to leave them for an extended period of time. Irwin tried to make light of the situation, to entice her with exotic vacations. On their fifteenth wedding anniversary, he purchased airline tickets to London. "Look what I have." He waved the tickets at Hannah.

"I can't go." Her face was ashen.

"It's only for a week. We haven't been alone in so long." He grasped her hand.

"Please, don't make me go," she whispered.

He caved in because Hannah was miserable. He didn't understand how she could give up a trip to England, but he realized asking her to leave the children was a lost cause.

The last time they went on a family trip to Puerto Rico, Ethan dunked Warren, in his clothes, under a burning, hot shower. Then Hannah insisted Nina stay in their room with her and Irwin sleep in the boys' room. To make matters worse, Ethan refused to sleep on the cot. Irwin shared a queen-size bed with Ethan snuggled next to him. Irwin kissed the top of Ethan's head and put his arm around him. He was glad that Ethan slept, but he tossed and turned all night. Since that incident, they hadn't taken a family vacation. There was no way he was going to be forced out of his own bedroom, again.

Just last night, after seeing the rope burns on Warren, he had dealt with the fact that Ethan had tied up Warren. He spoke to Ethan who was playing his guitar. "Why did you tie up your brother?"

"He kept boasting that he could jump rope better than me."

"That's not a reason to tie him up," said Irwin.

"I couldn't help myself." Ethan stopped strumming.

"You have to stop giving your mother a hard time." Irwin lifted Ethan's chin.

"She's too bossy," he said.

"She's still your mother," said Irwin.

"Why can't she be more like you?" Ethan frowned.

"She's not. You have to listen to her." Irwin frowned.

"It's easy for you to say," said Ethan.

"You could have cut off Warren's circulation," said Irwin sternly.

"Why are you getting so upset?" Ethan asked.

"I'm tired of your shenanigans!" Irwin shook his head.

"Okay, okay, I get it," said Ethan.

"I don't like it when you make me angry with you," said Irwin.

"I know Dad; I won't do it, again," Ethan pleaded. When Irwin saw his dejection, he suggested they play their guitars. Ethan's face lit up. They took out their instruments and played Dylan's song, "Times They Are a Changing." Music was an interest they both shared. He had taught Ethan to play the guitar when he turned eight years old. It calmed Ethan. When they played, Irwin felt a deep connection to him. At fifteen, Ethan was part of a band and playing his own music. Irwin wished he himself had the guts to become a musician but during the depression he was more concerned about putting food on the table for his mother and himself. So he started out as a mail sorter in the business he now owned.

Irwin didn't understand how Ethan could be so reasonable with him and difficult with the rest of the family. He wondered if the problem was that Hannah allowed Ethan to bully her. "You have to be firm but patient with him," said Irwin.

"It's stressful when he's physically hurting the other children," she said.

"He's easily upset. Give him attention before he misbehaves," he said.

"I've tried but he pushes me away," she said.

"Do you really mean it?" he asked.

"I'm being sincere, but he's always upset with me or Warren or Nina. The other two get much less of my time. I'm worried about them, too," she said.

"Are you saying I'm not concerned about Nina or Warren?" he asked.

"No, but it's difficult for me to divide myself among the three of them," she said.

"If you see the good in Ethan, he will behave," he said.

"I'm not talking about him being good or bad," she said.

"Everything that goes wrong isn't his fault," he said.

"I didn't say it was but when he's out, the others are calmer."

"That's not the point," Irwin scolded her. Why couldn't Hannah do a better job of managing the three children? She had to work harder to connect with Ethan, especially to soothe him. It wasn't Irwin's fault that the psychiatrist said Ethan had an attachment disorder. It was obvious to Irwin that Hannah couldn't connect with Ethan. Hannah needed to appreciate his talents in math, guitar and now art. He hated coming home to be a referee. Every night was another crisis. It was more than he wanted to handle.

But every morning, Irwin was lucky that he had Penelope at the office to talk to about his problems. He opened the door to his office to find her pouring him a mug of coffee. She looked gorgeous in a sheer while silk top and black skirt with high heels. Her silky black hair was smoothed back in a bun. She was everything that Hannah wasn't. His father would have called her a "fleisch mit eigen, a piece of meat with eyes." When he told Penelope that Hannah had breast cancer, Penelope burst into tears. "I can't believe this is happening to us."

"I don't know what I'm 'going to do," he said.

"What does that mean?" Penelope wiped her eyes with a tissue.

"I can't leave her now," he said.

"Let's not make any decisions, yet." She placed her arms around his neck.

Irwin pulled Penelope to him and kissed her. She smelled of jasmine perfume. She was intoxicating. She was gorgeous with her full breasts and long legs. When he walked down Madison Avenue with her, he enjoyed other men eyeing her. She knew how to put herself together. She looked stunning in expensive clothes. He looked forward to taking her to Bonwit Teller and Saks. They made such a handsome couple. She would appreciate the lifestyle he could provide for her. Not give him a hard time the way Hannah did. Penelope would be responsive to him in bed. She liked to please him. Since Penelope had no immediate family, she depended on him. He was attracted to her vulnerability. Penelope's twin brother and parents had died in a car crash when she was eighteen. He didn't give a damn that he was twenty-three years older than she was. At age fifty, he was tired of feeling guilty about his Porsche, the house in Great Neck and the lavish entertaining he enjoyed. He had already picked out the fifty-five-foot yacht that he was going to give Penelope as a wedding present. He'd name it the "Pen-Irwin."

At the beginning of the following week, Irwin accompanied Hannah to the North Shore Hospital. The last time he had been there was when Nina was born. He was happy she was a girl, a real charmer. At that moment, Irwin noticed he was walking ahead of Hannah. He slowed down to her pace. Her face was drawn and he put his arm around her. Hannah clung to him and trembled. He had never seen Hannah frightened. He bit his lip. He felt unsure of how to respond. His throat tightened. She buried her head in his chest. Her hair smelled like soap. "You're going to be fine." He rubbed her back.

"Do you really think so?" she asked.

"I sure of it," said Irwin.

"I'm glad you're here, Irwin," she said.

"Me, too," he said.

He kissed the top of her head. She hugged him. Her heart was beating fast. She was fragile. Irwin tried to stop himself from shaking. He was afraid for her. The only sick person he had loved was his father. He wished his father were still alive. He remembered, one day, accompanying his father to his furrier store and trying on the coats. His father laughed when he saw Irwin admiring himself in a black mink. He thought his father would yell at him for dragging the fur on the floor. Instead he said, "When you're older, I'll make you one, a special coat." His father kissed the top of his head. As he thought of his father's gentleness, he stroked Hannah's arms. Her lower lip trembled. Finally, she needed him. He would see Hannah through the surgery. He owed her that much and more. She was as good a wife and mother as she could be. It was nobody's fault that they had grown apart.

He remembered the day he met her on a blind date. He was waiting on the steps of PS 13 in Queens when she walked out of the building. She had a wide smile that made him grin. She was smart and taught him to understand Shakespeare. She thought he was educated even if he had attended college for one year. They were young and dreamed of being successful. He wanted to run his own business. Hannah longed for children. But it was rough with Hannah having three miscarriages. He couldn't stand to see her suffering. He agreed to adopt six-month-old Ethan, a gifted but demanding child. Since Irwin felt fulfilled parenting Ethan, he didn't want any more children. He was shocked when Hannah had become pregnant first with Warren, in 1958, and with Nina in 1960. At forty-one years old, Irwin felt too old to have young children. But when he hinted that he knew a doctor who performed abortions, Hannah blew up and told him he was being "selfish." She explained, "I have always dreamed of a big family." Irwin didn't want to disappoint her and resigned himself to her pregnancies.

Irwin knew Hannah struggled with Ethan—that she was trying to be a good mother to all the children. When Hannah tried to connect with Ethan, he frustrated her. This morning, Hannah was upset when he overheard her offering to make Ethan his favorite, a cheese omelet. "I don't like the way you make it. You use too much cheese."

"Tell me exactly how you want it."

"It's pointless; forget it."

"Please," said Hannah.

"No, I don't want eggs, anymore," said Ethan.

"I'm only trying to do something nice for you," she said.

Ethan didn't respond and walked into the dining room where Irwin whispered. "Go back in there and let your mother cook for you."

"I want you to make my eggs," said Ethan. Irwin shook his head. He thought about it, but Hannah would tell him he was encouraging Ethan's negative behavior. He didn't want to fight with her. Irwin avoided confronting Hannah with the knowledge Ethan and he had a special bond and enjoyed each other's company. She didn't complain, but he knew that she felt excluded.

Irwin wished he had that same closeness to Hannah. The feeling of wanting to be near her that he felt when they were young. He remembered sitting for hours on a park bench in Central Park to be alone with Hannah. As the sun went down, and the streetlights came on, they watched men hurrying home to their families. He imagined himself coming home to Hannah who would greet him with kisses. Hannah shivered. Irwin hugged Hannah to keep her warm. Irwin sneezed. "You're freezing." She took off her gloves to touch his cheek.

"Just a little," he laughed.

"Do you want my gloves?" she asked.

"No, but I want a kiss." When their lips touched, he realized Hannah lips were cold, too. "Let's go before we both freeze." He put his hand into her coat pocket and clasped her hand. When he walked her home, he was proud to be with her. Her admiration made him feel he could do anything. He wanted to succeed for her.

Since the younger children were born, when Irwin reached out to Hannah, she rarely reciprocated, hugged him or told him she loved him. He wished she were more loving. She was no longer interested in his successes at work. Hannah was happy with him because he provided a secure home for them. Her needs were simple. She was satisfied with their life. She didn't want more from their relationship. He was disappointed she rarely wore the diamond ring or the mink coat he bought for her. When he mentioned them to Hannah, she put them on but without enthusiasm. He encouraged her to buy new clothes, but she was happy in collared shirts and dark slacks. Penelope was more of a challenge. She was a highly emotional woman willing to put everything into a relationship. She would give him the attention he sorely missed.

During the week after the surgery, staying with the children proved to Irwin that he wasn't a family man. Starting with the weekend, he couldn't sleep late and have a leisurely breakfast the way he did when Hannah was home. During the week, he set the alarm clock to take care of the children. The house was silent. The housekeeper didn't come in until nine o'clock. Irwin had to admit that he missed waking to Hannah banging pots in the kitchen. First, he woke Nina who was slow to rouse. She threw her arms around his neck and he would kiss her hair that smelled like spring flowers, "Time to get up, sleepy head."

"Daddy, I hate to get up," she said.

"I'll carry you to the bathroom like a sack of potatoes," he said.

"Oh, Daddy." She hugged his neck. He carried her to the bathroom door.

· Then he checked to make sure the boys were up. Warren, an early riser, was already getting dressed. Ethan, who stayed up until all hours of the night, was difficult to waken. After rousing him, by giving him a big bear hug, he noticed a couple of empty Heineken beer cans on the floor. "Did you drink my beer?" Irwin asked.

"What's the big deal?" Ethan asked.

"You're too young to be drinking," said Irwin.

"All my friends drink," said Irwin.

"I don't care what your friends do!" Irwin exclaimed.

Irwin tried to remember when he had his first beer. He hated to admit it, but he and his friend had stolen a couple of bottles from Louie's Liquor Store. Afterwards, he had thrown up. He hoped the beer would make Ethan sick; also, in the meantime, he was going to have to remember to lock the liquor cabinet. He decided not to tell Hannah because she would overreact and think Ethan was an alcoholic.

Then he heard Warren coming out of his room and hurried downstairs to make the breakfast and lunches. Warren followed him into the kitchen with a big smile on his face and hugged Irwin. But then Ethan came into the kitchen and didn't answer when Irwin said, "Good morning." Ethan sat down at the table and glared at his siblings. "Warren's eaten all the Corn Flakes. He's a pig." Ethan scowled.

"I'm not a pig. There's plenty left." Warren shook the box.

"Stop fighting. Mom left a new box in the cupboard," said Irwin.

"I want Sugar Pops," whined Nina.

"Shut up, you're a big, fat cry baby," said Ethan.

"I want Sugar Pops," continued Nina.

"All of you stop talking, right now!" Irwin demanded.

They ate the rest of their breakfast in silence. While Irwin fumed, he imagined attending a breakfast meeting at work where everyone listened to him. He wondered what his colleagues would say if they knew that his children were rude to him. They wouldn't believe it. After breakfast, Nina opened her lunch bag and took out her sandwich. "I don't eat tuna fish," she wailed.

"Just great, now we are going to be late!" He grabbed the sandwich and made her a peanut butter one. Outside, they had missed their school bus. By the time he had dropped them off at school, he was relieved to be by himself. He hated to admit it but he understood Hannah's frustration. He awakened in a cheery mood but the children depressed him. They sapped him of his energy. He remembered how he had behaved as a youngster after his father died. Every morning, he brought tea and a blueberry muffin to his mother. "You're such a good boy, my little man." She stroked his hair with her magical hands. He was her prince.

During the children's school day, Irwin picked up tennis games at the Great Neck Estates Park and Pool. One morning, he noticed an attractive group of women in short tennis skirts as they watched him play; he grinned and hit the ball harder. He won every game. Afterwards, he walked down to the water. He imagined his yacht with Penelope standing next to him. The two of them, in blue blazers, white shorts and matching caps with the name of their ship emblazoned on them. Right now, he wanted to sail to St. Thomas and never come back.

In the hospital, fluorescent lights flickering, halls smelling of ammonia, Irwin forced himself to go into Hannah's room. Even though it was filled with colorful flowers from both him and their friends, it was a dreary place. The walls were dingy white. He hoped that she no longer needed a bedpan since the smell made him queasy. He had to believe that Hannah would be okay. After all, the surgeon said he had cut out the entire tumor. She was sexless. She wouldn't even miss her breast. In a few weeks, she would be as good as new.

In bed, Hannah was propped up on her pillows. She had a tinge of color on her cheeks. She had brushed her wavy hair. "I'm glad to see you," said Hannah.

"You're looking better," he said.

"Do you think so?" She gave him a shy smile.

"Absolutely," He touched her cheek. Irwin pulled her toward him. Despite himself, he felt drawn toward her. She was defenseless. He kissed the top of her head. He remembered when her hair was a deep chestnut color. He rubbed her cold hands. He told her about the children. He arranged to bring them to her window because the hospital rules were "no visitors under sixteen years old."

After seeing Hannah, he didn't feel like going home. Later, along with the women, Irwin waited at the school bus stop. He admired the ones with perm haircuts, tailored skirts and heels. He wished that Hannah could be like them. He resented that Hannah refused to be desirable. He dressed fashionably and couldn't understand why she didn't do the same. Irwin didn't expect her to care about what she looked like after she came home from the hospital. When he took her out, he liked to feel he was on a date. He remembered when they were young; Hannah would often go to the hairdresser, polish her nails and wear tight-fitting clothes. He wanted back the enticing Hannah.

The next day, during their visit, Warren and Nina cried at their mother's hospital window. Warren, red-eyed, and Nina with a dripping nose, looked like orphans. Warren pressed his face to the screen. "Come home soon," he said.

Irwin wanted to reach out and hold them, but he felt unsure. It was Hannah's job to comfort them, not his. She was in charge of the children. He put his hands in his pockets. He looked at the linoleum floor. He wished he could wait in the car.

"Where's Ethan?" Hannah asked.

"At home," he said.

"Why didn't he come?" she asked.

"He's fifteen. I couldn't force him," he said.

"He didn't want to see me?" Hannah asked sadly.

"Don't take it personally."

"I don't know how else to take it."

"We should go. You need your rest." Irwin backed away from the window.

"I don't want to leave Mommy," wailed NINA.

"Mom needs to sleep," said Irwin.

"Go with Daddy. Remember I love you," said Hannah. She turned to Irwin, "Just pick her up. She needs to be held."

Irwin picked up the sobbing Nina, and walked towards the car. "Mom is going to be fine. I told you the doctors made her all well," he said.

"Promise?" Her breath smelled of the chocolate mints that her mother had given her.

"Yes," he answered.

During the car ride home, Warren was silent. Irwin wondered what his son was thinking. Warren was a brooder like him. He was probably worrying about his mother. Warren felt close to Hannah, protective of her and Nina. Even at the risk of being hurt, he would put himself physically between Nina and Ethan.

Last night, as Irwin came into the television room to tell Nina to get ready for bed, Ethan said he was going to change the channel. Nina whined. Warren yelled "no" and blocked the screen. Ethan shook Warren. "Stop it, right now. What is going on here?" Irwin stepped between the two boys, but neither child answered him. Warren trembled. Ethan laughed. "Go watch in my room," Irwin said to Ethan. Warren's body relaxed when Ethan walked out of the room. Irwin asked Warren what happened but he shrugged his shoulders.

"Nothing," he said. Irwin was afraid to ask how many blows Warren had taken from Ethan to protect Nina. But as much as Irwin didn't like to admit it, he was relieved Warren, a trooper, hardly confided in him.

In the evening, when he went into Warren's room to kiss him good night, Warren tightly hugged Irwin. Are you okay?" Irwin asked.

"When is Mom coming home?" Warren asked.

"As soon as her body feels better," said Irwin.

"I miss Mom," he said.

"I know." Irwin held Warren. He felt as small in his arms as the day they brought him home from the hospital. Before the three miscarriages, every time Hannah had taken a pregnancy test, Irwin had been anxious for the results. He had been ashamed they couldn't produce a child. He had felt like a failure until they adopted Ethan. He had not objected strongly to Warren's birth because he wondered if he would feel differently toward his natural child. He was proud he had produced Warren, but he still felt closer to Ethan.

He looked down at Warren whose voice was muffled as he leaned against his chest. "The only good thing is that you stayed home." Warren continued to cling to him. Irwin kissed the top of his head. Irwin remembered his own father with his stale breath, bony arms and tissue paper skin. Irwin had prayed to God to make him well, but he still died of a heart attack. Irwin, watching his son's tears, wished he could cry. He was surprised by Warren's emotional outburst. Without talking, he held Warren, but he couldn't make it better for either of them.

A week later, he was relieved to get back to work where he was in control. His staff depended on him, lionized him for his creative talent and business acumen. His office was filled with junior members asking his advice or signing off on their ads. That afternoon, they delivered their new campaign to City Life Insurance. When he finished with their presentation that included acquiring the rights to the most famous comic strip character, Jumpy the Dog, the chairman of City Life slapped him on the back. "Terrific, I knew your company could do it."

"Thanks," Irwin grinned.

That evening, he especially dreaded going home because the day was exciting. After the presentation, he took everyone for drinks at the Four Seasons. The vice president of the City Life made a speech about Irwin being a "creative giant." The employees gave him a standing ovation. Their admiring eyes invigorated him. He toasted his staff's "ability to make my visions come true." As he looked around the room, he knew he had reached the pinnacle of the advertising world.

At home his life offered few rewards. Every night was the same routine. Hannah washed the dishes while he ate a late meal she had prepared. They made little conversation. After his dinner, he read Nina a bedtime story. Their time together was relaxing even though she liked to hear the same fairy tale of the "Twelve Princesses" every night. She leaned against him and he felt loved. Then he called Hannah to put Nina to bed since Nina needed the blankets tucked a special way to fall asleep and her mother to lie down with her. He complained to Hannah that she coddled Nina by giving into her bedtime ritual. He would check on Warren who, after homework, was usually working on a car model. He'd peek in on Ethan who would be playing his guitar or sketching. Irwin would have to encourage him to do his homework. Hannah, too tired to stay up with him, went to bed by ten o'clock. He watched the news until bedtime. The silence made him feel he was alone, in a jail cell. On these nights, he walked around the block to breathe the fresh air. Sometimes, he walked into town to call Penelope who comforted him.

Six weeks later, Penelope and Irwin were having a leisurely lunch at Lutece. He couldn't sleep the previous night when he refused to make love to Hannah who reached for him. He rejected her. He didn't want to admit her missing breast repulsed him. He felt ashamed of himself. But he wasn't physically attracted to her since he started dating Penelope over a year ago, even before the surgery. He rarely made love to Hannah. Last night, when she took off her clothes, she reminded him of a burn victim. Her skin was crispy. He was afraid that if he touched her, the surface of her skin would flake off in his hand. Underneath the scabs, the skin was raw. Bloody patches oozing pus. She looked deformed. Part of her body was missing, amputated. It reminded him of the army hospital where he visited his men. He had trained pilots during WW II. After a plane accident, some of the men's bodies were badly burned. Their moans seared through him. The sight of their singed skin made him queasy. He would leave the ward to vomit in the bathroom. He wanted to yell at Hannah to button her nightgown. He couldn't stand to see her without a breast. Her body smelled burnt. Her chest was torched and unrecognizable. He closed his eyes and prayed for her breast to appear. He couldn't make love to a war victim. He needed her to be whole. Not that her breasts were large but they were part of how he saw her. Penelope interrupted his thoughts. "You look piqued. What's the matter?"

"I need to make love to you." He rubbed her leg.

"Only after you leave your wife and we're engaged," she said.

"I can't wait." He kissed her.

Back in the office, the door shut, Irwin fantasized about Penelope. From the little he had seen, she had a terrific body. Like a kid in a candy store, he was not allowed to eat any of the sweets. He was frustrated and lonely.

The trouble with his marriage was that Hannah had come from the same deprived background that he had. At an early age, he had to nurse his mother who had suffered from a nervous condition after his father died. She spent a great deal of time in bed. Since she didn't like to be alone, he would rush from school to sit with her. He missed going outside to play stickball with his friends. As a teenager, on the way home, he would watch his friends flirt with the girls in front of Sam's Five and Dime Store. One time, he had stopped to talk to a girl, Lisa, who sat next to him in English class. When he arrived home, his mother was frantic. She cried until he promised to come straight home.

Hannah also had to parent herself when she was young. Her mother depended on Hannah and her sister to run the household. Both Hannah and he were serious people who didn't know how to have fun. During their courtship and early marriage, he enjoyed her enthusiasm. She came alive when he took her to a Broadway show or to dinner. Her excitement turned him on. He couldn't wait to marry her.

In the early years, she encouraged him to explore his creative side at work. When they adopted Ethan, he was proud to be a family. Then the younger children came along and drained them of energy. He felt empty. Hannah was no longer interested in him. As the children grew, he couldn't stand the constant bickering about Ethan. He was sick of having to defend him. His goal was to revel in his accomplishments and live in New York. He wanted a wife who enjoyed entertaining CEO's, authors and movie stars. Hannah was not capable of living the kind of life he now envisioned for himself. His first splurge would be a penthouse apartment in the Excelsior on East 57th Street.

Last week, he had a realtor show him an apartment that rented for two thousand dollars a month. From the living room and master bedroom, he had a view of the East River. He watched a tugboat pull a large ship out to sea. In the study, he imagined himself writing a book on how-to-succeed in advertising that he had been thinking about writing for the past five years. But his household didn't allow him the quiet he needed to write. Irwin tried to talk to Hannah. "We never have any fun. I want to do more in the city."

"I'm happy, Irwin. The city is too hectic. I like spending time with you at home." She gave him a hug. He didn't know what to say. She was naïve to think that they had a good marriage. When he looked into her trusting eyes, he didn't have the heart to tell her that he didn't love her anymore.

That evening, sitting in the den, Irwin tried to figure out what he was going to do about his marriage. He could hear Ethan yelling at Warren to "hurry up" in the bathroom. He prayed he wouldn't have to intervene, but when Ethan started kicking the bathroom door, he ran up the stairs. "What's going on?" Irwin asked.

"I have to pee. Warren's taking too long," said Ethan.

"We have four bathrooms in the house. Go into another one," he

45

said.

"Warren should get out. He's too damn slow," said Ethan.

"I don't care which other bathroom you use, but leave Warren alone," said Irwin. Ethan scowled at him. Irwin glared back. Ethan banged on the bathroom door, again.

"I'm not leaving. Warren, get the hell out of there." Ethan hit the door with his fist. "Stop it," wailed Warren from inside the bathroom. Irwin smacked Ethan across his cheek. Ethan, wide-eyed, looked at him with utter amazement. Irwin felt ashamed. "Oh my God," he said. He wanted to tell Ethan he was sorry, but he was unable to move. He couldn't believe that he had struck his own son. His father had never hit him. He felt wretched. Before he could apologize, Ethan slammed his bedroom door behind him. Irwin, taking deep breaths, tried to regain his composure. He would never have hit Ethan if he weren't disgusted. He didn't belong in this house. He belonged with Penelope. He had to leave soon. Otherwise, he was going to do something that he regretted more than smacking Ethan.

The following evening, as Irwin dragged himself onto the Long Island Railroad for home, he smelled Penelope's perfume on his clothes. He had spent a romantic lunch at The Copenhagen Restaurant with her. When he rubbed his fingers he could feel the softness of her skin. Reaching into his pocket, he took out the scarf she had given him and pressed it to his lips. The train was pulling him back to a life he no longer wanted.

As soon as he entered the house, he knew something was wrong. It was too quiet. Rusty, the dog, whimpered. "Come here, boy." Rusty cowered.

In the kitchen, Hannah was sitting at the table with her head bowed. Her arm was bandaged. She lifted her face drained of all color. She said the pain from the tetanus shot was excruciating. Rusty bit her because she stepped between him and Ethan. Hannah believed Ethan had antagonized the dog. Irwin thought something else made the dog turn vicious because Rusty was a timid animal. Ethan, upset, left the house. Irwin worried Ethan was missing. When Ethan was distraught, he lashed out. If Ethan fought with his mother, he must have felt misunderstood.

In the bedroom, Irwin threw his jacket onto the bed. Hannah had exaggerated Ethan's role in what happened. Ethan was only roughhousing with the dog. Irwin understood that aggression was important for competition, especially in advertising. He wondered if he could make a businessman of Ethan. He imagined Ethan, in a Brooks Brother's suit, taking the train with him to work. Ethan was bright enough to do anything he wanted, but he needed Irwin's guidance. Irwin had to go out and find him. His first hunch was that he must have gone to the club on the Sound. It was where they both went to calm down.

In the car, he realized Hannah couldn't keep Ethan safe. Irwin was going to have to take him when he left but Penelope would never accept him. Ethan would ruin their relationship. For the first time, he considered sending Ethan away to school. He couldn't stand the idea of being separated from his son, but he needed Penelope. They deserved a honeymoon period, a time to be intimate. As a new husband, Irwin didn't want Penelope to feel jealous.

After they made love, Penelope would want to wear the sheer negligees Irwin had bought her and lounge in bed. Irwin couldn't be the husband Penelope deserved if Ethan lived with them. Irwin would find the best private school for Ethan. He didn't care how much money it cost. He felt like a failure, but he didn't know what else to do. It would be best for everyone.

The Throg's Neck Bridge blazed with lights overlooking the Sound. The sky was alive with stars. Ethan was facing the water. With his back to Irwin, Ethan looked slender, as though he barely existed. Irwin slowly approached him. "What happened, son?"

"Mom got the dog excited and he bit her." Ethan shrugged his shoulders.

"That's not what Mom said," said Irwin.

"Mom's a liar," said Ethan.

"Mom came between you and the Rusty. She said you were provoking him."

"It's Mom's fault," said Ethan.

"You have to stop acting like this," said Irwin.

"I can't help it." Ethan lowered his head.

"You must try," said Irwin.

"Are you mad at me?" Ethan asked.

"I'm not happy you frightened your mother," said Irwin.

"Is Rusty okay?" Ethan asked.

"I didn't see him, but Mom needed shots," said Irwin.

"Do I have to go home?" Ethan wrapped his arms around himself.

"For the moment, but can you keep a secret I haven't told Mom?"

"My mouth is sealed." Ethan made believe he was zippering his mouth.

"I'm going to move into the city by myself," Irwin said.

"You mean leave Mom?" His eyes widened.

"Yes, we need a separation," he said.

"You can't leave me here with her." Ethan grabbed his arm.

"After I'm settled, I'll take you with me," said Irwin.

"Can't I go with you, now?" Ethan pleaded.

"Be patient; we'll work it out," said Irwin.

Irwin put his arm around Ethan. They silently watched the tips of the waves. In the distance, he heard a foghorn. Irwin imagined he was on his boat with Penelope and Ethan, the wind at their backs. Irwin was not sure what Ethan was thinking, but Ethan needed him.

After they came home, he told Hannah, "I'm too tired to talk." He went into the den and turned on the television. His head throbbed. He imagined Penelope massaging his forehead. He was revolted by the idea of lying next to Hannah's damaged body. He was helpless to make a better life for Ethan as long as he lived here. Hannah was incapable of being the mother Ethan needed. He wasn't a good husband to Hannah. Irwin wanted more than she was capable of giving him. He closed his eyes and tried to make his mind blank.

Irwin's eyes were still closed when Hannah entered the den and whispered his name. He prayed she would leave. He didn't want to hurt her. She was still recuperating from her surgery. The best thing for him to do was to say nothing. He gritted his teeth. But when she spoke in a complaining voice, he opened his eyes and glared at her.

She should have stayed away from him. "I'm not in a good mood. Leave me alone."

"I have to talk. What happened with Ethan?" she asked.

"Nothing," he said.

"Why are you shutting me out?" she asked.

Hannah was asking for trouble. She wouldn't stop talking. His cheek muscles pulsed. He had no choice. He knew how to shut her up. "I want a separation."

When she began to cry, he walked out of the room because he was afraid of blasting her, blaming her for driving him and Ethan away. After he had packed a bag, he climbed into his Porsche. Before pulling out of the driveway, he rolled back the top. It was a luminous full moon. When he looked at the house, he saw Ethan's light on. Poor Ethan! Irwin hated to leave him, for now, with his mother. Without really thinking about where he was going, he rode back down to the club. The only sound was the waves crashing against the sea wall. He breathed in the salty air. He felt invigorated. In the distance, he could see New York City, bright and alive, beckoning him.

Tilted: Ethan

~

Ethan stretches out his hand to feel Marion's warm body but she isn't there. "Damn," he says to himself. He forgot today Marion starts her job at Record Haven. He doesn't know why she needs a job. They're making ends meet, between his gigs and the money her parents send for living expenses. But Marion has decided to tell her parents about their living together. First, she takes the job because her parents may stop her allowance. Marion's plan doesn't make sense to Ethan because the less his mother knows about him, the better he feels.

Light pouring in through the half-closed blind illuminates the unpainted chest of drawers, the lopsided mirror and bookshelf built from crates. Kicking off the thin sheet, Ethan can't stand the heat. His shabby surroundings are part of a movie set he's tired of being on. Maybe he should call his dad and visit him and Penelope on Long Island where the food is good, the accommodations even better, especially the central air.

Last time his father grilled lobster, corn on the cob and served a good Sauvignon Blanc. Nearly drunk, Ethan fell asleep on the soft bed in their guesthouse. Early the next morning, the still pool water tempted Ethan to slip off his underwear and jump in. Looking up at the house, he saw the bedroom curtain move. He faced the window and then turned back to the pool where he dived into the cool water. Later, his dad told him, "It's not respectful to swim naked. You upset Penelope. Don't do it again." He apologized but secretly hoped Penelope had a good look at his well-hung penis, different from his father's shriveled one. Still, Ethan has to admit his father is distinguished with graying sideburns and trim figure. He stays in shape by playing tennis or golf at his club. But wearing an Armani suit with tasseled loafers like his dad is not for him. The advertising company his father built is filled with slick, dishonest people, except for his dad, of course. Ethan refuses to sit behind a desk, working nine to five, surrounded by "ass holes."

Ethan groans as he lifts his lanky frame off the mattress on the floor. He snaps the shade only to see a sooty rooftop, underwear on a clothesline and a heap of rusty cars in the distance, not exactly the beautiful New York skyline advertised in the ads his dad writes. The city makes him sick, but right now there's no alternative. He doesn't have the money to fly back to Los Angeles. If he closes his eyes he can see the boardwalk where he roller bladed or surfed. Across from the ocean was the "Red Parrot Restaurant" where he sometimes worked as a waiter when he was desperate. But then he ran out of money and places to crash. His father flew him home because he promised to complete two more courses and receive his college diploma. So far, Ethan has stretched college over seven years.

Ethan stares at his dark brown eyes and hawk-like nose in the mirror. Tying his long black hair back into a ponytail makes his face look thinner. Marion says he's "gaunt" and tells him to "eat more." He laughs because Marion is skinny, but calls herself "petite." He met her at New York University while sitting across from her at the library. He noticed her right away with her long black hair, pale skin and shapely legs. Sighing, she was struggling over a calculus book.

"Can I help you?" he asked.

"Why, have you taken calculus?" Marion asks.

"Yes. Of course," he said.

He had taken calculus as a freshman, but he was still able to figure out what she needed to know. He's good at math or any school subject when he makes a slight effort but the problem is school doesn't challenge him. He listens to the teachers drone on about information he already understands. In his last physics class at UCLA, he figured out formulas before any other student. The professor accused him of cheating. Ethan was so insulted he flicked his pencil at the teacher's face and was suspended from class for a week. But the teacher learned his lesson and didn't mess with Ethan when he returned.

Ethan picks up his guitar on the way out the door. He walks down the six flights to street level where he tosses the beer bottles left by slobs into the trash. Mrs. Gomez wearing bright red lipstick sits in the window of her first floor apartment while her kid whines in the background. He waves goodbye to her before putting on his sunglasses. Walking down the street, Ethan feels good. When he passes a blind man with a panting German Shepherd on the corner of Tenth Avenue and Fortieth Street, Ethan places a quarter in the man's cup. "Get your dog some water," he says.

At Joe's bar he opens the door and steps into darkness. He takes off his sunglasses and his eyes need a moment to readjust. The room smells of piss and beer.

"Hey, where have you been? I thought you were going to play last night?" Joe asks as he removes the apron covering his beer belly.

"Sorry, Marion was lecturing me because she had to get a job. She said I wasn't able to earn a decent living so she was going to have to help support the two of us."

"Women can be a real pain." Joe shakes his head.

Ethan and Joe strum their guitars for a while in silence. When Ethan closes his eyes to feel the notes, a sense of serenity fills him. Nothing else matters but the music. He felt the same contentment when his dad would sit on his bed to play their guitars together; too bad those days are long gone.

After they are done jamming, Joe offers him a beer and a burger. While they eat, ketchup drips on Joe's chin.

"I should go to class." Ethan wipes his face with a napkin.

"I wish I'd gone to college but I don't have a rich dad like you."

"Yeah, I didn't have a dad to hand me a bar to run," says Ethan.

"If I thought I could get through school, I'd sell it," says Joe.

"School is a pain in the ass," says Ethan.

Ethan looks at the pinball machine in the corner. The colored lights are beckoning him to play. "You're not going to play, again?" Joe asks.

"Just one game." Ethan leaves his guitar on the bar.

Ethan puts in a quarter and pulls the release. He presses the levers as fast as he can but he can't break his highest score. On the last ball, he picks up the machine and tilts it. Red, green and yellow lights flash and the machine makes a loud noise like a siren.

"Damn, Ethan. Leave the machine alone," says Joe. He comes over and pulls the plug.

"I can't help myself. I hate to lose," says Ethan.

"Go to school," says Joe.

Ethan leaves the guitar with Joe for safekeeping. As he walks in the direction of the university, he finds a copy of *The New York Times* on a bench and sits down outside his classroom. While reading an article about a couple who chained their son to a radiator, he is reminded of his days at the Jewish Residential Treatment Center, where his parents sent him after the final incident with the principal.

"Did you dump the milk on Jared's head or not?" The principal glared at him.

"He wouldn't get out of my seat," said Ethan.

"What difference does that make?" the principal asked.

"I've sat in the same seat in the cafeteria for three years. It's mine. Don't you understand?" Ethan screamed.

"I'm afraid you don't understand, Ethan. You're suspended for a week."

"You can't suspend me for something that's not my fault. Jared made me do it. He forced my hand," says Ethan.

"Jared didn't do anything to provoke you." The principal leaned over the desk.

"You can't do this to me," Ethan took off his shoe, aiming it for the principal's head.

The Center made him crazy. There were too many rules: when to get up, what to read, and when to study. A list of acceptable behaviors written in large block letters was laminated to every door. He'd close his eyes as he sat on the toilet so he wouldn't have to see the paper staring at him. Ethan had been a model citizen until they assigned him a roommate, Paul, who had big white pus pimples with yellow edges completely covering his face. Ethan's first thought was to buy him a pimple popper and astringent as a peace offering. But when the oaf plunked his suitcase down in the middle of the room and sat on Ethan's bed, they were in trouble. Paul had no sense of boundaries, especially when not to cross them.

"Listen, could you sit on your own bed?" Ethan asked politely.

"What's the difference?" Paul said.

"Half the room's mine and half's yours, so let's keep it that way," Ethan said.

Paul dragged his suitcase and lifted it onto his own bed. Inside it was filled with candy bars: Snickers, Almond Joys, Musketeers and Babe Ruth's, Ethan's favorite.

"You obviously have a sweet tooth," Ethan said.

"Don't think I'm going to share with you. I'll keep them on my side of the room." Paul sneered.

Every day Ethan picked up candy wrappers from the floor, the desk and the bathtub. When he asked Paul to clean up after himself, he just laughed.

One day, Paul clogged the toilet with his candy wrappers and it overflowed, truly disgusting. After the plumber left the room, Ethan asked Paul, "Can you spare a Babe Ruth?"

"I wouldn't give you a crumb." Paul bit into Snicker bar.

Ethan formed his hand into a fist. His face felt flushed. "Are you sure you don't want to reconsider?"

"Make me." Paul laughed.

Ethan jumped off the bed. With all his strength he punched Paul in the nose. Blood covering Paul's face and shirt, he ran screaming down the hall. Lying back on his pillow, Ethan noticed the splattered blood on his yellow shirt had turned into orange spots. He chuckled, opened the wrapper of a Babe Ruth bar and began to chew it. The chocolate tasted better than ever.

Right now, Ethan craves a Babe Ruth. He doesn't give a damn about class. At the corner grocery store with a faded awning, he chooses one. Since he's hungry, he bites into the candy while waiting on line. A squat foreign lady with black hairs growing out of a mole on her chin looks at him. She says, "You pay for that?"

"I'm going to pay. Can't you see I'm waiting on line?" Ethan sneers.

"You better pay! You not eat, pay!" she yells.

"What the hell is wrong with you?" Ethan throws a dollar's worth of change at her. He walks out while she's still screaming at him. "You're crazy," he yells. Walking on the street, he wishes he had pulled the hairs out of her mole, one at a time. He's never going back into that rattrap, again.

Ethan surveys the street to see if anyone else is going to give him a problem. A woman walks past him pushing a screaming infant. Children are annoying but if he ignores them, they leave him alone. That's what his own parents did, abandoned him at birth. Then his adoptive parents kicked him out when he refused to conform to their stupid rules like sitting with the family at dinnertime, going to school or taking out garbage. He liked to play his guitar, smoke a little weed and party with his friends. No one was going to control him and turn him into a geek.

His adoptive mother is a geek. When she was young, she earned a master's in literature but never used it because she married his father. She loves to pour over books on mythology. He hasn't talked to her in several months, not since his father forced him to thank her for the check she sent on his twenty-fifth birthday.

At the next pay phone, he closes the door to make a "collect" call.

"Hi, Mom, how's it going?"

"How are you, Ethan?"

"Could be better. The city is too hot, disgusting," Ethan says.

"Aren't you taking classes?" his mom asks.

"So what does that have to do with the weather?" Ethan asks.

"I just meant maybe it would keep your mind off being hot," his mother says.

"Stop pressuring me about school!" Ethan yells.

"I'm sorry I didn't realize I was pressuring you," his mother says.

"I have to go. You're dragging me down." Ethan slams the phone.

He is angry with himself for trying to connect with his mother. She doesn't understand him and never will. She's a lost cause, locked in her suburban world where people do what is expected of them. Since the divorce, his mother has gone back to school to become a history teacher. He can't imagine a more boring job except being a garbage collector. No, that job is interesting because garbage men sort through other people's junk and secrets. They can blackmail the customers whose garbage they collect, lucky guys.

His dad is lucky because he escaped with Penelope, a smart move since she is sexy—large breasts, tight ass. Too bad she reads *People Magazine* as though it's the Bible. On the other hand, he feels sorry for his dad stuck with a nitwit. After she finishes decorating the house they just bought in Kings Point, he wonders what they'll talk about. To cheer up his dad, he dials his private number.

"Nice to hear from you; how are classes?" his dad asks.

"School is great," Ethan says.

"I'm glad. I knew things would work out if you moved to New York, Ethan."

"Are you free for lunch? I'm starving." Ethan licks his lips.

"Not today but come by the office tomorrow. I know a new sushi place. You'll love it," says his dad.

When Ethan hangs up, he steps out of the booth with renewed vigor and stretches his long arms. Talking to his father makes him feel better because his dad understands him. He can already taste the sushi in his mouth, cool and sweet. Maybe he should phone his dad back and ask him to take Marion, too.

It's too bad that Marion has to work on such a warm day. At the Chinese take-out on the corner, he orders two egg rolls, fried rice and her favorite—shrimp with vegetables. The hell with class! His girlfriend needs sustenance. Outside the restaurant, he borrows a shiny red bike leaning against the wall. He figures any idiot who forgets to lock up his bike in New York deserves to have it borrowed. Weaving in and out of traffic Ethan feels like a rat going through a maze. Cursing anybody in his way, Ethan cuts in front of a Lincoln Continental. From the car, a bald man with a red face yells, "Asshole." His wife and two teenagers scream, too.

Ethan yells, "You want to see an asshole?" At the next red light, he stands up on the bike, pulls down his pants and moons them. He turns around to see their surprised expressions. He figures they never saw such a nice-looking ass. Cycling faster, Ethan leaves them in the dust.

He drops the bike in the alley outside Record Haven. In the air-conditioned store, he's touches his cool skin. He wonders if there's a correlation between body temperature and customers' willingness to spend their money. If so, they will be shelling out plenty of cash today. When he goes home, he will try to figure out on his computer the statistical correlation between the two. Since computers turn him on, during an internship in Los Angeles, he worked for IBM. When he found a glitch in their program, they gave him a bonus—one thousand bucks.

He watches Marion putting away CD's. She's wearing a sexy black shirt that shows off her ample cleavage and a short skirt highlights her great set of legs. He imagines taking her into the storage room to run his hand up her smooth thigh until he reaches wet, moist flesh, tasty. Ethan is also excited by Marion's silky hair that reaches down to her narrow hips. Last time, after a bath together, Ethan toweled Marion's body and brushed her hair. When Marion wrapped her legs around him, he screwed her while leaning against the sink.

Ethan stops daydreaming when a young boy with streaked blonde hair stands close to Marion. Leaning over the CD's, the boy is ogling Marion's breasts. The boy obviously doesn't know that Marion's body is his private property and the boy is trespassing. Casually, Ethan walks up to them.

"Hi babe," He pulls Marion to him.

"I didn't expect to see you." Marion laughs.

"I bought you some lunch." Ethan shows her the bag.

"I can't eat now. I'm helping a customer," Marion says.

"I can get someone else to help me, Marion." The boy lowers his eyelids.

"No, it's okay. Ethan is leaving."

"I am?" Ethan says.

"I'm working, Ethan," Marion says.

I'm not leaving but I'll go sit over there." He points to a chair. "Don't keep her too long." He glares at the boy.

Ethan wonders why the boy knows Marion's name. He shouldn't

be on intimate terms with his girl. Does he know she has a birthmark on her left thigh or her right breast is slightly bigger than the left one?

The crisp golf shirt and khaki pants reminds Ethan of Marion's father. Her parents flew in from Arkansas to see Marion and took them to dinner at a Chinese restaurant where Marion's mother wiped the benches with a napkin before sitting down. A painting of a dragon breathed fire on Ethan throughout dinner. Her father in his golf shirt and khaki pants had thin blonde hair with clear blue eyes, the kind that penetrated his soul. Ethan refused to make eye contact with him. Instead he stared at Marion's mother who twirled the toy umbrella in her drink. She ordered one apricot sour after another.

"What are you studying in school?" her father asked.

"I'm planning to go to law school," Ethan lied.

"What kind of law?" her mother asked.

"I want to prosecute criminals," Ethan leaned over the table.

Afterwards, when Marion and he were lying in bed, she asked, "How did you know that my dad wanted to be a lawyer? He had to take over his father's hardware store when my grandfather died."

"I didn't know but I could tell he wants you to be with some kind of white collar professional." He tweaked her breast.

"You're too funny." Marion grabbed his hand.

They both started laughing until Marion kissed him passionately, placing his hand between her legs.

Now turning around in his chair, Ethan notices a fat man behind the cash register. He is giving him dirty looks. He's probably mad because Ethan isn't buying anything. Standing up to look at the CD's, Ethan puts on headphones to listen to "Don't Look Back in Anger." Now that's a funny song because if someone pisses him off, he's going to get back. He never forgets an insult, not even a small one. Watching Marion and the boy, Ethan drums his fingers on the CD case. Finally, Marion walks over to him.

"How about eating lunch? I brought your favorite–Chinese. It's getting cold," Ethan says.

"Ethan, I don't get a lunch break for another half hour. Why are you here? You don't need to check up on me."

"Who's the boy?" Ethan asks.

"His name is David. I know him from my literature class."

"You know him?"

"Yes. I go to class with other boys. You're not the only boy I talk to."

"Well, I don't like the way he looks at you. He wants to get in your pants."

"Stop being annoying. He's nice to me."

At that moment the fat man comes from behind the counter to walk over to them. The pin on his shirt reads, "Tom-Manager."

"Marion, is there a problem?" Tom asks.

"No, this is my boyfriend, Ethan. He was just leaving."

Ethan sees Tom's eyes are covered with spidery red veins. He must have partied hard last night. Tom better not try to party with Marion. Ethan imagines punching him in the stomach but Tom will throw up mashed chips and sour beer from last night. But Ethan doesn't want to get dirty and the smell of vomit makes him puke.

"I was just going. I'll come back to have lunch with Marion."

"I don't care what she does on her own thirty minutes but now she is supposed to be helping customers." Tom says.

"Sorry, Marion, I'll be back in a half hour," says Ethan.

Ethan pretends to walk away but instead he goes into the alley. Surveillance is important. Ethan creeps out of the alley to lean against the wall across from the store. With a perfect view of Marion, Ethan plans on protecting her from David, a college kid who tallies the number of girls he screws.

Ethan isn't like David. He has been with only one girl besides Marion. Girls make him jittery. Since he can't figure out what they want, he stays away from them. Marion is different because she likes the same music and has a similar weird sense of humor. They have been to the Rocky Horror Show fifteen times together. The first time they had sex, he came before entering her. She didn't laugh but fondled him until he was hard again and finished the job. Because Marion is the only girl who turns him on, Ethan is never going to give her up, certainly not for a twerp.

A half-hour later on Marion's lunch break, they sit on a bench in a nearby park.

"You don't look too happy to see me." He offers Marion an egg roll.

"I'm glad to see you but you almost cost me my job. The manager says you can't come in while I'm working," says Marion.

"Isn't that against the law to kick out a customer?" Ethan asks.

"I don't know but I'm asking you to stay away from my work." Marion licks a piece of egg roll from her lip.

"What about that kid, David. Does he have to stay away, too?" Ethan asks.

"David didn't do anything. He's a customer." Marion shakes her head.

"I'm a customer too. I told you. I don't like the way he looks at you." Ethan takes Marion's hand.

"He is just a boy from class. Stop worrying." Marion leans over to kiss Ethan. Her breath smells of fried rice as he pulls her toward him. He feels her heart beating rapidly through her thin shirt and he cups her breast. She rubs his thigh.

"You turn me on, girl," Ethan whispers in her ear.

"Tonight, I'll turn you on more. Be patient," Marion smiles.

When they finish lunch, he waves goodbye. Walking back into the store, Marion is swallowed by the building. Ethan's heart races because he's afraid she may not come back and he can't be without her. He goes around the side of the building to look for the bike but it's not there, a bad sign.

He knows one way to keep Marion happy is to surprise her with a special steak dinner. Ethan walks to the butcher shop where Mr. Desa with hairy thick wrists stands behind the counter. He is chopping ribs with a cleaver that glints as he raises it in the air. His apron is a kaleidoscope of blood, neat colors ranging from orange to bright red.

"Hey, I haven't seen you in a while. Come on, I got a good steak for you," says Mr. Desa.

Ethan follows Mr. Desa into the freezer and swings the carcasses hanging from hooks on the ceiling. The meat feels moist to his touch. Ethan wonders if Mr. Desa sells horsemeat; it's supposed to be a tasty treat but he doesn't think Marion will enjoy it.

"This place is terrific." Ethan breathes in the smell of bloody meat.

"You think so? Maybe you want a job?" Mr. Desa asks.

"That would be cool. Would I get to use the cleaver?" Ethan asks.

"Sure, you crazy kid, every day—chop, chop, chop." Mr. Desa moves his hand up and down.

When they step out of the freezer Ethan rubs his hands together. "I'm freezing," he says.

"If you stay in the freezer too long, you could get frozen to death." Mr. Desa slaps Ethan's back.

Mr. Desa wraps two steaks for him. On the way home, Ethan looks on the street for David. Ethan's plan is to grab him by the collar and drag him into the butcher's freezer to leave him hanging from one of the hooks. The twerp won't chase after Marion any more.

Ethan is curious what frozen people look like, probably better than when they are dead. When he was thirteen, his grandmother died. He wanted to see her body in the coffin but the casket was closed. When he asked his mother if he could sneak a peek, she cried louder. His dad told him, "Jewish people never have opened caskets; Stop being so curious."

"I can't help it," Ethan shrugged his shoulders.

"You're upsetting your mother. Stop it right now. Do you hear me? I mean it!"

"Sorry, Dad."

Ethan imagines his grandmother's rotting body deep in the ground. He wonders what his dad would say if he becomes a butcher's apprentice instead of a college graduate. His dad would lecture him on "how are you going to support yourself when I'm gone?" Ethan hates that talk because he can't imagine his life without his dad.

When Ethan arrives home, he sets the table for two. He cuts

tomatoes and celery into small pieces the way Marion showed him. Snapping the ends of string beans, he places them in a pot while he chews on one of them, crunchy. When the phone rings, he picks it up and Marion is on the line. "Hello. I'm going to be late. One of the evening employees didn't show up."

"You can't be late. I'm making your favorite dinner-steak," Ethan says.

"You're sweet. But we need the extra money. I don't want Tom to be angry with me," says Marion.

"I don't care about the money. I don't give a damn about Tom. Come home!" Ethan yells.

"Don't yell at me. I can't help it, sorry," says Marion.

Before Ethan can say another word, the line goes dead. Standing in the kitchen holding the phone, he is astonished that Marion hung up on him. She has never done that before. Ethan slams down the phone. The job is already changing her to be more concerned about money than their relationship. She's like the wives in his hometown of Roslyn who own Range Rovers and wear three-carat diamond wedding rings. Their husbands work twelve hours a day to please them, commuting everyday to New York from Long Island. Husbands with weary faces, wearing soiled shirts and loose ties. Men, who can't wait to get home, crack open a Heineken, watch the sports channel and yell at their kids not to stand in front of the television. He doesn't want that kind of life for himself and Marion. He turns off the stove and places the steak in the refrigerator. If Marion continues her working, she'll leave him for a commuter or worse, try to turn him into one.

When he walks down the stairs, several of the stairwell lights are broken, again. He stumbles in the dark and collides with Mrs. Gomez on the first floor landing.

"Sorry, I didn't see you," he says.

"Don't worry. Why are you in such a hurry? Have to meet your girl?" Mrs. Gomez asks.

"Yes. I have to rescue her," says Ethan.

"Oh, you're a silly boy," laughs Mrs. Gomez.

Ethan knows there's nothing comical about the situation. Since Mrs. Gomez is divorced, she doesn't understand.

Outside Record Haven, he presses his face against the window to see Marion. Tom is busy ringing up a sale on the cash register. Marion is talking to another boy with their heads bent over the CD's. The boy shouldn't be flirting with her. Marion is oblivious of the fact that the store is a den of iniquity. She's too trusting, innocent and doesn't realize the boy wants to fondle her breasts. Marion and the boy are moving toward the aisle directly across from him. Ethan steps back into the alleyway. To his amazement, the red bike is back. It's a good sign. The bike is his friend and he rolls it out onto the sidewalk. Marion and the boy are standing outside by the front door. Ethan moves directly to the side of where Marion and the boy are standing. Marion's back is to him. The boy is drooling over Marion with his hand on her shoulder. He is going to molest her. When the boy steps back from Marion, Ethan picks up the bike with all his strength and hurls it at the boy. Marion screams. The boy falls to the ground. Howling, the boy cradles his legs. Ethan sees Tom, red-faced, shaking his fist as he picks up the phone.

"It's okay, Marion, you're safe," he says.

"What did you do? Have you lost your mind?" she screams.

Before Ethan can answer, police cars with loud sirens surround him. One burly cop throws him against the wall to handcuff him. The cop pushes his head down to fit him into the back seat of the squad car. When he looks out the window, he sees Marion crying with her thin arms wrapped around herself. He wishes he could touch the tears on her cheek, a good sign that Marion still loves him.

Warren: Add Out

~

Warren was attracted to Sylvia the first day he met her. When he was on the tennis team, she sat with a group of girlfriends and watched him volley. One day, after the team finished practicing, she entered the court. She flashed him a wide smile. "How about some pointers?"

"I'd be delighted," he said.

"You're so patient." She clumsily practiced serving the ball.

While he stood in back of her, he smelled her jasmine perfume in her long blonde hair that reminded him of a Japanese garden he never wanted to leave.

That day was the beginning of their three-year relationship. Although she wasn't a great athlete, he admired her energy. She marveled at his athletic prowess on the court. She told him she felt safe with him. They took dancing lessons. He learned to lead while she followed him gracefully as they moved across the floor doing the foxtrot. With her in his arms, he felt capable of anything. He was no longer the gawky boy who didn't go to his high school prom. Sylvia made him realize he could have fun. Her smile made him feel wanted, an emotion, which he had rarely felt as a child. At the end of six months, while at a dance lesson, he whispered into her ear. "I can imagine us waltzing at our wedding,"

"I can, too." She leaned into him.

Warren knew from that moment on that she was the girl he would marry. When he asked her to move in with him, she agreed. In the morning, he would rise early to make coffee for them. When he brought the mug to her side of the bed, she would thank him with a smooch. When they had been living together a month, Sylvia complained about how bossy her father was. She wished she didn't need his money, Warren said, "I'll take care of you.

"You will?" Sylvia snuggled against him. "I love you." She nibbled on his ear.

He kissed her luscious breasts. He couldn't believe he had such a terrific girlfriend. He imagined her in a lacy wedding dress that accented her tiny waist. They were under the hoopa overlooking Long Island Sound at his father's country club.

His father placed the carnation in the lapel of Warren's tuxedo. "She's a beautiful girl. A good catch," said his father. His sister, Nina, clapped the loudest when they left the room as husband and wife. His mother was relieved he wouldn't be alone. Finally, his dad was proud of him.

His dad and he have always had a precarious relationship. Too vividly, he remembers the evening that his mother told him and his sister, Nina, that their father was leaving the family. His older brother, Ethan, who fought constantly with him, wasn't home. Nina, seven years old, sat with her long brown hair covering her pixie face as she ate. Teasing her, Warren asked, "Does that hair make your hamburger taste better?" Nina's dark brown eyes lit up as she purposely chewed on strands of her hair. His mother had barbecued hamburgers; a charcoal smell filled the air. The orange sunset, casting a shadow on his mother's face, made it impossible for him to see her eyes. "Dad is moving out. After sleepaway camp, he won't be here."

"When will I see him?" Warren asked.

"None of my friends live without their daddies," Nina wailed.

"It's okay, Nina." Warren took her hand.

"I know, sweetheart. It's not my decision, but he will visit once a week."

His mother was right. After the summer, on Wednesdays, his father pulled up in his latest Porsche to take them to dinner.

The one activity he enjoyed with his father was tennis. The only time his father showed any patience was when he gave him a tennis lesson. He beamed when his father told him "terrific shot." They played weekly at the club. By the time Warren left for college, his father couldn't win a game off him. He encouraged him to try out for the tennis team. "You can beat the pants off anyone."

"I don't know, Dad. I'm not that good," Warren said sheepishly.

"Just try; that's all I'm asking." His father patted his back.

Since he didn't want to disappoint his dad, he attended the team tryouts. Much to his amazement, he was the only freshman to make the team. When he told his father, he said, "Maybe you'll become a tennis star. Won't that be something?"

"Sure, Dad." Warren hoped his dad was right.

Sylvia had admired his ability at tennis, but also his excellence as a student. Many nights, he had tutored her in chemistry and biology. Sometimes, when she became totally frustrated, he did her homework for her. She continued to brag to her friends that "our children will be smart like Warren."

Sylvia was less proud of him after he tore both his Anterior Cruciate Ligament's while playing tennis. He had been the star of the tennis team; now he could hardly volley. At the tennis matches, he had been known for his speed. He had reveled in the audience's applause. Sylvia would hang on him while the students congratulated him. He liked sharing the limelight with her. After the surgery, Warren obtained prescriptions for his pain from each orthopedist he saw, seven in all. He felt he could no longer control his legs, force them to play tennis.

The only place he felt competent was at the University of Miami's mental health center. He had already been promoted to chief crisis counselor. He oversaw three staff members and ran orientation sessions. As an undergraduate he had worked two jobs, one at the crisis center and another at a men's shelter, to make enough money to pay for his master's and their living expenses. Part of his goal was to put money away to pay for a diamond ring for Sylvia. Finally, after paying off the ring, he planned to ask her to marry him.

Limping to the car, he worried about how he was going to be able to drive downtown. Sylvia was looking for a dress to wear to an interview as a nutritionist at the health center where he worked. Recently, she complained that she wanted to do more on her own, but he found it difficulty believe her. He was also uncomfortable with the amount of money she spent on clothes since they were living on his monthly salary. At Saks, he found Sylvia in the dress department. Every time he saw her, he was overcome by how beautiful she was with her long blonde hair, size four waist and slim thighs.

She was a knockout. Her eyes widened when she saw him. "I didn't expect you."

"I figured I would surprise you." He kissed her cheek.

"I can pick out a dress by myself," she said crossly.

"You used to like me to go shopping with you," he said.

"Warren, that was over a year ago. I told you I need some space," said Sylvia.

"I'm sorry you're disappointed," he crossed his arms.

"We've discussed this before," she moved away.

"I thought you would like the company," he frowned.

"I don't have much time to find a dress. Can we talk about this later?" she asked.

"I guess so, but don't forget our dinner tonight," said Warren.

"I haven't forgotten. Please let me finish." She turned back to the dresses.

Warren couldn't work up the nerve to tell her that she needed to buy a less expensive dress. Instead he went to the perfume department where he found the kind Sylvia wore. He didn't want her to be angry with him. He charged it on his credit card. He hoped the card hadn't reached its limit. He had been putting off telling Sylvia that she had to get a job because all three of their credit cards were at maximum.

When he had first met Sylvia, he didn't know how much she liked to shop. She would beg him to go downtown with her. He remembered the day they went to look for an outfit for their senior prom. As she twirled around the mirrored dressing room, she modeled a white silky dress. Her cheeks were flushed and her eyes bright. "What do you think?"

"You look beautiful." He pulled her onto his lap and kissed her.

"I love you." She put her arms around his neck.

He bought the dress for her despite the expense. He wanted her to be the prettiest girl at the dance.

Warren limped back to the car. His parents were flying down this weekend, a delayed master's graduation celebration. He had hinted to them on the phone that he and Sylvia may be engaged. He hoped to ask Sylvia tonight at the Fountainbleu. He was especially looking forward to seeing his sister Nina's dark eyes light up when he gave her the good news. They had been best friends long before their parents' separation in 1967.

After his father had an affair with Penelope, his secretary, his mother wore dirty housedresses, barely climbed out of bed and was still for hours behind her bedroom door. When she came out, her eyes were red from weeping. Warren wanted to bang on the door and scream, "Get up. I need you," but he never did. He felt like a failure because he couldn't make it better. Instead when Nina came home from school, Warren helped her with homework and boiled hot dogs for them, seven nights a week. She relied on him. Now when Nina wanted to gross him out, she mentioned hot dogs. She was the only one who could make Warren laugh about that time in their lives. Nina still called him for advice on picking classes or to complain about boys. He told her to be patient.

He took two pain pills from the glove compartment and popped them into his mouth. His legs were throbbing, but he had a meeting at work with a couple of interns. He enjoyed his supervisory work and hoped one day to be the director of a mental health agency. Counseling clients made him feel important. When he arrived at the center, another staff member, Charlene, a tall brunette, greeted him with a hug.

Warren, holding his body stiffly, allowed himself to be held, but quickly moved toward his office. Charlene would date him in a second, but he would never cheat on Sylvia. He was surprised that Charlene was attracted to him since he had never flirted with her. He prided himself on being monogamous, but he wished he had his father's self-confidence with women.

The last time Warren flew in for spring break, he visited his father and Penelope in their penthouse apartment on 57th Street with views of Central Park. Dressed in a red silk kimono, Penelope, a tall, black-haired woman, sat surrounded by two howling Siamese cats. Her face painted with blue eyeshadow and dark red lips, she reminded Warren of a china doll hung to jiggle in the rear back car window. One of the cats jumped onto Warren's lap. He sneezed. "I'm allergic to cats."

"I would die if I didn't have Pierre and Jan." Penelope stroked the cat in her lap.

"Could you take the cat off my lap?" Warren asked.

"Just push Pierre off, gently," Penelope said.

The cat held steadfast, claws digging into Warren's flesh. "He won't budge. Take him off me, now," Warren gritted his teeth.

His father entered the room. "What's the matter, Warren?

"The cat is killing me. Take him off," Warren said.

"I'm surprised. Pierre is usually friendly." His father picked up the cat.

"I didn't know you were a cat lover," Warren said.

"They're good company for us," said his father.

"Really? I thought you liked dogs," Warren said disapprovingly.

"Penelope likes cats." His father's eyes narrowed.

Warren imagined taking Pierre and dropping him out the window. Then he'd watch Pierre fall the full twenty stories—blood and guts everywhere.

He never told his mother about the cats because she would have been upset. Warren had begged to have another dog but his mother refused after his father had Rusty put to sleep. Warren knew but couldn't prove that Ethan, his adopted brother, provoked Rusty to bite his mother. Ethan barred his teeth at Rusty and chased him around the yard. He hated Ethan for teasing the dog.

Warren imagined the warm snout of a dog nuzzling him awake in the morning. He'd name the dog, Chelsea, and train her to play catch. Recently, he approached Sylvia about it.

"You want a dog?" she asked, playing with his hair.

"Yes, I could take her on long walks," he said.

"I'll go with you," she said.

"It's not the same thing," he said.

"You could pet me." Sylvia, laughing, reached for him.

"You'll be my puppy?" He pulled her toward him.

"Woof, woof," laughed Sylvia. After kissing her, Warren realized he would have to wear Sylvia down until she agreed. He imagined being on the beach with Sylvia and their dog.

Warren finished his meeting with two counselors-in-training. They were both intelligent and understood during a crisis call to keep the client talking until he was willing to come in to the center. Warren spoke to them about their own counter-transference reactions. The more hopeless the client felt, then the more impotent they will feel as therapists. They should use their own reactions to better understand the client.

On the way home, Warren thought about his own sound advice. He wished he could be more objective about Sylvia. Recently, she was withdrawing from him, but the more she did, the more Warren felt the need to be with her.

Right after his surgery, Sylvia was frustrated that he couldn't participate in the activities they liked to do together. She insisted he play tennis even though his knees throbbed after one volley. She wanted him to go dancing, but he felt like a klutz. The more she pushed him, the more upset he became. He could rarely perform in bed. When he tried to explain to her how difficult it was for him, she pouted. He couldn't stand disappointing her. He took higher doses of his pain medication in the hope of recovering sooner.

When he reached home, Sylvia was not there. He was puzzled since she said she was coming straight home after shopping. He flipped through her date book to see if she was meeting a girlfriend, but it was empty. He wondered where the hell she was. He hated coming home to an empty house. It reminded him of when he was a child and his mother went back to school to become a teacher. Every sound bothered him, whether it was the buzz of the refrigerator or drip of the kitchen faucet. He was relieved to wait at the bus stop for Nina whose face beamed when she saw him and he felt calmer. She had turned into a smart kid, studying psychology and receiving straight A's her first semester of college.

In the bedroom, Warren took the black box out of the nightstand on his side of the bed. In the sunlight, the diamond ring glittered. Warren placed the ring back in the drawer, took out a bottle of pills and popped two more in his mouth. His mind wandered. On their honeymoon, he and Sylvia would sit on bar stools ai d drink margaritas overlooking the ocean. She would wear a flore l sarong that showed off her bronzed skin.

Warren was surprised when Sylvia woke him and she was not only fully clothed but also carrying a Saks bags. "Wait until you see what I bought," she said excitedly.

He patted the bed. "Come over here."

"Why?" she said coquettishly.

"You're damn sexy." He sat on the bed to pull her onto his lap.

"You really think I'm sexy?" She moved closer.

"Absolutely." He rubbed the back of her neck.

"I found the perfect dress for tomorrow's interview." She closed her eyes as he kneaded her shoulders. He studied her sculpted eyebrows and angled cheekbones. When he kissed her eyelids, Sylvia opened her eyes and rubbed her nose against his. He patted her rump as she went into the bathroom. He shook his head because just being near Sylvia made it impossible for him to say "no" to her buying sprees.

Leaning out the door, Sylvia held a pill bottle, Tylenol with codeine. "This bottle is empty? What are you doing? Popping them like candy?" Sylvia threw the bottle into the garbage.

"What do you mean?" His eyes widened.

"When did you open this bottle?" she asked.

"I don't remember," he said quietly.

"How often are you taking them?" She sounded worried.

"Only when my knees hurt." He reached for Sylvia.

"What does that mean?" she asked.

"I'm not a child. I'm handling it," he said.

"Just be careful. Don't overdo it. You're making it worse." Sylvia frowned.

"Okay, okay." He silenced her with a kiss.

That evening, he put on a new blue suit for their special dinner.

"Wow, you look handsome. I'm going to wear the red dress you bought me," she said.

His eyes followed her while she undressed. Lying on the bed, he watched her dab perfume behind her ears and between her breasts. When she realized he was watching, she came over to him. She undid his fly and caressed his penis, but he couldn't get an erection. "It's my fault, isn't it?" she whispered.

"No, I'm just worried about our future." He touched her cheek.

"Are you sure?" she asked.

"I wish we were both still undergraduates," she sighed.

"We'll have a fabulous dinner and act like undergraduates." He stroked her hair.

At the Fountainbleu, they sat at a table overlooking the ocean. A pianist played softly in the background. The waiters reminded him of ushers who were waiting to escort them down the aisle. Warren watched the crested waves crashing against the sea wall. The smell of the salt air invigorated him. The candles flickered making shadows on the table. He imagined the two them were movie stars. He had been planning this moment for over a year. The waves were applauding him. This night was the most important one of his life. Warren took Sylvia's smooth hands in his. They were soft with crimson nail polish. He leaned forward. "Will you marry me?"

"I don't know what to say." Sylvia withdrew her fingers.

"What's wrong?" asked Warren.

"I'm confused." She bowed her head.

"About what?" Warren whispered.

"I love you. I'm not sure about marriage right now." She clasped her hands.

"What exactly do you mean?" Warren asked.

"I need more time," said Sylvia.

"Time for what?" Warren's eyebrows slanted inward.

"We just graduated. I promise; just be patient with me." Sylvia leaned over and briskly patted his hand. Warren felt his skin shrivel like his grandfather's before he died. He saw himself lying on a hospital bed, oxygen mask over his mouth, as he admired Sylvia's lined face. He couldn't imagine being married to anyone else. He fingered the black box in his pocket, but said nothing.

On the way home, Sylvia turned on the radio while they rode in silence. Warren couldn't believe that Sylvia turned him down. The only explanation was that he had become a poor lover since his injury. He realized even though Sylvia hadn't complained, she was disappointed in him. He remembered she had actually started playing tennis with Brad, a law student. He questioned what would happen if he stopped taking the drugs for his knees, but he couldn't stand the discomfort.

The next day, Sylvia left early for her interview. On his way to work, Warren saw her sitting on a bench with Brad. Warren stepped behind thick bushes. He wondered what happened to Sylvia's appointment. Brad and Sylvia were deep in conversation. Her face was glowing. Their knees were touching.

Warren slowly walked to their bench. He wiped his sweaty hands on his pants. Sylvia was engrossed in conversation with Brad who thought he was cool because he drove a red corvette. He imagined tying Brad up, driving him in his corvette to the nearest cliff and pushing the car off the ledge.

Warren realized he was not being reasonable. He took deep breaths and concentrated on his warm feelings for Sylvia. He said, "Hi," in a casual voice. He leaned down to kiss her on the mouth but she turned her face. He planted his kiss on her cheek.

"We're waiting to be interviewed." Sylvia clasped her hands.

"Brad's interviewing for a job, too?" Warren frowned.

"Yes. They've two openings." Sylvia bit her lip.

"Really?" Warren asked.

"It's just a coincidence." Sylvia said.

Warren looked into Sylvia's sea-green eyes to see if she was lying but he was unable to tell. They reminded him of Ethan's turbulent eyes. "I'm going to work. Walk me."

"I wish I could but we have to leave in a minute." Sylvia flashed a wide smile.

"I'd really like you to come with me." Warren glared at Brad.

"You can go," Brad said quietly to Sylvia.

"Who's talking to you?" Warren said angrily.

"Please, I have to go to this interview. Won't you be late for work?" she pleaded.

"I know, but I really wish you'd come with me," Warren said loudly.

"You can't lose your job. We need it." Sylvia touched his arm.

"I'll go, but I'm not happy about it," Warren said bitterly.

"I promise I'll phone you after the interview." Sylvia said with sincerity.

"Definitely, call me," he said.

During a counseling session with a female student, he concentrated on the freshman's fear of going home with poor grades. By the end of the hour, she was coping better with the feeling her parents would be disappointed. Warren felt helpful, but his confidence faded, after the student left and he had not heard from Sylvia. He limped to the bathroom where he sat on the toilet seat. He rubbed his knees, sharp jabbing pain. Warren wondered if he had been blind to the fact that Sylvia was fooling around with Brad. His mother hadn't known his dad was sleeping with Penelope. Maybe, while he was busy working to take care of her, Sylvia was sleeping with Brad. Yet, she couldn't be fooling around because he would never touch another woman. He prided himself never to cheat on a girlfriend and on being loyal. He didn't want to live alone like his mother. He couldn't imagine making a meal for one or sleeping alone. He didn't know how his mother could stand it. In the middle of the night, Sylvia's slight snoring comforted him.

Warren paced in the office. He ran his hand through his wavy hair. He had to speak to someone. The only person to call was Nina. He prayed she would be home as he telephoned her. As soon as she picked up the phone, he relaxed. Warren told her about Brad and Sylvia. "I think they are fooling around."

"That's terrible. I'm sorry," said Nina.

"What am I going to do?" His voice cracked.

"Maybe it's not true," said Nina.

"I have a bad feeling about them."

"Try talking to Sylvia before you get too worked up," said Nina.

"What if she gets upset?" Warren asked.

"It doesn't matter. You need to know the truth," said Nina.

After limping to the car, Warren drove home. His stomach rumbled. On the side of the road, he opened the door to throw up. He stopped at a Mobil station's bathroom to clean his face. He was disgusted with his own weakness. He wished he were more "manly" like his father. Penelope never upstaged him. Back in the car, he realized that Sylvia didn't know Warren meant business. He would be firmer with her like his father was with Penelope. He would insist they get married. He wouldn't wait any longer. They need to find a justice of the peace this afternoon. She would complain that she wanted a big wedding. After they were officially married, she could have any damn wedding ceremony she desired. She would wear her white dress embroidered with violets. He would buy her white roses. She would be virginal in front of the judge.

At home, Warren found Sylvia tossing clothes in the closet. She wore a short tennis skirt that showed off her fine legs. He wished he could wrap his arms around her and make all the bad feelings between them disappear. He knew his judgment was clouded by his emotions for her but he couldn't help himself. "Let's talk," said Warren.

"I wish I could, but I don't have time. I'm late." Sylvia tossed a pair of red shoes.

"Where are you going?" He picked up the shoes.

"I'm going to volley with a friend," said Sylvia.

"What friend?" Warren threw the shoes on the floor.

"I'm going to play with Brad," she said shrilly.

"I don't want you to play with him, anymore," Warren said angrily.

"Don't tell me you're jealous?" Sylvia laughed.

"Yes, I am. Don't go," Warren gently squeezed her arm.

"You're acting like a baby." Sylvia moved away.

"No, I'm not." Warren followed Sylvia to the front door. She slammed it behind her. He felt like a puppy swatted with a newspaper.

He was being ridiculous, but he couldn't stop himself. He couldn't block out the image of Sylvia and Brad volleying. He pictured Brad, lean and muscled. The way Warren was before his accident. Brad served the ball to Sylvia who laughed and stepped toward the ball. When she missed, Brad comforted her. As his hand grazed over her behind, Sylvia snuggled against him.

Warren took a glass of water and popped two pills in his mouth. In bed, he imagined following Sylvia to her rendezvous and confronting Brad, "Get the hell out of my girl's life." Brad would start running. Sylvia would yell at Warren. "What is wrong with you? Stop following me! I hate you!"

Warren wished he could call his father for advice, but he would not understand. He would tell him to stop sniveling and take control of the relationship. But he didn't know what that meant. He wanted to believe Nina was right that he was blowing things out of proportion. Sylvia was only playing tennis with Brad, nothing more. Tennis didn't mean they were touching.

When Warren opened his eyes, he looked at her pink slip hung on the doorknob. Sylvia's dress was crumpled on the floor and the Shalimar bottle remained uncapped. Limping across the room, Warren slipped her dress on a hanger, but he wondered what would happen if he stopped cleaning up after her. He imagined a pile of clothes heaped to the ceiling. Her placed her silky blue dress to his nose and smelled her perfume. He remembered giving it to her. After she had dabbed it on her neck, he kissed every part of her body as they made love. Then they took a walk on the beach to watch the sunrise. He could still feel Sylvia's arms wrapped snugly around his waist. He wanted to feel that way, again. He needed to please her, but how? He knew she wanted a cashmere sweater. Then he glanced on the bookshelf and noticed the cookbook she had bought him for his birthday. Leafing through the pages, he calmed himself by thinking about cooking. He decided to make her favorite food, lobster, as an apology.

Warren took two more pills to steady him. He walked slowly to the car because he felt like a cripple. On the way, he passed a couple playing tennis. He stopped to watch them. The girl had long blonde hair like Sylvia. For a moment, he thought it was Sylvia. He wished he could go back to the time before his accident when he was who

Sylvia needed. He hated his knees. He wished he could have the knees of the young man on the court. Then his life with Sylvia would be the way it once was.

Their apartment was near the University of Miami. Although he knew he was in no shape to drive down US 1, he had no choice. The glare of the sun hurt his eyes. He had difficulty staying in his lane. He pulled over when a car honked him. Then he continued on to the fish store. Inside, it was spotless. Warren stared at the bright red lobsters with their claws wrapped in rubber bands. They looked sad. "Poor guys can't move," said Warren.

"How many you want?" Kim asked briskly.

On the way home, holding the bag, Warren listened to the rustling of the lobsters. He couldn't believe he had to kill these poor lobsters that never did anything to him. Warren wondered if they were siblings. The lobsters probably had names like Jim and Harriet. Their mother must be scurrying along the ocean bottom looking for them. Warren will boil only one for Sylvia and bring the other back. But he knew if he told Sylvia, she would think he was nuts.

Warren placed the bag of lobsters in the sink while he boiled a pot of water. He concentrated on chopping tomatoes into the salad. The lobsters were noisy and for a brief moment, Warren thought about smashing them with a hammer. Instead he poured more cold water over them and they revived, thrashing their claws at him.

Setting the table with the china dishes Sylvia's mother sent them, Warren remembered her parents' visit, three months ago. It was weird when her mother started to rearrange the utensils in the kitchen drawer while her father looked over the apartment. He was a distinguished-looking man with salt and pepper hair, a lawyer for a large pharmaceutical company. He reminded Warren of his own father. "How the hell are you going to support a family?" he asked.

"We'll be comfortable," said Warren.

"Warren is taking good care of me." Sylvia took Warren's hand.

"What does that mean?" Her father frowned.

"Stop cross-examining us. We're not getting married," said Sylvia.

When her parents left, Warren climbed into bed and didn't say a word to Sylvia. He was furious she hadn't told her parents they were discussing marriage. He didn't understand why it was a secret. Warren wished he had told her father to drop dead when he questioned him. That night, in bed, Sylvia put her arms around Warren. "I didn't like my dad bullying us."

"What's the big deal if he knows we are talking about marriage?" Warren asked.

"My dad has nothing to do with our relationship." Sylvia stroked his thigh.

Warren turned over to kiss her. He couldn't stay angry with her for long.

While Warren worked in the kitchen, Sylvia came home. Her cheeks sweaty and her knees streaked with dirt, he imagined washing her knees as he did for Nina when she hurt herself. "Great. You're making lobsters, how sweet," said Sylvia.

"It's my way of saying forgive me," said Warren.

"I'm sorry I blew you off," said Sylvia.

Warren pulled Sylvia to him to kiss her. "I stink. Wait till I shower," she said.

"Just one kiss," said Warren.

"Okay, but I warned you." Sylvia gave Warren a deep kiss.

"You taste like mints," Warren said.

"I do?" Sylvia smiled coyly.

"I could eat you up," said Warren.

"Maybe later." Sylvia flounced into the bathroom.

Warren felt nervous. He wanted to be close to Sylvia, again, but was not sure how. He wiped his sweaty hands on his pants. He took a vial from his pocket and popped two pills in his mouth. He whispered to the lobsters, "Wish me luck."

Freshly showered, Sylvia entered the kitchen. Her skin glowed. She smelled like Jasmine. He tried to kiss her, but Sylvia turned toward the lobster pot, "I'm starving. Throw in the lobsters."

"I can't, poor little guys." Warren shook his head.

"You're kidding, right? How can you feel sorry for lobsters?" Sylvia frowned.

"I think they are siblings." He stared in the sink at the lobsters.

"What are you talking about?" Sylvia laughed nervously.

"They seem attached to one another," he sighed.

"You're joking?" She stepped away from him.

"Sure." Warren put his hands in his pockets.

"They're only lobsters! Right, Warren?" Her eyes widened.

"Of course." Warren tried to sound positive.

They both looked into the sink at the squirming lobsters. Sylvia gave him a quizzical look. "You're going to let me do the dirty work?"

Warren shrugged his shoulders. "Would you?"

"Sometimes, I don't know what to make of you." Sylvia dumped the lobsters in the pot. She didn't even try to comfort or say goodbye to them. Warren frowned. He couldn't believe Sylvia's callousness, but maybe she was right. It was odd that he felt attached to them, but they were defenseless. He was angry with himself that he couldn't even save them.

During dinner, Sylvia's chin was covered with butter as she ate all her lobster. Warren picked at his. He couldn't look at the empty shell on her plate. Warren had murdered his best friends. He said out loud, "I should have bought a tank and kept them as pets."

"You're joking, right?" Sylvia stopped eating.

"Sure, listen Sylvia. We need to talk about us." Warren leaned toward her.

"What do you mean?" Sylvia put down her lobster claw.

"I asked you to marry me. We've graduated. I'm supporting you. My parents are coming down and I need an answer." Warren crossed his arms.

"Maybe after I have a job, get settled." Sylvia played with her fork.

"How long do you expect me to wait?" Warren said sternly.

"Is that what you're upset about, that I don't have a job." Sylvia banged the fork.

"You don't get it, do you? I thought you loved me." Warren grabbed her fork.

"I do love you, but you've changed," said Sylvia.

"What the hell does that mean?" He glowered.

"You've been acting strange since your accident," said Sylvia.

"I can't help it if I'm not physically well," he said.

"I'm doing the best job I can handling your accident."

"What about spending all your free time with Brad?" Warren said.

"We have fun together. He doesn't want a lobster as a pet." She laughed.

"You're not funny! Are you fooling around with Brad?"

"We're only playing tennis," she said.

"Listen, I've problems but I've taken care of you for two years, treated you like my wife." Warren drummed his fingers on the table.

"I never promised we'd get married," said Sylvia.

"Why the hell are we living together, playing house?" Warren shouted.

"Don't scream at me." Sylvia stood up and walked into the living room.

"I'm trying to talk to you." Warren followed her.

"You're depressing me," said Sylvia.

"I'm depressed because you won't marry me," said Warren.

"It's not my fault. Why don't you see a psychiatrist?" She glared.

"So it's my entire fault? You're guiltless." Warren threw up his arms.

"You're impossible. I can't talk to you." She shook her head.

"I'm trying to get through to you."

"I can't help you," she said.

"What does that mean?" he asked.

"I don't have to answer you. I'm leaving." She moved toward the door.

"Don't go." Warren blocked the door with his body.

Let me out," Sylvia yelled. "You're screwed up, popping pills. Now talking to lobsters."

"I'm screwed up, what about you?" Warren looked into Sylvia's cold eyes.

"My only problem is you," she said.

He moved away from the door. "You win, bitch."

"You're a bastard," Sylvia slammed the front door.

Warren hurried to the window and watched Sylvia climb into her red Explorer and drive, tires screeching, out of the parking lot. He thought about dragging her from the car, but he took two more pills from the nightstand. He sat on the couch, rubbing his knees. All he had wanted was to have a romantic dinner and reconnect with Sylvia. Instead he was alone. Warren punched the sofa cushion. He wondered if Sylvia ever loved him. He had become Sylvia's servant, someone to massage her ego, a large one. He couldn't believe that she didn't feel the least bit sorry. He remembered the times when they would fight and make up. Cuddled under the blankets, they would apologize to each other and go out for a late night movie. Their relationship had gone haywire. He shouldn't have said anything, but she pushed him. He couldn't believe she called him a pill pusher.

Sylvia never met his brother, Ethan, stoned most of the time. Warren was relieved that he hadn't seen him in several years. He shivered and wrapped a blanket around himself. He wished he hadn't called her a "bitch," but he couldn't help himself. Ethan had called him a "bastard" all the time. But Warren promised himself he would never act crazy like Ethan. He should have told her what Ethan did to Rusty. For the first time, he wished Ethan were here to threaten Sylvia. Why did Sylvia have to be so self-righteous?

In the bedroom, Warren picked up a bottle of red nail polish on the bed stand. He imagined Sylvia scratching his back with her perfectly manicured nails. Then he felt Sylvia's hands choking him. He felt foolish thinking that Sylvia would hurt him. He pressed her sweaty tee shirt to his nose. He opened the black box and slipped the ring on to his wedding finger, but it was too small. He placed it on his pinkie.

He wondered whether his mother had contemplated killing herself when his father abandoned them. That could have been the reason she spent so much time in her room. Warren wished he knew what death felt like. He could use a rest. He wouldn't have to see his father's disappointed face when he realized Sylvia and he were not engaged. If he were dead, Sylvia would miss him and feel guilty when she discovered him sprawled out on the bed.

Then again, Sylvia would probably not come home. He cringed when he thought about her with Brad. He took the pills from the drawer and hugged them to his chest. He shivered and curled up under the blankets.

Suddenly, he remembered Nina was arriving before his parents' early tomorrow morning. She would probably come straight to the apartment before stopping at her hotel. If Nina were the one to find him, she would be traumatized. She was a good kid who loved him. She would be lost without him. He had to be strong for her. Then he thought about his mother who had been doing better. She was teaching high school and making a new life for herself.

Warren slipped the ring off his pinkie and flung it across the room. He wasn't going to let his family see him as a loser. He replaced the bottle of pills in the nightstand.

The phone rang. It was not Sylvia. One of his counselors at the crisis center had an emergency. She was crying because she didn't know how to handle a male caller threatening to commit suicide. He spoke with assurance as he told the staff member what to say to calm down the student.

Fooling Around: Nina

~

When Nina enters the dorm room, Susan, her roommate, is sitting at the typewriter while a stranger lounges on the bed. When he stands to meet her, she realizes he's tall with inviting blue eyes, the color where the sea is lucid and infinite. He's wearing a Polo tee shirt and jeans that show off his muscular build and Nina wonders if he lifts weights. His broadness is comforting. Their eyes lock and Nina has the feeling they have met before. He's wearing the same Old Spice cologne as her father and brother, Warren.

She can't figure out what a good-looking man is doing in their dorm because Susan goes out with upper classmen who have private rooms. Despite her curiosity, Nina's annoyed she can't wash her hair and change into sweats. She wishes they would both leave. Susan, dressed in a skintight leotard and jeans, continues typing and stuffing potato chips into her mouth. "Ralph, this is Nina. Say hello, squirt, to Ralph."

"You're roommates? She's young enough for you to baby-sit." Ralph smiles.

"I can't help it if the dorm screwed up." Susan clicks clacks away.

"Don't listen to her; she's typing my psychology thesis. She's just cranky." Ralph leans close to Nina.

"She's always cranky," Nina whispers to Ralph. "I try to ignore her."

"She's a good typist; that's all I care about." Ralph winks at Nina.

"Hey, you two, stop whispering." Susan brushes the crumbs off her shirt.

"Sorry, I was just saying what a great typist you are," says Ralph.

"See, Nina, I'm a nice person," says Susan.

"She may be a great typist but she's a slob." Nina turns off her record player. The Bee Gees album and several records are out of their jackets. She picks up Susan's lacy pink underwear using two fingers and drops it on Susan's bed. "Thanks, Nina. See how well

I'm training her?" Susan looks at Ralph.

"I wouldn't brag about it," says Nina.

"See how the kid picks on me?" Susan pouts.

"She's right. You're a slob." Ralph drops a dirty sock into Susan's lap.

"Hey, don't be mean or I won't type." Susan throws the sock on the floor.

"Me? I'm a nice guy." His eyes brighten.

"When you want to be," says Susan.

"What does she mean?" Nina asks Ralph.

"Stop upsetting Nina." Ralph puts his hand on Susan's shoulder.

"I'm not upsetting her." Susan puts her hand over Ralph's.

"Well, you're making me uncomfortable," says Nina.

"I told you. Now apologize." Ralph takes away his hand.

"Sorry." Susan sticks out her tongue at Ralph and continues typing. Nina frowns. She's not sure what is going on between Susan and Ralph, but she is relieved that Ralph defended her. She can't stand Susan's nastiness. Nina can't understand how the University put the two of them together. They have nothing in common. As Nina turns off *All in the Family*, she watches Ralph's reflection on the screen. He has the same height and large frame as her brother, Warren. She gravitates to broad-shouldered, muscular, tall men with light eyes. She adores Warren and hopes Ralph is also kind. For a moment, Ralph stands over Susan's shoulder to watch her type. Nina gazes at Ralph and wills him to look at her. She wishes Susan would disappear. She wonders if there is something between Ralph and Susan. But Susan has never mentioned him. Not that Nina talks to Susan about anything important. Susan likes to be the center of attention and can't keep a secret. As she scrutinizes both their faces, Susan is absorbed in typing and Ralph turns to stare at Nina who blushes and looks toward the window. She closes the blinds, but hopes Ralph is still watching her. The snow is forming into clumps and piling up, sealing their cave-like room off from light. "The snow is getting heavy."

"Do you think it is safe to drive?" he asks.

"I don't know," says Nina.

"Great, how am I going to finish this paper if you go home? I can't read your handwriting." Susan whines, "Nina, be a sport. Let Ralph sleep over so he can tell me what the hell he's written."

"She has such a way with words," says Ralph.

"Hey, don't make fun of me. You're the one who waited until the last minute for me to type it. I'm trying to save your ass." Susan leans over to pat his behind but Ralph moves away.

Nina lowers her head to hide her smile. "Where would he sleep?"

"He could sleep with me." Susan throws Ralph a kiss.

"That's not a good idea," says Ralph.

"Why not?" Susan asks.

"You move around too much," says Ralph.

"You two have slept together?" Nina asks.

"Not really," says Susan.

"Listen, she's just talking. All talk. Don't pay attention to her." He paces.

"Are you sure?" Nina bites her lip.

"I'm positive. I'm not lying to you." He touches Nina's hand.

"I wouldn't want to get between the two of you." Nina stares at Ralph.

"There is nothing to worry about," Ralph says seriously.

"We could push the two beds together and sleep side by side," says Susan.

Nina looks from Susan to Ralph. She's still trying to figure out what Susan meant when she said, "not really." She can't stand the thought of Ralph touching Susan's body. Susan bites into another potato chip and offers one to Ralph. He pushes her hand away.

Nina wishes Ralph would feed her chips. "I guess you could stay," says Nina.

"Ralph, you had better behave yourself. I'm the only one who's had a boyfriend. You'll have to fool around with me." Susan chuckles.

"You've never had a boyfriend? Is she telling the truth?" Ralph asks.

"Why the hell don't you mind your own business, Susan! You

don't know anything about me. Forget it, Ralph, go home." Nina backs away from Ralph.

"Listen, don't pay attention to Susan. She thinks she's humorous. The truth is the weather conditions are too awful to drive home." Ralph looks at Nina with worried eyes.

"I was just kidding. See the kid has no sense of humor," says Susan.

"I have a sense of humor but you're not funny," says Nina.

"Okay, girls, time out. The snow is horrible. I'm afraid I may get into an accident. If you don't want to put the beds together, I'll sleep on the floor," says Ralph.

Nina doesn't know what to make of the change in Ralph. He looks contrite. He reminds her of Warren after Ethan yells at him for no reason. Warren ends up feeling guilty and she comforts him. She doesn't want anything to happen to Ralph. She can't allow her feelings for Susan to get in the way of doing the right thing. She has to admit she would like to know him better. She's thrilled that he's standing up to Susan. His forcefulness interests her but scares her, too.

Nina and Ralph peer outside. The window registers zero visibility. Nina can't see the cafeteria, a short walk from her dorm. If Ralph has a car accident, she would never forgive herself.

"I'm sorry, Nina. What I said was nasty. Be a sport and let Ralph stay. I'll even help make up the beds. I promise I'll keep my hands off him," says Susan.

"Listen, I was a Boy Scout. I'll behave myself. Susan is the one you have to worry about." He places his hand on Nina's shoulder.

"You're not that sexy. Don't flatter yourself. I've some work to do. You two will have to entertain yourselves. But don't get too cozy, Ralph," says Susan.

"I'm going to be a gentleman." Ralph salutes Nina.

"If he gets out of line, just smack him." Susan's eyes gleam.

"Okay," Nina laughs. In the parking lot, the cars are covered with snow. She imagines Ralph's car skidding out of control and hitting a lamppost.

Ralph and Nina sit crossed-legged facing one another on Nina's bed and play gin rummy. Ralph furrows his brow, concentrates on every card. "Gin," he says.

"I can't believe you won, again. That's the fifth game! What's your secret?" Nina notices his thick fingers with smooth rounded fingernails.

"It's concentration," says Ralph, placing his finger under her chin.

"What do you mean? I'm paying attention." Nina keeps still.

"I'm concentrating on you," says Ralph.

"You're a regular Casanova!" Susan stops typing.

"Be nice," says Ralph.

"You act nice," said Susan.

"Stop worrying, I'm behaving like a gentleman." He pats his own back.

Susan shakes her head and continues to type. Nina's face feels warm. She hopes Susan is wrong about Ralph being a playboy. He seems sincere. She decides to ignore Susan and turns toward Ralph to whisper, "Well, if you're not keeping an eye on the cards, how are you winning?"

"Am I winning?" Ralph leans toward her. His torso is close enough for her to see the hairs peeking out of his partially unbuttoned shirt. She'd like to touch him but instead she reclines against the wall. Self-conscious about her body, she thinks her thighs are fat and her breasts small even though her best friend, Patty, has reassured her that she has a good figure. Last time they shopped, Nina fit into a size eight pair of jeans that Patty couldn't zipper. "Hey, what are you two whispering about? I'm almost done and I want to play, too." Susan wiggles her bottom on the chair.

"We're just playing gin, nothing exciting." Ralph winks at Nina.

"We'll don't forget about me." Susan stands up and stretches. Her belly button is exposed. Nina wishes she was big breasted like Susan who has an endless stream of boyfriends. Susan is not afraid to flaunt herself. Nina has always had small breasts like her mother. Nina examines her breasts every month because her mother is afraid she will develop breast cancer the way she did. For a moment, Nina imagines she is parading naked in front of Ralph while he whistles.

But Nina knows she is a prude. She likes to wear overalls instead of skirts. At home, Nina's family wrapped themselves in terry cloth robes to go to the bathroom. Her parents before they divorced always closed their bedroom door. One time, she rose early in the morning and entered their bedroom without knocking. Her father struggled to put on his underwear. "Get out. Knock," he yelled. She ran back to her room and stayed in bed until her mother came to wake her. Now, she can't remember whether her father was naked.

Nina looks at Ralph and closes the top button of her blouse. It is important to cover up. She recalls once when she opened the bathroom door without realizing Ethan, her sixteen-year-old brother, was about to turn on the shower. She saw his private parts. "Get the hell out." He threw a bar of soap at her.

"I'm sorry," said Nina as she slammed the door. Her brother's skinny torso and penis shocked her; it was so unappealing.

"Stay out of here!" Ethan screamed.

The only time her mother talked to her about how sex occurred was when she turned eleven years old. She showed her a book, *Where Do Babies Come From?* Her mom couldn't make eye contact with her and Nina was embarrassed to ask questions. She couldn't remember ever finding her parents snuggling in bed. A quick embrace was their standard greeting.

Susan turns on the lava lamp and joins them on the bed. Nina notices she has unbuttoned the four top buttons of her blouse and is not wearing a bra. Nina focuses on Ralph who keeps looking at Susan's chest. Nina wonders what it would like to be admired for her breasts. She wants Ralph to think she is sexy. She wishes she had the nerve to unbutton her shirt and slip into her tightest pair of jeans.

She is fascinated by how self-assured Ralph appears as he deals the cards. She hopes he's not cocky. When Ralph catches Nina watching him gawking at Susan, he chuckles. Nina freezes. She feels stupid. She stands up to put on the record player and takes deep breaths. Susan requests "Lay, lie, and lay across my big brass bed..." Nina isn't interested in listening to Dylan, but doesn't want to fight.

She wants Ralph to think she's easy-going. Susan croons the song while she takes out glasses and a bottle of red wine.

"Just a little," says Nina who hates the taste. Sometimes she would catch Ethan at her parent's liquor cabinet. He would threaten to beat her up if she told on him. She kept silent because she didn't want to tangle with him after seeing him smack Warren who protected her from Ethan as best as he could. But Ethan was definitely dangerous. "Don't be a baby. Drink up," says Susan.

"It won't hurt you. Come on. It's fun." Ralph pours himself a second glass.

"Just a little drink to loosen you up." She pours a glass for Nina.

"It's good for you," says Ralph. Susan and Ralph clink their glasses.

"I guess." Nina takes a small sip. She grimaces.

"You'll get used to the taste. It's delicious," says Ralph.

"I said she was young." Susan shakes her head at Ralph.

"Stop talking about me like I'm not here," says Nina.

"I told you to stop being disagreeable." Ralph glares at Susan.

"I'm not upsetting her. You're being a jerk, not me," says Susan.

Nina feels she's watching her parents fight. Her palms sweat. She wishes her brother, Warren, was here to tell her what to do. He took care of her after the divorce and helped her with her homework in grade school. He's always given her solid advice about boys. She wishes she met Ralph somewhere else. She can't concentrate on him because Susan is being a pest. She wonders how Warren would handle Ralph. She will call him later. He's been depressed since his girlfriend, Sylvia, left him.

They play gin with Ralph sitting between the two of them. Ralph's knee is touching Nina's. She imagines sitting in his lap. "How the hell do you keep winning?" Susan pours herself another class of wine. "Are you cheating?"

"That's not very nice," says Nina.

"Of course I'm not cheating. I'm a better player than you," says Ralph.

Nina watches the two of them while she nurses one cup of wine.

She notices Ralph's full lips. "He's playing by the rules," says Nina.

"See, she thinks she has to protect you. She doesn't know that you can take care of yourself." Susan laughs at Ralph while he shakes his head. Susan refills her glass. Susan had drunk most of the wine. Susan's eyes begin to close. She leans against Ralph and plants kisses on his cheek. "You need to lie down," Ralph says firmly.

"Lie down with me." Susan pushes her chest into him.

"I'm not interested." He stands up.

"Are you sure?" Susan reaches for Ralph's cheek.

"I'm positive." Ralph turns the side of his face.

Susan curls into a ball. "I feel like I have a hammer banging on my head."

"Sorry, she's drunk. Let's put the baby to bed," Ralph whispers to Nina.

"Good idea," Nina grins.

She's relieved that Ralph isn't responding to Susan. She'd leave the room if they started to make out. She can understand why Susan encouraged Ralph to kiss her. His lips are red and full. A mouth meant for kissing. For once, maybe she will get the guy. She is flattered by Ralph's attention, but puzzled by it. Last time that they went to a school dance, Susan danced with three times as many boys as she did. Susan left with one of them, a football player, and didn't come back until the following morning. After pushing the beds together, they tuck the covers around Susan. "She's a load," says Ralph.

"She's heavier because she's drunk," says Nina.

"She's too big for me." He shakes his head.

"Really?' Nina asks.

"I like petite woman," he rubs her hand.

Nina blushes. She doesn't know what to say. He kisses the top of her head. "Now go get into pajamas. I'm tired."

"Okay, I'll be right back." Nina retreats into the bathroom to change into her nightgown. She wishes she owned a black, silky negligee. Instead she slips on her bright red and blue flannel nightgown, a gift from her mother, one that makes her look like an

American flag. Her mother wanted her to go to a commuter college but Nina refused. It's 1974, but her mother acts like it's still the 50's. All the pajamas her mother buys for her are granny style. Nina brushes her jet-black hair in to a ponytail. Her dark brown eyes stare back at her in the mirror while she checks her face for pimples. Thank goodness, her olive complexion is unblemished. She wonders if she should put a little rouge on her angled cheekbones or lipstick to make her thin lips appear plumper. She decides against it because Ralph might think she's odd. For a moment, she sees her father's second wife, Penelope, thick mascara, rouged lips and red lipstick. Her dad couldn't have picked a more different woman. Her mother never uses makeup, dresses in polyester pants and wears flat heels. Penelope is totally possessive of her father and their pampered life. Penelope would not be with her father if he weren't rich. Every time Nina visits their apartment, she sees Penelope has added to her Tiffany collection. Nina couldn't believe Penelope had a portrait done of her cuddling her Siamese cats. When she asked her dad why he wasn't in the picture, he just laughed. "It was a gift for Penelope." Nina wonders if her father is ever jealous of the cats. Nina wants to have a boyfriend who will like her for herself.

At that moment, Susan walks into the bathroom. The whites of her eyes are covered with spidery veins as she stares in the mirror. She smells like sour milk. Her hair resembles a bird's nest and her yellow negligee droops. "I feel sick." She runs to the toilet.

"Are you okay?" Nina yells into the stall.

"What do you think of Ralph?" asks Susan.

"He's nice," says Nina.

"Nice? I think you dig him," laughs Susan.

Before Susan can say anymore, Nina hears Susan throwing up. She doesn't know what to do about Ralph. Maybe she's in over her head. She's not sure if she can handle Ralph, but on the other hand she's drawn to his "take charge" personality. She's uncertain about going into the room but Ralph's intensity is pulling her back. His blue eyes are like a crystal ball about to tell her secrets she has never heard before. His powerful arms will protect her. She shivers at the image of Ralph lying next to her. She's curious about his body and wants to see more of it. She is not sure she's making the right decision, but she has to find out. Ralph yells into the bathroom, "Nina, what's happening?"

"Susan's throwing up." Nina steps out of the bathroom.

"She didn't look too good when she got up." He nudges her toward the room.

Back inside, Ralph sits on the bed and pats the mattress. "Let's lie down."

At that moment Susan walks in. "I've got to sleep. My head is killing me."

"Sorry to hear that, Susan." He winks at Nina.

"Hopefully you'll feel better in the morning," Nina tries not to laugh.

"Don't patronize me. You're lucky I feel too sick to respond." Susan climbs into bed.

Ralph waits until Susan lies on the edge of the bed and faces the door. When he beckons to her, Nina realizes she is being foolish. Nothing bad could happen with Susan in the room. For the moment, she is relieved Susan is there. "Where should I lie?' Nina asks.

"Next to me," Ralph rests in the middle of the bed between Susan and Nina. He turns on his side facing Nina who is against the wall. She notices his muscular chest and yearns to rub her hands through the hairs but doesn't dare. "Come here." He puts her hand on his chest.

"Are you sure?" Nina whispers.

"You're adorable. Your hand feels good," he sighs.

"I feel funny," Nina whispers.

"It's okay." He pulls her closer.

"What if Susan wakes up?" Nina frowns. She wishes Ralph wasn't quite as self-assured. She thinks about leaving, but she doesn't want to make a scene.

"She won't." Ralph gently rubs her cheek.

"How long ago were you in college?" Nina is consoled by Ralph's touch.

"I'm older than you," Ralph whispers.

"How much older are you? Nina asks.

"I'm twenty-nine." He kisses her earlobe and neck.

"Twenty-nine years old?" Nina is confused. Her ear tingles. Ralph's kisses are exciting, but she's not sure how she feels that he is eleven years older. He is about the same age as her brother, Ethan. Her lips tighten. He doesn't look old. He could be too sophisticated for her. He might expect her to be competent in bed. She feels embarrassed to tell him how inexperienced she is, but maybe he's willing to instruct her. "Don't worry. I like you. I'll take care of you," he says.

"I feel funny about this." Nina blushes.

"I promise there is nothing to worry about," says Ralph.

"Okay," Nina says softly.

Ralph turns around to look at Susan snoring. "She's really out. How can you stand the noise?"

"She always snores when she's drunk." Nina laughs. "She's drunk a lot."

Ralph cups Nina's face. "You're beautiful."

"Am I?" Nina whispers.

"I wish you were older," Ralph rubs her cheek.

"You make it sound like I'm a child," says Nina.

"Aren't you?" He kisses her hand.

"No, I'm not," Nina says.

"Don't you want to date boys your own age?" Ralph twirls her hair.

"I want to date someone who cares about me. Age isn't important," Nina says.

Ralph gives her a deep kiss. The roughness of his tongue excites her. She arches her body toward him. "You're delicious," says Ralph. Nina laughs. He probes the inside of her mouth with his tongue. Nina moans.

Susan sits up on her side of the bed. "You two are disgusting. What are you going to do? Fool around while I'm in the bed?" She stands up and puts on her bathrobe. "I'm going to sleep next door. I can't take the two of you. Ralph, you're worse than Nina. She's jailbait. What the hell is wrong with you?"

"She's eighteen. Stop talking about her like she is an idiot." Ralph sits up.

"I can make my own decisions," says Nina.

"Well, you're making the wrong one." Susan slams the door as she leaves. Nina's face feels flushed. She's not sure if she has made the best choice. She's surprised Ralph is interested in her. He's so mature. She feels grown-up lying next to him.

"Don't listen to her. She's just jealous," he says.

"Do you think that's what she meant?" Nina asks.

"What else could it be? She's been after me since last semester. She's just angry that I like you better," says Ralph.

Nina tilts her head. She can't believe that she won over Susan, the beauty queen. She imagines introducing Ralph to her freshman friends. They will be envious she caught a graduate student. Now, they will have intimate conversations in bed. But still, she feels she's doing something wrong. It is crazy but she wonders if she stole Ralph from Susan. She would never rob another girl's boyfriend. She hates Penelope for luring her father from her mother.

"It's okay, you've haven't done anything wrong," he says.

She sighs. Before she can worry anymore, Ralph reaches for her. He trails his mouth down her neck to her breast and he starts to unbutton the front of her nightgown. Aware of his strong male odor and her hot skin, she allows him to massage her breasts. "Why don't you take off your nightgown?"

"I'm not sure if I should," whispers Nina.

"Why not? We're alone," says Ralph.

"I don't know you very well," said Nina.

"We're together, now," says Ralph.

"That's not what I'm talking about. I mean we haven't dated. I don't know anything about you," said Nina.

"Consider this our first date." Ralph kisses her neck.

"I know that's exactly what I'm saying. Going to bed with someone is not my idea of what I'm supposed to do on a first date."

Her neck feels hot where he kissed her and she wants him to touch her, again.

"You taste good." He nibbles on her ear lobe.

She laughs. Ralph grins. Nina closes her eyes. She feels confused. Her mother has always stressed that she should go to bed with a boy she loves. Her mother never said anything about intense attraction at first sight but her mother fell in love with her father on their first date. Both of them were virgins on their wedding night. Later, her father told her that he should have slept with her mother first. He would have known they were sexually incompatible. She refuses to be in the same position as her mother. She wants to sleep with her boyfriend before she marries him. "Will you take me to the freshman dance next weekend?" Nina asks.

"I'll take you anywhere you want." Ralph pulls her closer.

"Really?" She looks into his light eyes. He seems truthful. Her flesh is moist. She kisses him back. Ralph squeezes her too tightly. She gasps. "I don't know if this is a good idea."

"Sorry, I didn't mean to hurt you. Listen, we're alone. Susan is gone. I thought I'd go nuts if she stayed any longer," Ralph says.

"It was embarrassing, but I feel bad she threw up," says Nina.

"There's nothing to feel upset about," says Ralph.

"Do you ever feel guilty?' Nina asks. She thinks of all the times she wanted to tell on Ethan and didn't. Especially when she saw him choking the dog from her bedroom window but she was too frightened to yell for help.

"Not about Susan leaving and having you to myself," Ralph whispers.

Nina gently moves away. She needs a little more time to feel comfortable. "Tell me about yourself? Where you live? What's your favorite food?"

"I live in an apartment in Queens. I love Chinese food." He caresses her hair.

"I like Chinese food, too."

"Add that to the list of things we will do together." He strokes her arm.

"It sounds great." She imagines the two of them at the Red Dragon cuddling in a booth. She runs her hand through his thick hair.

"You smell sweet." He presses against her. Nina can feel his hard torso. She doesn't know what to do. She feels stupid. "My body really likes you," he says.

"What do you mean?" Nina asks.

"I'll show you. It's not scary. I promise." He places her hand on his penis.

"I don't know if I'm ready." She moves her hand away. She wonders what happened to Ralph's underwear. She's never met a boy who didn't wear underwear. She hopes he is not a freak who exposes his body to girls in the park.

"I can't believe I just met you." Ralph puts her hand back between his legs.

"I'm not good at this." She gently massages him. She feels like an idiot. The only other boy she ever gave a hand-job was a boy she dated at the end of senior year in high school. They were both so nervous that she didn't worry what he thought of her.

"You're doing fine. It's okay if you massage me harder," he says.

"I'm afraid I might hurt you." She moves her body closer to Ralph.

"I promise you won't." He nibbles her ear lobe.

"I feel like an idiot," she whispers.

"Don't say that about yourself. You're beautiful," he says.

"I'm more attractive than Susan?" Nina asks. No boy has ever called her sexy.

"You're adorable, naturally pretty. I'm being serious. I'm not just fooling around with you. I want you for my girlfriend." Ralph strokes her hair.

"You do?" asks Nina.

"Yes, I love your dark eyes. Your hair is silky," he whispers.

"But I'm not blonde," she says.

"I don't like blondes. I like you. I'll take you on plenty of dates."

"I'll be your only girlfriend?" Nina tilts her head. She's not sharing Ralph with anyone the way her father had Penelope, while he was still married to her mother.

"Yes. None of them are as pretty as you." He grins.

"How many girlfriends have you had?" Nina asks.

"I don't think that's crucial to discuss, right now," says Ralph.

"Maybe it is important." Nina hesitates.

Ralph slowly rubs her back. "You need to relax. Imagine the two of us holding hands on campus. You'll be the best looking girl at the freshman dance."

Nina closes her eyes. Ralph's hands soothe her. She drifts back to Puerto Rico where she was having a massage at The Dorado Hotel's sauna while on vacation with her dad and Warren. Her body is slick with oil. She imagines Ralph's naked body being rubbed next to her. The room is steamy, soft Caribbean music plays in the background and she reaches for Ralph.

"How do you feel?" Ralph's hand slips under her nightgown to stroke her buttocks. "Why don't you take off your panties?"

"Not yet." Nina burrows in Ralph's chest.

"I promise I'll make you feel better." He kisses her hair.

"I'm embarrassed," she says.

"You don't have to be. From the little I have seen, you're terrific-looking. No need to hide in your nightgown." He rubs her thigh.

"That feels good," she whispers.

"How about the nightgown?" Ralph kneads her buttocks.

"I'm not very pretty," Nina says quietly.

"I think you're beautiful. Please let me help you," he says.

"You'll take me to the freshman dance?" She puts her hands on his shoulders.

"I'm not going anywhere. Later tonight, we'll go out for a snack at Leo's Diner." Ralph unbuttons her nightgown.

"Really?" She rubs his back. Nina wonders if her friends will see them at the diner.

"Can you help me?" Ralph starts to lift off her nightgown.

"Susan might walk in." Nina holds down her nightgown with her hand.

"Susan is sleeping. I promise she won't come in." Ralph clasps her free fingers.

"Are you sure?" Nina asks.

"I told you you're lovely. Let me see if I'm right." He works off her nightgown. She helps lift it off her head. "Perfect." He sucks her breasts.

"You think I'm pretty?" Her breasts tingle.

"Absolutely." He slips off his jeans.

Nina's eyes widen. She has never seen a man completely naked. His body looks foreign to her. His erect penis is huge. She can't imagine how it will fit into her. Her mouth is dry. She wants a drink of water but is afraid to move. Ralph seems unaware of her feelings as he moves against her. His penis is rock hard. "You're wonderful. Your body feels great." He strokes between her legs.

"What you're doing feels nice," she says shyly.

"I want you to feel as turned on as me," he smiles.

"I'm not any good at this." Nina's not sure how much pressure to apply to massaging Ralph. Suddenly she thinks about a conversation she had with her father when he told her that it was "her job to find a husband in college." She has to please Ralph for him to be her boyfriend. She wants to continue, but she feels awkward.

"Your body is wet." He kisses her and guides her hand back onto his penis. She looks at Ralph's face. His eyes are closed. Beads of sweat have formed on his forehead. He is lost in his own world. He's not paying attention to her. She wishes he'd open his eyes and kiss her, again. She loosens her grip on him. "Keep going, I need you to help me," he whispers.

She wonders why he's not touching her body. She feels cold and wants to put her nightgown back on. Maybe he doesn't find her attractive. He thinks her body is fat. She's unsure what to do. She wants to pull her hand away but she's afraid Ralph will be angry. He will think she's a tease. Warren had a girlfriend, Sylvia, whom he ended up hating because she was a tease. She wants Ralph to like her, but she's no longer in a sexy mood. She feels like his plaything. Any girl could be holding him. She wishes Susan would replace her. She can have him. Ralph wouldn't even know the difference. She can't believe she's about to make love and she's alone. Finally, Ralph opens his eyes. "What's the matter? Please don't stop."

"I don't feel right about this," says Nina.

"Look how eager I am!" Ralph says.

"I'm not very excited," says Nina.

"I'm sorry. We're just getting started. Be patient." He reaches between her legs.

Nina keeps her legs closed. "Don't." His body smells foreign.

"You're just nervous because it's the first time. Relax." Ralph runs his hands down her back to her buttocks. "I'll be gentle."

Her body feels like it is floating. "Your hand feels good."

"I'll take care of you, trust me." Ralph's mouth trails down to her vagina.

Nina moans. She sees blue rings, each one larger than the next. She's in heaven. Maybe, she jumped to conclusions about Ralph. He's a wizard. He trails his mouth back up to her lips to kiss her. "Your turn, doll." He guides her hand back to his penis.

"Okay," Nina touches Ralph gingerly. She tries to relax by imagining the lapping of waves on a sandy beach.

"Now hold me tighter." His grip is strong over her hand.

"Like this," she asks sheepishly as she rubs him.

"Good girl," he says.

Nina can't move her fingers away. She stares at Ralph who is in a trance. His face is ashen. He looks dead. She's fondling a cadaver. She stops herself from laughing hysterically because she doesn't want to upset Ralph. Instead, she closes her eyes and wishes Susan would enter the room. "Doesn't that feel great?" he asks.

"What?" Her eyes open wide.

"Turning me on, but could you rub harder?" he asks.

"I'm doing the best job I can." She imagines her hand is a knife slicing him.

"I know you can do better." He tightly squeezes her wrist the way Ethan did when he was mad.

"You're hurting me." She will take the knife and stab him in the gut.

She looks at him. His eyes are cold like her brother, Ethan. She can't wriggle her hand free. "Stroke me," he commands. She tries to arch her body away from him. But he pulls her and presses against her. She is boxed in. Her body trembles. His knees have her pinned against the wall. Her heart quickens. She takes deep breaths. Ralph thrusts his hips and enters her. She imagines his sperm is blood pouring out of him. Her head throbs. Ralph opens his eyes. "That was nice. You're a good girl." He climbs off of her.

She doesn't answer him. Her body is paralyzed. Ralph lies on his back and hums. She refuses to look at him. She reaches over to the nightstand to take a tissue. She wipes her sticky legs. When she touches his scum, she wants to puke. She slips into her nightgown and glances at the clock. It's six A.M. She must shower; let the warm water engulf her. She imagines scrubbing her body, cleansing herself. She has to rub away Ralph's odious smell. She wonders if she should call Warren. If he were here he would protect her. "Next time it will be better for you, too." Ralph pats her leg.

"I'm sure it will," Nina moves her leg away. She can't believe Ralph thinks there will be a next time. Her mouth fills with bile. He is definitely nuts. She clasps her hands and looks up at a large crack in the ceiling. She prays it will fall on his head. Her body is icy. She's too tired to scramble under the blankets. She wants her mommy to place the covers up to her neck, safe. She whimpers. Then Ralph turns to her with a beatific look on his face. "Don't be upset. You'll get the hang of it."

"I guess," says Nina in a low voice.

"Come on. Let's see my girl smile," he says.

SECTION TWO

~

Trapped Hearts

Whither Thou Goest

~

Rachel presses her face against the window of the pawnshop to watch the owner put her ring, a gold band with a single ruby, in the showcase. As she moves her hand into the sunlight, only a pale circle of skin reminds her of the ring her mother gave her. She shoves her too exposed hand into her pocket. She's just another nineteen-year-old girl with limp brown hair, blue eyes and angled cheekbones. The tight gray tee shirt makes her look stick-thin. Her head aches because she's hungry. Janis, who usually brings home sticky buns from the diner where she works, didn't leave any on the counter this morning. Feeling the four crisp one hundred dollar bills in her pocket, at least, Rachel can pay her half of the month's rent. She licks her dry lips while deciding to have waffles with strawberries at Tom's Restaurant on Broadway.

After breakfast, as she walks down One Hundred and Twentieth Street, Rachel massages her ring finger. When she eventually visits her mother, Rachel can report that a man in a hooded jacket stole the ring. He pulled it off her finger at knifepoint. Rachel turns around to see if anyone is following her. No one looks suspicious, only an old man stinking of wine scavenges through the garbage. She hands him five dollars and says, "Eat breakfast." He grunts as he shuffles in his ratty sneakers to the next row of garbage cans. She wonders why he would rather eat crap than a good meal like her mother cooks. The old man has obviously never celebrated Shabbat. It has been too long since Rachel ate cake-like buttery challah, brisket in tomato sauce and roasted potatoes. She can hear her mother's voice blessing the candles.

The studio apartment smells of night sweats. It's eleven in the morning but the shades are drawn and sunlight seeps through the cracks of the blinds. Strands of light fall on a lump lying under the covers. Rachel briskly picks up Janis' black lace bra to place it on a chair. Rachel hadn't known what a slob Janis was until they moved in together a year ago. Janis sits up in bed. Her long blonde hair is disheveled. "I'm so tired. My feet are killing me from work."

"Long night? I didn't hear you come in," Rachel says.

"This group of college kids ordered one of practically everything on the menu. When they were all done, the bastards left me three dollars," says Janis.

"So much for college kids being smart." Rachel flips open the window shade only to see the fat man in the building next door. He's wearing an undershirt and boxers as he sits at the table. With a grizzly beard and bulging stomach, he looks worse in the morning. He reminds Rachel of a book her mother read to her about a boy swallowing everything he sees until his stomach bulges and he can't walk. When the doctor arrives, he reaches into the kid's stomach and pulls out galoshes, a rooster and a tricycle. The gross man doesn't look dangerous, but Rachel pulls down the shade.

Wearing a too tight tee shirt and bikini underwear, Janis sticks her plumb feet towards Rachel. "Rub my feet and I'll pay you a million."

"Okay, but then I have to go to the laundromat," says Rachel.

Rachel kneads Janis' toes and thick ankles. Janis moans the way she does when they have sex. Usually her reaction turns Rachel on, but today she's thinking about her ring. Then she realizes that Janis' leg is almost as fat as that of the man's across the alley. Rachel imagines she is nursing Janis back to health. Her mother planned on her becoming a nurse. Rachel remembers holding a cool cloth to her mother's forehead. "Do I really make you feel good, Mommy?"

"Like a little nurse." Her mother kissed her fingertips.

"I love you, Mommy."

Janis thumps Rachel's knee with her foot. "Earth to Rachel, hello, come in."

"Sorry, I was just daydreaming," says Rachel.

"About me, I hope." Janis runs her foot across Rachel's outer thigh.

"Listen, I have things to do." Rachel starts to stand up.

"Please don't stop. I feel like a cripple." Janis nudges Rachel's knee with her foot.

"Okay." Rachel continues to knead Janis' toes.

"Wonderful." Janis sighs.

Rachel watches Janis close her eyes, relaxed. She wishes they could sit here forever, calmly. But Rachel's forehead throbs above her eyebrows. She closes her eyes and leans against Janis. "What hurts?" Janis caresses her hair.

"I've a terrible headache," says Rachel.

"I'll rub it," says Janis.

"Great," says Rachel. Janis' hands feel cool on her skin like her mother's.

"You're my girl," Janis whispers.

"I hope so," Rachel says wistfully.

Janis reaches for Rachel's breasts. "Not now," says Rachel.

"What's the matter with you?"

"I'm not in the mood. My head's killing me," says Rachel.

"You're never in the mood." Janis grabs her arm.

"That's not true. You're hurting me." Rachel pulls Janis' hand off her.

"Hurting you? What about me?" She slaps Rachel across the face.

"Stop it," yells Rachel.

"I don't get you, at all." Janis goes into the bathroom and slams the door.

Rachel dumps the dirty clothes into the laundry bag. She yells, "Goodbye," even though she wants to sneak out, but the last time she ran out Janis didn't speak to her for days.

She can't explain to Janis what she's feeling because her mind is numb, a frozen screen. She wants to lie down with Janis in a grassy meadow, feel the breeze on her body, and be part of nature. She recalls the day when the two of them took a picnic lunch to the botanical gardens. They lay side by side in the meadow and watched the clouds. "That one looks like a lion," said Rachel.

"I'm a lioness and if you're not careful, I'm going to pounce on you." Janis outlined Rachel's lips with her finger. They snapped pictures of each other as they stood in the rose garden. Rachel sent one of the photographs to her mother. There is one of the two of them hugging that is pasted on their refrigerator.

Now her life is moving in slow motion; she's lucky to move one foot in front of the other. Everything is out of whack. She needs the ring her mother gave her back so she won't lose her balance. Rachel wishes Janis cared about her the way she did before they lived together.

When Rachel returns with the laundry, she changes into a clean tee shirt and khaki jeans to go to work. She looks around the apartment for some sign of Janis. Her half-filled cereal bowl with a cockroach crawling on the rim sits in the sink. Rachel squishes the bug in a napkin and throws it in the garbage. The apartment is too quiet. Janis says they don't have enough money to fix up it up, but she can't stand the drab grayish walls. The couch has a large coffee stain. The windowpanes are dim with soot. She thinks about the frilly pink curtains in her bedroom at home. But then she remembers her mother yelling at her for accidentally smearing them with chocolate pudding. Her mother tore them down. Janis used to leave her a note. But recently she is less reliable and is spending more time with her friend, Deirdre, a masseuse with long black polished fingernails. The sight of her nails makes Janis' skin itch.

She hurries down Broadway to Chin's fruit stand. On the way she salutes the Indian totem pole painted red and green in front of the cigar store because it makes her feel better. One time when she forgot to salute, she stepped in dog crap. She touches the tips of every fire hydrant she passes. The faces around her whiz by and she wonders if she is living in a dream world. By the time she arrives at work, Mr. Chin is waiting impatiently for her. "You are late. Need to wash apples." He points to the back room.

"Sorry, I'm going," says Rachel.

In the back of the store she rinses apples in a big bowl. The cold water chills her hands. She looks at her ring finger and wonders if anyone has bought the ruby ring; a couple looking for a wedding ring maybe admiring it at this very moment. If not, when she has enough money, she will buy it back. Rachel takes the bowl of apples from the sink and replaces it with peaches. Knowing what is expected of her and being able to do it, she likes the monotony of her job. Mr. Chin's youngest daughter, Ling, enters the room. Her face is moon-shaped and smooth with lips like fresh cherries ready to be eaten. Ling, age six, climbs onto the stepstool next to Rachel and they wash peaches together. Ling's small hands are delicate in comparison to Rachel's larger ones.

Rinsing the fruit with Ling, Rachel remembers helping her mother wash the vegetables for the salad when she was little. Side by side they stood at the kitchen sink, each in their aprons. Her mother said, "Wash the whole celery stalk thoroughly."

"I did, Mommy." Rachel showed her the stalk.

"This celery is filthy." Her mother took a piece of sludge and smeared it on Rachel's hand. "No dirt, no dirt," she kept saying.

"I'm sorry, Mommy," wailed Rachel. Before she knew what was happening, her mother had slapped her arms until they were swollen.

She massages the bruise where Janis smacked her that morning. Just thinking about being hit causes Rachel's body to ache. She steadies herself against the sink as the sound of the water washes away terrible thoughts of digging her nails into her mother's skin until she bleeds.

Rachel wanted to lash out at her mother. What stopped her were the pictures of her parents taken in Germany. Her father, with tired eyes, had half-smiled for the camera; his baldhead was shaped like an almond. His shoulders, concave, were unable to bear any weight. Her mother was pencil thin, eyes vacant, with her hands held behind her back to hide her missing pinkie, a small nub in its place, smooth as a newborn's head.

Once, in her mother's bedroom, Rachel found her weeping. She squeezed a pair of white gloves in her hand. "My gloves don't fit. My hands used to be pretty."

"Can I help you?" Rachel asked.

"No one can help me," she said.

"What happened to your pinkie?" Rachel asked.

"I wish I were dead," said her mother.

"Don't say that. Where would I be without you?" Rachel hugged her mother.

"Better off, much better off." Her mother went into the bathroom and returned with her rose-scented hand cream. She stood by the window, slowly rubbing the cream into her thin fingers, one at a time. She stared at the apple tree Rachel's father had planted before he died. Rachel didn't remember much about him, except that he spent summers working in the garden. His slight figure bent over the stalks as he picked tomatoes. Her mother continued to plaintively hum a tune. If Rachel tried to speak to her in this trance-like state, she never responded. At these times, Rachel felt her mother was a ghost, unable to be touched. She could put her hand right through her, a scary apparition. In the living room, Rachel would turn on the television just to hear another human voice.

At seven o'clock when Rachel's work is done, she gathers the bag of overripe peaches that Mr. Chin gives her and heads for home. It's her turn to cook. At Bee's Fish Store, she stops to pick up two fillets of salmon. She will prepare Janis' favorite meal. In the apartment, she finds a note from Janis. "Sorry I upset you. See you at ten, love Janis."

Rachel is relieved that Janis apologized. She recalls how sensitive Janis can be. The time Rachel had the flu and Janis placed cold compresses on her head throughout the day, even missing work. For her birthday, Janis baked her favorite chocolate cake and filled the room with balloons. Janis fed Rachel the cake with her fingers and they made love, gently. Then there was the time they rented a rowboat in Central Park, made silly quacking noises and fed the ducks. Rachel can't stand when Janis is angry with her. The silence reminds her of when her mother wouldn't speak to her. Rachel would lie on her bed and watch her own body float away. For a moment, she didn't exist. When she was younger, she read books on reincarnation. She hoped to meet her father in her next life. For now, she wants to make the most of her relationship with Janis. Rachel turns on the television for company.

Rachel is cooking at the stove when Janis comes in. She points to the table set with candles. "Wow, I should fight with you more often."

"Listen, I'm sorry I blew you off," Rachel says.

"I can live with it, sometimes," Janis says.

While Janis changes out of her waitress outfit into a tee shirt and shorts, Rachel imagines running her hand over Janis' soft skin, caressing her large breasts. She stares at Janis' nipples. They are round and dark just like her mother's.

Janis lights the candles while Rachel puts the food on their plates. When they sit down at the table, Janis reaches for her hand. Rachel lifts Janis' fingers to her lips, kissing it. "That feels good," says Janis.

"I'm glad," laughs Rachel.

Then Rachel notices the wax from the candle is dripping on the table. She takes her hand away to scratch the wax off with a knife. "You'll ruin the table," Janis says.

"How can I ruin a Salvation Army table?"

"I did see a nicer one this afternoon."

"Where were you?"

"Before work, I saw it on the way to the park with Deirdre," Janis says.

"How can you stand her? She gives me the creeps!"

"I think she's funny. You're jealous? Wow! Great!"

"I don't like her to paw you. Why does she call herself a witch?"

"Maybe she thinks she can put a spell on someone. I'd like to put a spell on you, right now." Janis places her toes over Rachel's.

"Then what?" Rachel grabs Janis' foot, playfully.

"I'd do nasty things to you." Janis sticks her foot in between Rachel's thighs.

"Not too nasty," Rachel says.

"What happened to your ring?" Janis reaches for her hand.

"I pawned it."

"I'm sorry you had to hock it. But you have to help with the rent."

"I've always contributed."

"The rent went up last month. You need to pay more."

"You'd throw me out? Even though I have nowhere to go."

"Stop worrying; we have the money now," says Janis.

"I don't want to fight. I just miss my ring." Rachel rubs her bare finger.

"I'll make you feel better." Janis pulls her up from the table. Rachel imagines she is still wearing the ring, as the two of them lie down. Rachel runs her hand through Janis' silky hair. When Janis sticks her tongue in her mouth, Rachel smells the fishy salmon. It reminds her of the fresh fish her mother would bring home from the market. She pictures the fish with bulging eyes, half dead, flopping around, bewildered. Rachel tries to concentrate on Janis' soft flesh, which feels strange, alien from her own small breasts and lean frame. Rachel remembers being attracted to Janis when they met. Janis was slim and affectionate. They were always caressing one another. Now, when Rachel runs her hand over Janis' flabby stomach, she squeezes her love handles. Working at the restaurant, Janis brings home leftover cream pies that she eats all the time. Janis climbs on top of Rachel, rotating her hips. Her body feels too heavy. Moving her mouth slowly down Rachel's belly, Janis' lips feel like suction cups making reddish circles on her skin. Rachel wheezes and tries to push Janis off of her.

"What's the matter with you?" Janis abruptly sits up.

"I don't know. I can't breathe," Rachel holds her stomach.

"What the hell are you talking about?" Janis frowns.

"I feel like I might throw up." Rachel's mouth is filled with bile.

"Making love with me makes you feel sick?" Janis stands up.

"It must have been the fish we had for dinner." Rachel rocks.

"You're nuts, you know that?" Janis hurriedly pulls on her shorts.

"I'm sorry. I need to rest." Maybe if she doesn't move, Janis will go away. She closes her eyes to play possum like she did with her mother. "Rachel, wake up," her mother whispers.

Rachel could hardly open her eyes. Her body didn't want to wake up. She needed to sleep.

"Baby, Mommy needs you." Her mother climbed into bed and kissed her cheek, arms and flat chest. Then her mother began to cry. Rachel opened her eyes.

"It's okay, Mommy," she said.

Her mother coaxed Rachel to put her hand on her mother's breast. They were soft and squishy, not like Rachel's own flat chest. Rachel did what her mommy asked because she wanted her to be glad.

She needs to make Janis happy, too. She opens her eyes when Janis touches her. "Come on. Let's try, again. Give me a little kiss."

Rachel allows Janis to kiss her but her lips feel bruised. Rachel flinches. "What is the matter with you?" Janis tightly squeezes Rachel's arm.

"Let go!" says Rachel.

Janis tries to push her tongue inside Rachel's mouth. "Kissing you is like kissing a store mannequin." Janis pulls away.

"I'm just tired," says Rachel.

"I'm tired, too, tired of you." Janis' nails dig into Rachel's skin "Leave. Come on. Get up. Get dressed!" Janis dumps Rachel's clothes on her lap.

"I've nowhere to go," says Rachel.

"That's not my problem." Janis pokes her arm.

"Please, I'll be good. Come on. Sit down," says Rachel.

"You're driving me crazy just like my mother did," says Janis.

"I'll do anything to stay," pleads Rachel.

"Stop whining. Just get the hell out!" Janis flexes her hand into a fist.

Gathering up her clothes, Rachel dresses in the bathroom. She isn't going to tangle with Janis. When she's mad, the best thing to do is leave her alone. Rachel hears Janis pacing the floor. Janis calls Rachel, "a bitch." Rachel shivers. Janis is not calming down. Rachel prays she can make it out of the apartment without a fight. For a moment, she imagines charging into Janis, crashing her into the furniture, throwing Janis out of the apartment.

When Rachel comes out, Janis is drumming her fingers on the table.

"Don't say a word, just go."

Janis' eyes are fiery. Rachel quickly walks past her.

The bright lights on Broadway make her squint. She pulls down the brim of her Yankee cap. She doesn't know where she is going but her sneakers keep moving. A group of boys stand on the corner to whistle at girls passing in mini-skirts. A bum pees against an abandoned brick building. The city is out of control. Maybe that is why Janis' flare-ups have worsened over the past months. Janis reminds her of a raging pit bull.

When Janis acts mad, she scares her more than her mother. Her mother's behavior is more predictable. Rachel can usually calm her mother. She thinks about going back to her mother but Janis is the reason she can't go.

When Janis started coming over, her mother complained. When they turned on the radio while lying on the bed in her bedroom, her mother would knock loudly on the door. "Turn it off. I can't think."

"What the matter with her?" Janis asked.

"She doesn't like loud noises." Rachel lowered the radio.

"Weird," Janis whispered in Rachel's ear.

"I know," laughed Rachel.

When she talked to Janis on the phone with the door closed, Rachel heard the wood floor creaking on the other side. One time, she yanked open the door to catch her mother. "Leave me alone. I hate you. I'm seventeen. I don't need a nursemaid!"

One night, when she came home at ten minutes after her twelve o'clock curfew, she found her mother pacing the floor. "How do I know you're safe? You could have been murdered."

"It's okay, Mom. Nothing bad happened," said Rachel.

"You can't go out at night." Her mother lips chattered.

"I'm fine." Rachel grasped her mother's hand.

"What would I do without you?" Her mother sat down on the couch where she rocked methodically, tightly wrapping her hands around her own body.

"You're fine, Mom," Rachel whispered.

"My baby, my baby is safe. I couldn't live without you. Is that wrong?" Her mother caressed Rachel's face, arms and breasts.

"I know, mom," Rachel said woodenly.

"You love me, don't you?" Her mother's eyes clouded over like window shades being lowered as she put her arm around her. Rachel, feet dragging, followed her into the bedroom because it was the only way to soothe her. In the morning, she crept back to her own bed so she wouldn't have to face her.

Drizzle intercepts Rachel's troubled thoughts. Rachel ducks under a gray awning at Joe's donut shop. She enters and perches on a cracked vinyl stool at the counter. She faces a waitress with bony wrists. "What can I get you?"

"A cup of hot chocolate and a glazed donut," Rachel says.

"They're rock hard. Take a vanilla frosted, instead," says the waitress.

"Okay, "Rachel smiles at the girl.

While sipping her hot chocolate, Rachel watches the waitress sitting at the cash register. She gazes at the rain. When a young man walks in, she kisses him. He laughs and murmurs something in her ear. Rachel fingers her donut. She doesn't want to embarrass them but she can't help staring. She wishes that Janis could be gentler.

In the beginning, over two years ago, Janis was kind. She took Rachel in when she couldn't stand living with her mother, anymore. They would cook dinner together and cuddle in front of the television every evening. But Rachel's feelings began to change after Janis had slapped her. She recalls why Janis hit her. Rachel constantly worried that her mother would drop by the apartment and realize her and Janis were intimate. One night, her mother, weeping, called and Janis answered the phone. She heard Janis say, "Rachel can't come to the phone. She's busy. Stop calling her."

Rachel grabbed the receiver. Her mother said. "I need to see you. I'll take a taxi to visit."

"Mom, I love you. I'll visit. Please don't come here."

"Why can't I come see you? Why does Janis hate me? What's going on between you?" her mother asked.

"Nothing is wrong. Stop worrying, I'll come this weekend," said Rachel.

When Rachel put down the receiver, Janis said, "Why didn't you let me handle her? If you go back, she'll make you feel guilty."

"I didn't know what else to say to make her stop crying," said

Rachel.

"Our mothers don't want us. I need you." Janis pulled Rachel onto her lap.

"I worry about her." Rachel placed her head on Janis' shoulder.

"Stop thinking about her. I'm glad my mother didn't snivel when I left home." Janis laughed.

"I never said anything bad about your mother. Let's drop it." Rachel pushed herself off Janis' lap.

"My mother doesn't act like a crybaby when I call her," said Janis.

"Stop it!" Rachel covered her ears.

"What's the matter? Did I hurt your feelings, poor baby?" said Janis.

"Why can't you just drop it?" Rachel's eyes fill with tears.

"Don't tell me you're going to cry?" Janis laughed.

"Your mother isn't upset. She abandoned you," said Rachel.

"I told you to shut up!" Janis slapped her across the face.

"I hate you" Rachel locked herself in the bathroom.

"I didn't hurt you." Janis banged on the door.

"Leave me alone," Rachel looked in the mirror. Her cheek was burning.

In the diner, Rachel puts her hand to her cheek and looks at the mirror on the wall. Supporting her head with her elbows, Rachel tries to think about the good times with Janis, like the summer night, surrounded by Chinese lanterns, on a boat ride up the Hudson when they embraced each other and talked until morning. They attended a Madonna concert in Central Park where they danced. Two bodies becoming one. Janis is a part of her. The more she thinks about Janis, the more Rachel has to talk to her. Leaving the donut shop, she finds a phone booth on the corner of Eighty-Ninth Street. The phone rings for a while before Janis picks it up. "Hello," says Janis in a sleepy voice.

"It's me," Rachel says.

"Where the hell are you?" Janis asks.

"I'm at Eighty-Ninth Street," Rachel says.

"Why don't you come home?" Janis says.

"What are you talking about? You told me to leave," Rachel says.

"I changed my mind. Come back," Janis sounds annoyed.

"You want me back?" Rachel asks.

"Are you being dense? Isn't that what I just told you?" says Janis.

"I can't come home. I'm too confused." She slumps against the phone booth.

"Confused about what?" Janis asks.

"About me, about you, about my mother," Rachel says.

"I can solve the equation. Your mother is nuts," Janis says sarcastically.

"There are reasons she has problems. You know, stuff she would like to talk about, to tell someone but can't. She is afraid she won't be understood or forgiven." Rachel tightens her hold on the receiver.

"You're not making any sense. Come home. I need to sleep," says Janis.

"I didn't think you would understand. I have to go now. There's no time left." Rachel gently puts the receiver back in its cradle but wishes she could smash it into tiny pieces. To stop her hands from trembling, she sticks them in her pocket.

The fog makes her invisible. Rachel walks down the stairs of the subway station. The platform is empty except for a black man playing on his harmonica, "When the Saints Go Marching In." She knows the song because she played it on her flute in the high school band. For a moment, she sees herself wearing the school uniform, yellow shirt and brown skirt as the band marched down Queens Boulevard on Memorial Day. Her mother stood at the curb. She waved an American flag. Delighted to see her mother who didn't go anywhere but to work at the shoe factory, Rachel waved back.

As the subway whizzes by on the next track, the flicker of the overhead lights makes Rachel blink. Maybe she never marched in a band. Maybe her life with Janis is a dream. Maybe nothing happened between her mother and her. Maybe Rachel doesn't exist.

Only her mother exists for her. Her flesh is warm to the touch, alive. She needs to be cradled. She wonders what her mother is doing now. Since her watch says one-thirty, she must be in bed, not that she truly sleeps. Her mother lies on the edge of the mattress, waiting for something bad to happen. She catnaps.

Rachel's shoulders ache as she leans against one of the columns. Her teeth hurt from grinding them. Her eyelids droop. When the train stops in front of her, she enters and sits down. Out of habit, she watches for the names of the stops. The train is taking control of her life. When the subway stops at Queens Boulevard, she steps out and walks up to the street, passing Jahn's, the ice cream store, where she used to buy her vanilla milk shakes.

The houses on Elm Street are dark. The lamppost lights cast long shadows on the sidewalk as she walks down it. She touches the tops of the fire hydrants. She waves to Mr. Weaver's statue of an eagle with beady eyes on his front post. She pats the face of the redheaded gnome on Mrs. Reiner's lawn in a game she has played since she was little.

After she opens the wrought iron gate, she looks at the brick, squat, one-story home to see if it's changed. It still has the same frayed yellow awning over the porch. On the side of the house, she picks up a fake rock, twists the back of it and takes out a key. Slowly she opens the back door leading into the kitchen. Inside, the only sound is the grandfather clock chiming two. She stands in the living room, midway between her room and her mother's directly across. She shivers and wraps her arms around herself. Her mother is breathing, rhythm soft and steady. The sound is comforting and familiar to her, like a flute. She enters the bedroom where the warm sheets smell like lavender and she slides into bed next to her mother.

I Don't Give a Damn

~

Today we are going to a fair at Central Park. The sun is warm enough that my mother carries her cardigan, but doesn't wear it. She is thin, jutting collarbone and always cold. I take her frail hand in the park to maneuver us through the crowd. I spy the ice cream stand. We lick our cones while watching a juggler and a mime. I dab the vanilla dot on my mother's hollow cheek with my napkin. She tugs my hand to ride on the merry-go-round. "Are you sure you are up to it?" I ask.

"Yes, I feel fine," she says.

"You look pale." I say when we come off the ride.

"I'm chilly." She places her sweater over her thin shoulders.

"I guess the ride was a bad idea," I say.

"I have to find a bathroom." Her face is dark.

"Sure." I put my arm around her to navigate through the crowd. It is wall-to-wall people. I yell at a bicyclist blocking our path. My mother takes deep breaths. The music is so loud that I can hardly think where to go. She places her hands over her ears. The smell of frankfurters, cotton candy and popcorn surround us. Her eyes are watery. "I'm going to have an accident." My mother's hands tremble.

"Hold on," I say. The sun is hot on my back. I stop at the next apartment building. I tell the doorman with bushy eyebrows, "My mother is sick. Do you have a bathroom?"

He starts to say, "no" but then he looks at my mother's blue lips.

"The super's apartment." He takes us inside.

I stand guard outside the bathroom door while watching the super's son glued to Sesame Street on television. I wish I still sat on my mother's lap to laugh at Cookie Monster. My mother groans inside the bathroom. I talk through the door. "Mom, are you okay?"

"Just a few more minutes," she says.

"I'm right here if you need me." I concentrate on the minute hand of my watch to avoid the puzzled face of the super who keeps peeking out of the living room. I pray my mother will feel better. I feel stupid for allowing her to come to the park because I should have known it would be too much for her.

When she comes out, my mother is haggard. "I'm sorry for the inconvenience," she says to the super. She buttons her sweater and smooths down her skirt. In the hallway, she asks, "Do I look okay?"

"Of course, Mom." I don't tell her that her face is pasty, but I straighten the collar of her shirt.

Outside, the sun glares down at us. The sidewalk is crowded. As we walk toward our apartment on West End Avenue, my mother leans on me and I put my arm around her. Her breath is sour. "I wanted to be with you," she says.

"Don't apologize. You didn't do anything wrong," I say.

"We can go another time when I'm better," she says.

"That would be fine," I hesitate.

The doorman, Tony, takes one look at my mother and hurries to press the elevator button. Inside the elevator, she steadies herself against the side. For a moment, I wish we lived in a new building instead of this prewar one that my mother loved the moment she saw it. A building with a super fast elevator, not one that creaks as it slowly reaches for the fifth floor. In the apartment, I yell for Riva, our housekeeper. I sigh with relief when she runs down the hall. "What is it, Missus?" she asks my mother.

"I'm not feeling well. Can you help me to bed?" She leans on Riva who is smaller than she is, but plumper.

I walk behind them to my mother's room and close the damask curtains while Riva takes out my mother's silk pajamas. "No problem, we get you comfy in no time," says Riva. Listening to Riva's soothing voice, I feel less worried. I try not to look at my mother's skinny limbs, but when Riva helps her into pajama pants, I notice how emaciated she has become. Her skin is red and flaky. "Everything aches. Be gentle," says my mother.

"I go slowly." Riva unbuttons the pajama top and helps my mother into it.

I stand near the window and watch a mother and child enter

Central Park. I remember when we roller skated through the park. My mother was as fast as I was and we passed everyone. I saw the men admiring my mother, blonde hair blowing and green eyes alight. She would smile and whip by them. I wondered if the men thought she was a tease. She liked to be noticed when we skated because she always wore makeup and a bright sweater with slimming pants. She argued with me to dress better, but I told her, "I can't skate in tight pants." She'd shake her head. I wondered what it felt like to be adored by my father and noticed by other men. I didn't think I would ever know because I have a thick body with small breasts and hardly any waist. I can't imagine anyone staring at me except to giggle. In junior high, when my mother wasn't home, I'd squeeze into her clothes. One time, brimming with self-confidence in her red gown, I sashayed around my room. But when I looked in the mirror, I saw an overripe tomato bursting out of its skin. I felt hopeless, but I prayed when I grew up, my baby fat would disappear and I would develop a womanly figure.

I stand by my mother's bed when Riva leaves the room. The light on the antique nightstand throws shadows of lions prowling. Hopefully, they will protect my mother who reaches for me with icy fingers that feel small in mine. I notice she is no longer wearing her ring. She rubs her bare finger. "It doesn't fit, anymore. I haven't taken that ring off in twenty-four years," she says.

She gives me a weak smile and I ask, "Do you need anything?

"A cup of water," she says.

When I go into the bathroom, I shake my head at all the medicine bottles lining the shelf. There are pills for sleep, for pain, for her to go to the bathroom and for stopping her from going to the bathroom. In bed she sits up, but when I give her the cup, her hand shakes and she spills the water on her pajamas. "Damn," she says.

"It's okay." I wipe it with a towel.

"I'm so clumsy," she says.

"Me, too." I smile. My mother pats my arm. I hold the glass for her while she drinks slowly. I remember being little when she held the cup for me, a pink "sippy" cup. I wish I still had the cup. I would give it to her. She wouldn't have to worry about wetting her pajamas.

I go into my bedroom and listen to Riva singing Spanish songs in the kitchen. I can smell her cooking chicken potpie, my favorite, for dinner. I wish I were still little because Riva and I always had supper while my parents were at a party or just out dancing. When my parents glided across the dance floor at my Bat Mitzvah, all our guests watched them. My mother had a diamond choker around her neck. Her bare shoulders were milky white. She wore a sequined black dress that accented her thinness. My father held himself proudly as though he were escorting a queen. He had eyes only for my mother while she threw kisses to her guests, as she twirled across the room. I stood by the side of the dance floor. Even as I smoothed down the pink satin dress my mother picked for me, the material kept bunching up. I felt like my decrepit grandmother who wore brown, sack-like dresses on all occasions. I wanted to hide under the table. No one would notice I was missing even though it was supposed to be my special day. When I gave my mother a piercing look, she just laughed and whispered into my father's ear. Then the two of them came over and dragged me onto the dance floor. I stepped on my mother's foot, but she didn't yell at me. When I looked into her clear blue eyes, she made a graceful curtsy. When I bowed back, without tripping, I grinned. The guests clapped and for the moment, I was the star.

I open the drawer of my nightstand to survey my candies: Snickers, Hershey's and M and M's. I close my bedroom door before I eat a Snickers bar. My mother will probably not get up, but I don't want to take a chance because she worries about my weight, especially how I fit in clothes. The last time we shopped was a year ago, when I turned sixteen. We visited the Chalet Ski House on Broadway to buy new ski outfits for our trip to Aspen. My mother tried on an aqua one-piece snowsuit that fit her perfectly. "You look great," I said.

"Do you think? It's not too big?" she asked.

"Big? Where? I asked.

"Funny, funny," my mother smiled.

Reluctantly, I tried on a shapeless, gray outfit. "What do you think?"

"Don't you want something with color, jazzier?" She held up a fuchsia outfit.

"If I wear that I will scare everyone on the mountain."

"No, you won't."

"Mom, not everybody is a size six, okay?"

"All right, I know I can't win." My mother shook her head.

But we never made it to Aspen because my mother had such a bad stomachache she was crippled with pain. She was barely able to climb out of bed so that my dad could take her to the doctor.

After the medical tests were completed, when my parents sat me down in the living room, I knew something was wrong because Dad kept biting his lower lip. My mother's eyes averted my face. "What's wrong?"

"I have pancreatic cancer, but I'm going to beat it." My mother said in her cheerleading voice.

"It's in an early stage," my father added.

"I start chemotherapy next week."

"Are you sure you will be okay?" I frown.

"The doctors assure me I will be fine."

"How do they know?" I take my mother's hand.

"Don't be a worry wart." My mother hugged me.

That weekend, the three of us stayed home and watched old movies. *Casablanca* was my favorite. I sat between my parents and held their hands. I couldn't help comparing my father's stubby fingers to my mother's slender ones. I didn't want the movie to end. I imagined that as long as our bodies were joined, nothing bad could happen to us. Our bodies gave us sustenance. If we stuck together, we formed an impenetrable wall. Nothing could slip through us.

While snacking on a Hershey Bar, I take my homework out of my knapsack, but I decide against doing my calculus. My art assignment is to make "a drawing that tells about you." After I find a piece of poster board on the shelf, I go into my father's study to collect a stack of medical magazines. I cut out the colored pictures of different body parts. I paste eyeballs, a tongue, a kidney, a stomach, esophagus, arms, legs and hands in different places. I write captions under each picture with India ink.

"I look at my mother's yellowish eyes. I cut out the tongue of her doctors who aren't helping her. I vacuum out all the pus-colored cancer in her stomach. Her arms and legs are atrophying because I can't help her. Her skin is lusterless. I pump golden air into her lungs to help her breathe better."

I am being dramatic, but I didn't care. I drip blood everywhere.

Riva calls me into dinner. My parents are already sitting at the kitchen table. I'm surprised my parents are eating with me because my mother still looks pale. Riva dishes me out a large helping of chicken potpie. She looks at me with affectionate eyes.

"I'm afraid I ruined Rachel's day." My mom pushes her fork through her food.

"Mom, don't say that."

"I felt sick at the park. I had to use the super's bathroom at 325 Central Park West. I was so embarrassed."

"Why did you take your mother to the park?" asks my dad.

"What are you talking about?" I say.

"She's not strong enough."

"Please, stop fighting." My mother holds her stomach.

"Are you okay?" I ask my mother.

"I don't feel well," she bows her head.

"Riva, could we eat in the bedroom?" he asks sharply.

My father starts to help my mother from her chair. Her slippers have fallen off and her feet are bare. "Wait," I bend down and carefully put back her slippers. I notice her toes are bluish. I know that's not a good sign. She's not getting enough circulation to her toes. I want to remind my father to put on her special socks that are attached to an ankle pump. The socks will help to circulate her blood, but I don't want to alarm my mother. "I'll be better company tomorrow," says my mother.

"Don't say that. You're good company." My eyes follow her out the door. Riva brings their dinners and comes back to sit with me. I bow my head. "Did my dad put on the special socks?"

"Yes," said Riva.

"What am I going to do?" I whisper.

"You be strong for your mother," she says.

"The Internet says my mom's disease is hard to treat," I answer.

"I know your mother for sixteen years. She is strong lady. She get well," says Riva. While I hold Riva's callused hand, I remember one day when my parents and I were sitting at the table while I talked about my school day. Dad, a surgeon, told a dirty joke he heard in the operating room. My mother blushed and said, "Really, David." But she couldn't hide her smile. My dad gave out a belly laugh, the kind that is contagious. Once the two of us started laughing, it was a free-for-all.

The next morning, before I leave for school, I try to talk to my dad at breakfast. The room is bright with vases of lilies of the valley that my mother has delivered every week. I wish we were at our country house where the backyard is filled with wildflowers my mother and I like to pick. I lean over to smell the flowers. "They're beautiful," I say.

"Right." My dad doesn't lift his head from reading *The New York Times*.

"How's Mom?" I ask loudly.

"She had a rough night." He looks at me with tired eyes.

"Can I say hello?"

"She's asleep."

"I did an art project for school. Do you want to see it?"

"I don't have time this morning, maybe later."

"Great, just great."

"What's the matter with you?"

"Nothing."

"Don't exhaust your mother today."

"I didn't tire her out. The disease did that to her." I cross my arms.

"You don't have to be rude." My father frowns and gets up from the table. I shake my head. I look for comfort to Riva who is washing the dishes, but she hasn't heard our conversation. My dad has no idea what I'm feeling and I don't think he cares.

At Riverdale Country Day, my art teacher has questions about my poster because she calls me to her office during study hall. Mrs. Alexis, a dark-haired, energetic teacher, has a distraught look on her face. "Could you tell me how this picture represents you? She asks.

"It's how I feel all the time," I reply.

"What do you mean?"

"My mother has pancreatic cancer," I say quietly.

"I'm sorry."

"Not as sorry as me," I mutter.

"You could talk to the school counselor, Dr. Goldstein."

"That won't help," I whisper.

"Why not give it a try?"

"I'll think about it," I say hopelessly.

"I'm going to have to call your parents," she says.

"I don't think that is a good idea!" I get up and slam the door behind me.

I imagine going into the art room, ripping the poster into shreds and making a bonfire out of it. I hate myself for having drawn it. Now, I am going to be in deep trouble with my parents, at least with my dad. He's going to angry with me for upsetting my mother. I can't stand what my mother's illness has done to my family. I'm sick of bickering with my dad. My mom isn't herself. I don't recognize her lined face. She looks sickly even with makeup. When I look in the mirror, my cheeks are rosy, healthy-looking. My eyes are deep brown without being bloodshot. I never thought being chubby was a good thing, but it protects me from being chilled. I wonder what my mother thinks when she looks at me. Does she wish she were still young with her whole life ahead of her?

That night, my parents call me into their dimly lit bedroom. My mother takes up very little room in the king-size bed. She weighs much less than I do, maybe eighty pounds. Her pajamas hang on her. Large blue veins show through her papery skin. Dark circles make her eyes sunken. She pats the bed for me to sit down. My dad stands near the foot of the bed. The room has a medicinal smell that reminds me of my mother's hospital room where she goes every time the doctors find blood in her stool. Last time, they operated and took out half of her stomach because she had a blockage. She's too damn thin because her stomach doesn't absorb much food. I avoid looking at the rows of pills that have been moved from the bathroom to her vanity table. Instead, I imagine the ruby and emerald glass bottles filled with perfumes and the cosmetics that I tried on when they were out for the evening. "We received a call from Mrs. Alexis and Dr. Goldstein," says my father.

"They mentioned a poster," my mother starts.

"Why did you do it?" my father follows.

"I was upset about Mom last night," I defend myself.

"It sounds like an emotionally charged piece," says my mother.

"I think seeing Dr. Goldstein would be helpful," adds my father.

"I told you, no way," I exclaim.

Over the next few weeks, I try but can't concentrate on school because my mother is too weak to climb out of bed. The room is dark now all the time. Then, one afternoon, when the curtains are open with light streaming into her room, I find her tailor, Mrs. Liana. I worry that something is wrong because Mrs. Liana never makes house calls. My mother is trying on her pajamas, a size zero. I remember I went with Riva to pick them up after we special-ordered them from the Countess Lingerie Store. "You're too skinny. Need to eat more." Mrs. Liana is holding a pincushion.

"No matter what I eat. Food runs through me," says my mother.

"She eats like a pig. Last night Riva made her a banana milk shake." I try to laugh.

"It's true," says my mother.

My mother is unsteady and I go over to help her. She is a skeleton with shrunken breasts and no waist. She is stick-thin like a girl before puberty. She is wearing a wig but underneath she is bald, smooth like a Buddha's belly I want to rub. When Mrs. Liana leaves, I help my mother climb into bed. Then I lie down next to her and hold her hand. We both fall asleep.

I dream that I visit a medicine man in Wyoming. The sky is cloudless and clear blue. A herd of cattle is grazing. Inside a log cabin, a man with leathery skin and long gray hair is sitting by a fire. "Rachel, I've been expecting you," he says.

"Do you have the potion for my mother?" I ask.

"Of course," he says.

I am relieved when he hands me the bottle filled with swirling liquid smelling of chicory. I carefully carry it back to my mother. When she drinks it, her face changes to the way it was with plump red lips, soft cheekbones and a curvy body.

When I wake up, the room is pitch black. It takes me a moment to realize that it's a dream and not reality. I'm angry because I want my mother better. I wonder if my artwork upsets my mother. Maybe she understands what I'm feeling. I am angrier with my father who pretends that I have nothing to worry about, but he's wrong. I'll drag him onto the Internet and show him all the gruesome facts. Then he will see what an uphill battle we are facing. He never includes me in anything that goes on with my mother. I wonder what he is really thinking.

I find my dad watching a Yankee game in the study. He is sipping a glass of red wine. My mother complains that he can't be in the house without the television on. We both hate sports on television. I don't mind a live Yankee game at Shea Stadium because I love the hot dogs, peanuts, and ice cream with waffle cones. "Dad, why don't we go to a game."

"You're kidding, right?"

"No, I'm not."

"Leave your mother alone?"

"Riva will watch her."

"Do you hear yourself?" He shakes his head.

"I'm joking. I wanted to see how you would answer."

"Don't you care at all about your mother? Are you that selfish?" he asks.

"Now that's funny. I spend every afternoon with her. What about you?"

"I don't have to justify myself to a sixteen-year-old."

"Right, that's your favorite line when I want to talk about Mom."

"Look, I'm tired. I just need to sit here while Mom is sleeping. I want to watch the game in peace. Go do your homework."

"Maybe I'll do another poster for art."

"You really want to upset your mother?" he asks.

"Why are you saying that?" I ask.

"Do you know how upset she was by your poster? Have you lost your mind?" He makes a fist.

"I may have lost my mind but I still have my heart!" I run out of the room.

"What the hell is that supposed to mean?" My father yells after me, but I slam my bedroom door. I can't believe how insensitive my father is. He goes to work and forgets about my mother, but I can't. I don't want to block out my feelings. I can't anesthetize myself. He thinks I should be like him, but he can go to hell.

I take out a photograph album of my family. My parents were kissing each of my cheeks as I ate a piece of chocolate birthday cake on my first birthday. Our eyes glowed as we stared into the camera. I have a picture of my dad teaching me to water-ski. My mom must have snapped the photo while my dad helped me on with my skis. I look at a picture from two years ago where the three of us were holding our skis on a mountaintop in Aspen. We laughed at the camera. My mother's complexion was ruddy and her snug ski outfit was bright yellow. But then I remember the two of us had a private instructor, Todd, blonde, blue-eyed and a real hunk. My mother was a competent skier, but she kept falling down and Todd would lift her up. At lunch, my mom said, "Todd's adorable."

"I don't want to hear this," I squirm.

"Being married doesn't mean I can't notice an attractive man," she assures me.

"Okay, Mom, I agree he's cute, but so what?" I challenge her.

I guess I made my mom feel bad because she didn't fall once for the rest of the afternoon. From the adoring looks Todd kept giving my mother, I knew he was disappointed.

The problem with having an attractive mother is everyone notices her and I feel like an ant. I remember when my mother chaperoned my sixth grade dance. She wore a low cut green dress. My date, Jeff, kept staring at my mother while we were dancing. Finally I said, "She's a little old for you."

Jeff accidentally stepped on my toes. He stammered, "I don't know what you're talking about." He blushed.

Later, in the car, my mother said, "Jeff's a nice boy, very polite."

I nodded, but didn't bother to enlighten her that my date had a crush on her, not me.

The next day, when I come home from school, I go into my parents' room. Since I hear my mother splashing in the tub, I walk into the kitchen for a snack. Riva has baked my favorite oatmeal chocolate chip cookies. The room is warm. "These are delicious," I say to Riva.

"I know you like. I make cause I hear yelling last night between you and father," says Riva. She wipes her hands on her apron and squeezes my shoulders.

"I can't help it. He makes me so mad," I answer.

"Father not good at being useless. He sees mother sick and he can't do anything so he is angry." Riva takes out the ironing board.

"I'm angry, too, but I'm not yelling at him," I say.

"You yell last night," says Riva.

"Okay, Okay, I'm guilty." We both laugh.

Then, my mother screams. We run down the hall. "I can't get up," cries my mother from the bathroom. Riva and I open the door. My naked mother is lying on the floor. She is wet, shivering and curled into a ball. When we lift her up, her body is all bones with sharp curves. Riva wraps a towel around her while I caress her baldhead and pray her thick hair grows back. My mother loved to wear her blonde hair in a ponytail tied with a ribbon. For my Bat Mitzvah, she wore her hair in a bun covered with a net of tiny pearls that made her look regal. I remember smoothing my own limp hair and wishing I had her luxurious hair. We help her on with pajamas. I realize her body is hairless. I rub her thin arms to warm her. She asks me to massage her weak legs and bluish toes with lotion. Her feet are unfamiliar to me. I remember when she would drag me with her for pedicures and she picked bright colors that accented her slender toes. Her body looks like my grandmother's before she died. Then I tuck her into bed while Riva goes for a heating pad. "I'm sorry," she says.

"You can't take a bath unless someone is with you."

"I'm such a nuisance."

"You're not."

"Don't tell Dad I fell. He worries too much about me."

"Let him worry."

"It's hard for him."

"I love you." I wrap my arms around my mother's slender shoulders.

"I love you, too," she replies. Her breath smells stale, but I kiss her.

In the kitchen, I lower my head onto the table. I try not to think about what could have happened if she were knocked unconscious trying to climb out of the tub by herself. I hear my father's key in the door. When he sticks his head in the kitchen, my voice cracks when I say, "Go check on your wife."

He runs down the hall. I close my eyes and rest. When I look up, my father is standing at the kitchen door. "Mom says she is feeling better. Are you okay?"

"No, I'm not okay. When Mom fell in the bathroom, she couldn't get up," I say.

"Damn, I told her not to bathe without help." He runs his hands through his hair.

"She could have really hurt herself."

"I know," he says.

"Mom is getting worse."

"Don't tell her that."

"Mom didn't want me to tell you that she fell."

"I don't know why Mom is trying to protect me." He shakes his head.

Then my mother calls, "David" and my father flies out of the room. I hear the two of them arguing. "I'm worried you're going to fall and hurt yourself. You need a nurse," insists my father.

"I can't stand the lack of privacy."

"I know, but how can I go to work if you're not safe?"

Then, my mother starts to cry and the door of their bedroom closes.

I want to rescue my mother. In my mind, I bang on their door until they let me in. I crawl into their bed. I refuse to leave.

The next day, after school, I am not surprised to see a tall black woman wearing a white uniform in my mother's room. Her dangling earrings are a row of silver stars that sway as she plumps my mother's pillows. "Here, darling," the woman says to my mother.

"I have two angels. Claire, this is my daughter, Rachel," says my mother.

"It took me all morning to persuade her to take a bath."

"After a bath, my skin hurts." My mother stares at her chapped hands.

"You smell good." I kiss her cheek.

Claire goes into the bathroom and I hear the water going down the tub drain.

My mother leans against the pillows. "I hate being sick. I can't take much more of it."

"Mom, don't say that," I grab her hand.

Then, my mother coughs, an echo down a hollow tunnel. She closes her eyes and takes her hand away from me. Her lips are cracked and bloody. I reach for the lip ointment, but my mother shakes her head. I wrap my arms around myself. Claire comes out of the bathroom and picks up the cough medicine with codeine by the side of the bed. She pours the liquid and feeds it to my mother. "She has to rest," Claire whispers to me.

"Okay," I lower my head. I don't want to leave, but Claire leads me out of the room.

From my bedroom I can hear my mother coughing. I close my door. I sit at my desk to make a sketch of my mother and me. I sketch us in bright acrylic colors. My mother's skin is healthy, beige with a pink glow to her cheeks. Her eyebrows are sculpted and her lips deep red. I draw myself a chubbier version of my mother. We are on

Rollerblades in Central Park. The sun is yellow with an orange halo. Then I scribble over our faces and I draw another picture of us in charcoal. My mother's face is gaunt, sharp-lined. The sky is dark and threatening rain. I'm confused. I love my mother. I hate that she is sick, but part of me is relieved that she won't be flirting with ski instructors and my dates won't be salivating over her. I rip the picture in half and lie down on my bed. I weep into my pillow. I feel evil. I can't believe myself. I keep seeing my mother the way she is now, frail. When she was well, I wished she wasn't my mother because men acted like she was royalty and I was her handmaiden. My rational mind tells me it is impossible to put a hex on my mother, but part of me worries that I could have caused her illness. I know this sounds crazy. I feel unbalanced.

That night I can't sleep because thoughts about my mother's sickly body won't leave my mind. She is the thinnest person I know. When her skin is pressed too hard, it turns black and blue. Claire gave her a sleeping pill before she left for the evening. She is resting peacefully. I wonder if her coughing can bruise the inside of her chest. My father is watching television. When I stand at the door of the den, I see that my father has a lost look on his face. His lips are moving as though he is talking to someone, but he is alone. In the evenings, my mother would sit with him while he watched the ball game and make breezy conversation about her day. He keeps shaking his head as though he is arguing with someone. I have been too hard on him. He misses my mother, his best friend. I walk to his lounge chair. "Dad," I whisper.

"What?" When he looks at me, his eyes are red-rimmed.

"I'm worried about Mom," I say.

"Me, too," he sighs.

"What's going to happen to her?" I put my arm on his shoulder.

"I don't know." He pulls me onto his lap and holds me the way he did when I was small.

The next morning after he leaves for work and before Claire arrives, I hear my mother weeping. When I look in the bathroom, she is standing over the sink. In her pajamas and bathrobe, she stares into the mirror. She doesn't notice me as she struggles to place her wig on her head. Her veined hands are shaking. Her baldhead shines. Her lips are still bloody and she licks them. "Mom, can I help you?"

"No, go away." She flicks her hand.

"I have nowhere to go," I whisper.

"I want to be alone. Can't you see that?" she asks.

"Please let me help you." I step closer to her.

"No one can help me." Her voice quakes.

"I can try." I touch her bony arm.

She scrutinizes my image in the mirror. I hold my breath. She says, "Be careful. My skin feels tender." She bites her lip and hands me the wig. I watch her grateful eyes in the mirror as I gently adjust the hairpiece. When I am done, she tilts her head. "You did a good job," she says.

"You look terrific." I kiss her gaunt cheek.

"Sure." She puts her arm around me and we gaze tenderly at our joined reflection in the mirror.

Photographs

~

Melissa turns away from Leo in class to study the composition of her artwork while he's working on a vivid composition of two people intertwined. She paints shadows on her canvas to darken her parents' faces. She quickly draws herself as she built a castle, buckets overflowing with sand while her parents watched from the porch swing. Her body was tawny from playing on the beach. When she overheard her father telling her mother how beautiful Melissa was, she dug deeper in the sand. When the water edged closer to the fortress, she dug a moat and yelled to mother and father for help. With arms entwined her parents descended the steps to aid her.

With a fine-tipped brush, she draws her mother with ivory skin and a white cotton shift. She appeared paler in contrast to her deeply tanned father who draped his arm around her. Melissa wishes she could go back to being six years old when her family vacationed in East Hampton, Long Island.

Leo stands next to her canvas. "I like the different tones on the parents' faces, but maybe accentuate their features. Why not add a little blush to the mother's lips?"

"Do you think I need to?" Melissa asks.

"It would make the mother's face more feminine."

"I'll think about it," she smiles.

Leo moves to the back of the studio to put his easel away. Melissa inhales the familiar oil smell as she snaps her paint box shut. Melissa and Leo are sophomores, friends since the first month at Parson's School of Design in New York. Leo is everything her father isn't. Tall, lanky with long black hair, he wears his T-shirt untucked and his blue jeans are torn at the knees. After she leans her easel against the wall, they say goodbye to their classmates. Melissa pulls back her hair. She rubs her baggy jeans, splattered with blue paint. After buttoning the top button of her blouse, she makes sure it's neatly tucked into her bell-bottoms. "The last model was too chubby for me, like Reuben's women," says Leo.

"I wish I could paint like Reuben," Melissa sighs.

"You have your own style." Leo reaches for her hand.

"You think I'm improving?" Melissa places her hands behind her back.

"Absolutely. I love your paintings." Leo smiles.

"Are you being serious?" Melissa asks.

"I wish my paintings were as realistic as yours are." He touches her shoulder.

"I wish I had your sense of color." Melissa's shoulder feels cold.

"That's why we're a good match. What are you doing this afternoon?"

"I have homework."

"I do, too. We could work together," He says earnestly.

"Maybe another time."

"Are you positive?" Leo calls after her as she descends the subway stairs.

She smiles as she waves goodbye. But while waiting for the subway, Melissa wonders what's wrong with her. She has fun with Leo, is attracted to his lean frame but when he touches her skin, her body turns icy. She has the impulse to run away from him, to hide. It isn't just Leo who makes her feel this way, but any boy. In high school she barely dated. She felt self-conscious. Boys never seemed interested in what she had to say but only in her shapely figure. Leo is different, easy to be with. He carefully studies her paintings to offer her helpful suggestions. Their pictures are of people searching for answers, but he paints in vibrant colors. He can do with a paint brush what her father can do with a camera: capture the essence of a person. She hopes to paint as well as Leo before she graduates. His talent and ability excite her.

When she arrives home, she flips on the hallway light to walk through the narrow passage to her bedroom. Her mother likes a dark apartment. She opens the curtains to allow in the sunlight and throws her purse on to the pink canopy bed that holds a Snoopy dog that Leo won for her when they went with a group of classmates to Six

Flags Amusement Park. She turns on the radio to an oldie channel playing "Free Man in Paris" by Joni Mitchell. Her black cat with white paws, Midnight, jumps onto the bed. "You missed the sun, poor baby." Melissa strokes the purring cat.

A poster of Degas's dancers from the Metropolitan Museum of Art hangs on the wall above her bed. She remembers the day she first saw the ballerinas with her father. As he explained the pictures, he seemed fascinated with them, too. Her desk is cluttered with watercolors and brushes. For a moment, she picks up an unfinished India ink drawing of Central Park with children bicycling. 't's such a lively scene that she can hear the children laughing. A faded photograph of her family standing in front of their old beach house sits on the bookshelf next to a book of Henry Moore sculptures, a present from her father for her birthday. She listens to her messages on her answering machine. "Hi, this is Dad. I'm back from Hawaii. Kate and I would love you to come tonight to dinner. Call me." Melissa frowns. She wonders what her mother is doing for supper.

She goes into the study where the bookcases are filled with Baldwin, Chekhov, Dickens and Kafka, her mother's favorites. Papers are strewn across the large desk where her mother who works as a freelance journalist is typing on the computer. Her black-framed glasses make her seem older than forty-nine. Dressed in a brown turtleneck and matching pants, she blends in with the oak-paneled room, no contrast except for her fiery red hair. Melissa smooths her brown hair that is like her father's, "Dad invited me to dinner. I'm not sure I want to go. His girlfriend drives me crazy."

"I know what that feels like. Don't go if she upsets you," says her mother.

"I wish I could just ignore her."

"I can't help you with that, sweetheart. I couldn't handle the girls, either." Her mother touches her shoulder.

"Do you have time to eat with me if I stay?" Melissa asks.

"I wish I could, but I've a deadline. Tomorrow night is better."

"You have to eat."

"Don't worry about me."

"You promise to eat if I go to Dad's?" Melissa rubs her mother's shoulders.

"Yes," her mother laughs.

Then kissing her mom's cheek, soft and fine. Even though it sounds silly, she wants to dance with her mother across the wood floors, both women unfettered.

In the kitchen, she pours herself a Coke. She fingers the moldy Jarlsberg cheese and smells an open can of tuna fish in the refrigerator in hopes of finding something edible. She resorts to munching on a carrot. Her father is a good cook. She wonders what he is making for dinner. She doesn't like to admit it but she is curious about what her father is photographing now.

When she was four, her father gave her a box of acrylic paints. He set up her easel on the beach and took photographs of her while she worked. She painted the ocean with bold swirling strokes. After he told her mother she had "a natural ability," he encouraged her mother to arrange for private art lessons. Now Melissa can't go a day without picking up a brush, a pen, or a piece of charcoal.

But recently, her thoughts are about Leo—the intense look on his face when he paints, eyebrows slanted. She wishes she were able to express herself. Yet nervousness holds her back. This morning she wanted to hold his hand, even kiss his soft lips. She keeps him at "arms length" because she is afraid of becoming too attached.

After calling her father, Melissa changes into a pale, blue-buttoned shirt and khaki pants. She brushes her straight black hair into a ponytail. She refuses to wear cosmetics. One day, her father actually dragged her into Saks. When she found out the gift was a "make-over," she pouted.

"Cosmetics will accent your bone structure." He cupped her chin.

"I'm not one of your models, Dad." She stepped back.

"You could be. You're more beautiful than all of them," he lamented.

"Stop it or I'll leave," she said sternly.

"Okay, I'm sorry. Let's go to Serendipity's for a hot fudge sundae." He linked arms with her to cross the street.

Melissa walks down Broadway to his apartment. She hasn't seen her father for a few weeks. She hopes he doesn't pressure her to see her latest painting. When she was younger, she enjoyed sharing her sketches with him but now he feels like an intruder. She's developing her own style and doesn't want her father's critique.

The air is humid. She buys a frozen cherry ice from a street vendor to soothe her dry throat. Passing Leo's apartment house, she wonders what he's doing. Maybe if she finishes dinner early, she'll call him. She looks for his window in the hope of catching a glimpse of him. It's Friday and she knows tonight his family celebrates Shabbat.

Last Friday, invited for Shabbat, Melissa sat at the long mahogany table with Leo and his three sisters, ages ten, twelve and fourteen. She recalls the high-pitched excited voices of his sisters and mother saying the blessing over the candles. His father's baritone voice rang out when he said the prayer over the wine. After the motzi over the challah, Leo broke a piece of it for her to eat. "May your week be a good one, filled with fun," He winked at Melissa.

"A blessed week for all of you," said his mother.

Then his parents hugged each other followed by placing kisses on the tops of all their heads. Over dinner, laughing at his sisters' silly jokes, Leo's eyes brightened. When he caught Melissa staring at him, he asked, "What's the matter?"

"No, I'm having a good time. I wish my family was n ore like yours," she said.

"You can come over as often as you like." He squeezed 'ier hand under the table.

If she had her charcoal pencil, she would have sketched his tall father with large hands placed on his mother's petite shoulders and his three sisters with rosy cheeks, dark eyes and wide smiles as the family sat around the table. Leo's long arm leaning over the table to chuck a piece of challah at his youngest sister, Rivka, for asking, "Is Melissa your girlfriend?" Melissa choked on the pot roast when Leo told his sister to "mind your own business." But she's not sure where she would place herself in the picture even though she is Jewish. Her parents never go to temple except on Yom Kippur and Rosh

Hashanah. Melissa's saddened by the thought that maybe she doesn't belong in the picture, at all.

By the time she walks the eight blocks to her father's apartment, she wonders if she should have asked Leo to come. He has been asking to meet her father, but she is afraid her father will embarrass her. She takes a deep breath and rings the bell. Kate opens the door, "hi, kiddo."

"Hi, nice trip?" Melissa asks.

"Fabulous. Your dad and I had a wonderful time."

"Great," Melissa fakes a smile.

"You know how good your dad is with a camera," Kate grins.

"I know," says Melissa reluctantly. The truth is that she can't stand Kate, only ten years older than she and acting chummy as if Melissa's her younger sister. Kate is wearing a silk shirt and tight black skirt. Her red hair is drawn back into a bun. Standing six feet tall, she looks regal as she invites Melissa into the living room. When Kate bends to pick up her glass from the coffee table, the outline of her panties shows off her firm buttocks. Melissa averts her eyes to look at the photograph on the wall above her. It's not much consolation, a photograph of one of her father's models sitting in a canoe. Melissa appreciates the placement of the model, the lighting and the backdrop, Central Park. But if she had her paints, she would put the model in a lilac jumpsuit with a parachute in the background.

"I'm thirsty. Can I have a drink?" Melissa asks.

"Sure, help yourself. I just squeezed some fresh orange juice."

The pitcher is filled with frothy liquid. Orange peels cover the kitchen counter. She pours herself a tall glass. Then she shoots the peels into the garbage, scoring points. Kate is definitely the biggest slob of all her dad's girlfriends. There have been plenty of them, too many to count. The one outstanding feature is they are all beautiful and redheaded. Taking a piece of ice from the freezer, Melissa unbuttons the top of her shirt to place on her warm skin, refreshing.

Her father in a white shirt with neatly pressed khaki shorts enters the kitchen. He's small, rotund with a chubby face and a thick head of graying hair. He has strong arms from lifting weights at the gym.

He takes the ice out of her hand to hold it to her chest. "Dad, I can do that myself." Melissa frowns.

"It's so hot. I was just trying to be helpful." He doesn't remove his hand.

"You're not funny." Melissa forcefully takes his fingers away.

"You're such a prude." He laughs.

When Kate enters the kitchen, she looks at the two of them. "What are you two love birds up to? I'm hungry." She thumps the cutting board on the counter and takes several onions from a bowl.

After Melissa buttons her shirt, she sits on a stool by the counter. She glares at her dad, but he ignores her and pours three glasses of wine. With a tinge of guilt at accepting the wine, Melissa sips her Chianti that her father has served her since she turned thirteen. Her mother would be furious if she knew because she never drinks anymore. But after a few sips, Melissa relaxes.

In the dining room, her father holds out the chair for Kate. They exchange an intimate look. The walls are covered with gorgeous females who have brought her father fame. One black and white photo is of a nude woman sitting on the back of a camel. The lighting accents the woman's voluptuous breasts. Another one is of a woman draped only in a sheer orange fabric. She looks mysterious and alluring. The angles of the shots makes Melissa feel the women are enticing her with their sexy bodies to take off her clothes and join them. The nude on the camel motions her to climb aboard. The woman draped in orange wants to entangle her in the fabric. The photographs are fascinating. Her father is watching her admire them. Her skin prickles. He winks. She ignores him. She takes a forkful of stir-fry and swirls it. "The food's delicious."

"It's a recipe from a chef that cooked for us in Hawaii." He smiles at Kate.

"How was the weather?" Melissa sips her wine.

"The weather was great but the water was rough!" Kate's cheeks turn bright red. "I was knocked over by a huge wave during a shoot."

"Made for a fabulous shot." Dad laughs.

"Did you forget that I almost drowned? I can't swim," Kate says hysterically.

"I never knew anyone who couldn't swim," says Melissa.

"Come to think of it, neither have I." Her father toasts Melissa.

"Stop making fun of me!" Kate turns to her father.

"Listen, I jumped in to the ocean to save you, didn't I?" Her dad turns to Melissa. "You should have seen her arms flailing."

You are being inconsiderate." Kate retreats into the kitchen.

"Now look what we've done." Her father leans toward her.

"We didn't do anything. She's doesn't seem that upset." Melissa grins.

"I know her. She's very sensitive." Her father stands up.

"She'll get over it. Give her time." Melissa shrugs her shoulders.

"I didn't think she would leave the table." Her father closes the kitchen door behind him.

Melissa stands up for a closer look at one of the proofs propped against the wall, a new addition. She grimaces when she recognizes Kate wearing only the bottom half of a string bikini while leaning over a park bench. Kate's body is flawless. Her father has not only captured Kate's gracefulness but also her beauty. She wonders if the picture would look better if she painted Kate in a long silky black dress surrounded by white roses. Melissa hides the picture of Kate in the drawer of the china cabinet.

The photos and her father's pompousness are the reasons she never brings her friends to her father's apartment. She tells them he is a successful photographer but the nudes on his wall embarrass her. She wishes he would pick other subjects, maybe scenes of orange-banded sunsets. Then she could introduce Leo who has asked to meet her father, even bring Leo to one of his openings. She thinks about sharing her feelings with Leo but she's not sure how he will react. Her father is so different from Leo's dad, a family man. She's also afraid that if she introduces Leo to her father and Kate, Leo will be enthralled with them. It's a risk she's not willing to take.

On the cocktail table, she fingers a photography book of her father's work. Inside it is a series of scenes of the beach where they had their cottage. The sunset accents the solitary nature of the cottage.

One picture is of her naked while she shovels sand into a pail; another photo is of her nude as she runs on the beach. Her father has caught her innocence with the camera. She wishes she could capture that simplicity in her painting. She's uneasy looking at herself naked, but she finds it reassuring that she was only three when the pictures were taken, too little to be self-conscious. Even though the book is well regarded, she wouldn't want Leo to see it. She snaps it shut.

It has been over fifteen minutes since her father went into the kitchen. Their voices are getting louder. Kate is telling her father to stop treating her disrespectfully. He tells her to stop acting "childish." Kate tells him he is "insensitive." Their conversation is a familiar one that her parents had when they were married.

Melissa telephones Leo. He arranges to meet her at the Starbucks on the corner of Eighty-Fifth Street and Broadway. She writes a note, leaves it on the dining room table and slips out the front door, closing it softly behind her.

Inside the coffee shop, she sees Leo sitting at the back table. Freshly showered with his hair brushed, he looks handsome. When Melissa sits down, his eyes are inviting. "My dad and his girlfriend had a fight."

"When am I going to meet your dad?" Leo takes her hand.

"Why do you want to meet him so badly?"

"You've mentioned how much his photos have affected your work."

"I'm trying to develop my own style now."

"You will. Be patient." He takes Melissa's hand.

"Really? Do you promise?" Melissa laughs.

"Absolutely," Leo puts her hand to his mouth.

"I don't know anymore than when I started." Melissa removes her hand.

"You do, I promise." Leo's face softens.

"I wish I had your confidence." Melissa leans closer to him.

"If you spent more time with me, dated me, we'd both feel better."

"I'm not ready." Melissa averts her eyes.

"I don't understand." Leo says sadly.

"I don't either, Leo. I wish I did," says Melissa.

For a moment, she imagines Leo embracing her with his soft hands touching her body, everywhere. But she stops herself by rubbing the rim of her mug with her finger and concentrating on the bitter taste of the coffee. She wants to push Leo's hair away from his forehead to admire his eyes. She imagines outlining his angled cheekbone with her hand. She longs to wrap the strands of hair on the nape of his neck around her fingers.

At one o'clock in the morning when they leave, clouds dust the full moon. On the corner, Leo hails a cab. Despite her protests, he pays the driver and tells him "take my girl home safely." When Melissa opens her mouth to say "thank you," Leo leans over, kisses her on the lips and she allows his smooth tongue to probe the inside of her mouth. Melissa pulls back, wide-eyed. "It's okay, Melissa, it felt good, didn't it?"

"You caught me off guard."

"I can live with that, can you?" he whispers.

"I'm not sure."

"I wish you would let me kiss you, again." He leans toward her.

"Not now." She moves her head and he pecks her cheek.

"Hey, you two lovebirds, let's go," says the cab driver, a man wearing a leather cap.

"Okay, take her." Leo's voice sounds like a caress.

Melissa leans against the back seat of the cab. She touches her warm lips. She doesn't know what's happening to her because she wants Leo to kiss her, again.

In class the next day, Melissa arrives early to set up her easel and locates it in several locations but she's unable to find one she likes. Taking out the painting of her family on the beach she mixes a deep blue for the ocean. She wants to work on her canvas and forget about the model. Once she starts a painting, she hates to stop until it's completed. Not that she's ever totally satisfied with her work but sometimes she has a temporary sense of accomplishment. Chewing on the wooden tip of her brush, she stands up to move her canvas.

When Leo comes in, he places his easel next to hers. Carefully lining up his paints, he leans over to say, "I'm glad you called me last night. I had fun."

"You're a good friend," she says.

"Just a friend?" Leo touches her shoulder.

At that moment a young woman with frizzy red hair in a white robe enters the class. Quickly undressing, she sits on a chair placed on a raised platform in the middle of the room. One breast is larger than the other is. Her hips are small and her skin is white, too pale like her mother's. Hands sweating, Melissa mumbles, "She s okay," when Leo asks, "What do you think of her, cute?" When the model stands erect, her breasts with pale nipples are full. Every time Melissa lifts the brush to paint, her hand shakes. Her canvas is empty. She imagines painting delicate strokes to outline the woman's body and filling in the figure with a tinge of flesh-colored pigment. Looking over at Leo's composition she sees he's painting the model with a vibrant reddish-pink. She's lovely.

Melissa excuses herself and hurries out of the studio. She sits on the steps of the school with the sun beating down on her. Her head throbs. As she closes her eyes, she doesn't know what's happening to her. Melissa remembers being overwhelmed as a child. Her body sweats. She bows her head to re-play the afternoon her family had built the castle on the beach. She rolls the camera in her mind to that evening when she watched the bright stars while lying in bed. Quieted by the sound of the waves lapping against the shore, Melissa had drifted to sleep. Awakened by shrieking noises coming from her parents, she had run to their room.

The brightness of the light rushing out into the hallway from their bedroom had stopped her from entering. She observed them without being seen. Her father, naked and covered with hair, had circled the room while snapping pictures of her mother. Her mother with legs apart had fondled her body everywhere. Her mother had moaned while she called her father's name. "More," her father had yelled as he began to stroke himself. Climbing on top of her mother, they had begun to move, gyrating.

Melissa peed, liquid dripped on her legs. For a moment, she

couldn't move. She didn't understand what was going on, but she was mesmerized. Then, her father began to groan, too. Whatever they were doing was ugly. She ran back to her room, threw her wet pajamas in the back of her closet and put on a fresh pair. She wanted to yell for her mother but she was afraid her father would be angry. She hated her father with his hairy body for getting on top of her mother, hurting her. She couldn't understand why her mother let him. Her own body felt icy. She covered herself with another blanket. She felt it was wrong to have looked into their room. She promised herself to be good, never speak or think about what she had seen.

Melissa wipes the tears off her face as she sits on the steps of the school. She tries to make sense of the memory. Her father had been turned on by her mother's pose. Her mother had seemed to enjoy it, too. She doesn't understand how her mother could have willingly participated.

Dad hadn't stopped with her mother. He had gone on to photograph other models. Back in Manhattan, behind the bedroom door, she had overheard her parents fighting about his sexual conquests. Night after night, her mother had cried and her father had yelled, "It's none of your business what I do with my models." Finally her mother had made him leave.

On the steps of the school, she turns around to Leo who is softly calling "Melissa." He sits down next to her. His shiny black hair falls in his face. "Are you okay? Are you mad at me about last night?"

"No, it was my fault." Melissa bows her head.

"It wasn't anyone's fault. We didn't do anything wrong." Leo touches her knee.

"I don't know about that. I'm not feeling well." Melissa looks at Leo.

"Should I stay with you?" Leo places his arm on her shoulder.

"No, I'll go home." She wishes she could lean against him, but instead she tells him, "Go back to class. I'll be fine."

As Leo moves back to the studio, she imagines running after him and telling him to come with her to her father's house. Maybe, Leo will understand her feelings. She has to ask her father what is wrong with him. Why can't he be monogamous? Leo's parents have been married for thirty years. They are content. She wanted siblings and a secure home. Instead her dad flits from one model to the next. She recalls that her dad and Kate mentioned they were going to Philadelphia for a shoot. Deciding she has to confront her father the minute he gets home, she hails a cab.

She uses her keys to let herself into the apartment and throws her jacket on the couch. The quietness makes her feel nervous. She begins to walk around the apartment. For the first time she closely examines every single picture. Disrobed, exposed, vulnerable girls stare down at her, begging for attention. She notices a photo of a naked model curled up in a fetal position and another one of a sad-eyed woman sitting on a swing. Her father played on their vulnerabilities. His words and caresses must have spellbound the models to strike these poses. Seduced by him, the models never had a chance. Now she sees her father is a predator.

In his bedroom, she notices Kate's sheer red baby doll pajamas lying near her father's thong underwear on the floor. Along the wall, a picture of a woman with long, blonde hair and doe eyes stares at Melissa. She halts in front of a photo she has never seen before, hidden on the wall in a dark corner of his bedroom. It's a picture of Melissa when she was eleven years old. She lies naked in a sandpit with her legs open, exposed, in the same position as her mother in the bedroom years earlier. The longer she looks at the picture, the more she remembers that day.

Early in the morning, Melissa and her father had gone for a walk before the beach was covered with lounge chairs. Seeing a large hole in the sand, Melissa jumped into it and grabbed her father's foot. "Come in. There's room for two of us."

"Lie down, Spread out your body. The light is good." Her father readjusted the camera around his neck.

"I don't want my picture taken now."

"Just one picture," Her father moved his foot away from her hand.

"Okay, just one." Melissa made herself comfortable in the pit.

"Take your swimsuit off. You're so beautiful." He towered above her.

"Dad, I don't want to do that anymore." Melissa bit her lip.

"You look lovely. It's just a photograph," he squatted by the side of the pit.

"I'm too old to be photographed naked," she cried.

He continued coaxing her while she took off her bathing suit and spread her legs. She wouldn't look at him. But, walking home, he began to hum and she yelled. "Don't develop that picture. I hate it. No more pictures of me. I'm too old. Mother agrees with me." Her father had promised he would destroy the photo.

He had lied to her and had developed the film. She takes the picture into the darkroom where she lays it on the bench. She knows now what she has to do. After finding a hammer, she grips the handle firmly to smash the glass of the picture. Blood drips from her arm but she doesn't care. Her father will never see her unclothed again. Sprinkling the shreds of the photo into the garbage, she feels powerful, capable of anything.

She has to destroy the negative of her in the sandpit. Her fingers are throbbing, but she stretches her hand to open the metal drawers. The drawers are filled with negatives of models posed in erotic positions. Some photographs are of her father having sex with the models. One negative is of Melissa, ten, soaping herself in the shower when she didn't even know her father was there in the bathroom. Several of the pictures are of her naked mother bashfully posing on the beach in front of their cottage. When she locates the one of herself in the sandpit, Melissa carefully immerses it in water. Then she soaks all the negatives of her and her mother.

Women will do anything for her father when they fall under his spell. He's a great artist, but the models need protection from him. His fame is based on exploiting his models. She will draw bold colors over the bodies hanging on the walls. Bright yellow, reds, and blues will enhance the photographs. She will cover their nakedness. They will no longer be victims. Melissa takes all the negatives and cuts them up with scissors. She can feel the pain of the models dissolving. She wonders if she should take her father's appointment book to call them. She wants to tell them they can start over with a clean slate, innocent. They don't have to worry about the photographs. Their husbands or boyfriends will never know what happened. They can erase him from their minds.

After she has emptied the drawers of the cabinets, Melissa slips on her jacket. She can't stay in her father's apartment a moment longer. In the street, she is startled it's dark; the moon is out and streetlights are lit. The street is streaked in amber. Cars whiz by her. She wonders what her father will say when he arrives home. He will probably call the police to investigate. She's not sure if he will realize the meaning of the missing picture on the wall or even remember it. Her father will think another artist, a competitor jealous of his work, broke into his apartment. He's always complaining other photographers are trying to copy him.

As she passes Starbucks, Melissa can smell coffee beans being roasted but her hands are too sore to hold a cup. Through the plate glass, she sees a couple kissing. They remind her of Leo. Wondering what he is doing, she moves in the direction of his apartment.

When Leo opens the door, he is wearing only blue jeans. His chest is smooth, hairless. She stares at his torso. "I was just about to take a shower. I'll put on a shirt." Leo lowers his eyes. She is unable to speak. He ushers her inside and helps take off her jacket. "My family went to temple, a concert. I had too much work." Leo reaches for a shirt.

"I wondered where everyone was." Melissa looks around the living room.

"What happened to you? Your arm is bleeding." Leo's eyes widen.

"I hurt myself." Melissa holds her arm.

"It looks nasty. It needs to be cleaned and bandaged."

"It's not too bad." Melissa flinches when he touches her arm.

"Yes, it is. Come on." Leo moves down the hallway. In the bathroom, he searches for an antiseptic ointment and Band-Aids. "Here they are. The cut needs to be washed."

She sits on the rim of the tub while Leo gives her a damp cloth to place over the gash. Leo asks hesitantly, "Do you want to clean it yourself?"

"I don't think I can." Melissa looks into Leo's concerned brown eyes.

"What should I do?" Leo picks up the antiseptic.

"I want you to clean it. Will you?" Melissa whispers.

"Are you sure?" Leo bends over her.

"Yes." says Melissa.

Gently, Leo rinses her cut with warm water and applies the antiseptic. "Ouch." Melissa flinches.

"I'm sorry. I didn't mean to hurt you." Leo sounds worried.

"It's okay. None of it's your fault. It's my fault." Melissa bows her head.

Leo places a large Band-Aid over the cut. When he's done, his slim fingers rest on her arm. He quizzically looks at her. "How did you get hurt?"

"I was working with my dad's negatives. He wasn't home." Melissa murmurs.

"What happened?" Leo asks.

"They were damaged." Melissa hangs her head.

"A burglar broke into your father's apartment when you were there? Did you call the police? You're lucky you weren't hurt. Your father is going to be a maniac when he finds out."

"It wasn't a burglar," she whispers.

"What are you talking about?" He squats in front of her.

"I'm not sure I can explain it." Melissa avoids Leo's eyes.

"Did you have something to do with the pictures being destroyed?" Leo gasps.

"I may have." Melissa stammers.

"You ruined your dad's photos?" Leo is wide-eyed.

"Do you think I'm evil?" Melissa asks.

"You're not a bad person," Leo says.

"You don't hate me?" She begins to sob.

"I could never hate you," he whispers.

"Really?" She stares at him.

"There must be a reason for doing what you did," Leo says

tenderly.

Melissa looks down at the black and white design of tiles on the bathroom floor.

Leo starts to move his arm away but she reaches for his hand and squeezes it. Leo pulls her trembling toward him. With bodies intertwined, Melissa knows she will purge herself.

Little Blessing

~

I lie on the bed as he pounds with his tiny fists. Gently, I rub my belly and hum, "Hush Little Baby." I know Joshua hears me because he kicks my stomach. I sing another verse and wait for his reply and he kicks me again. He has strong legs like his father.

Blue veins ran though the surface of my taut skin like strands of ink. I was seven months pregnant; my toes were plump, unrecognizable to me when I set my feet on the wood floor. I slipped into Abe's cushioned slippers, more comfortable than my own. In the kitchen, Abe muttered to himself while he searched for clean silverware in the drawers. When I opened up the dishwasher for him, he kissed the top of my head and I could smell his musky cologne. He still had his thick shoulder-length brown hair that he wore in college over a decade ago. "What are you going to do today?" he asked.

"I should finish my drawing. But I'm too tired," I said.

"Sweetheart, we'll get through this," said Abe.

"Speak for yourself," I said.

In the living room, Abe pulled me onto his lap where I wished I could stay until our son was born. I felt I had betrayed Abe, who had always dreamed of a big family. He had learned patience by living with five siblings in a two-bedroom apartment in the Bronx. At temple, every Saturday, dressed in hand-me-down starched white shirts with frayed edges, he sat for hours. He had spent his lifetime waiting.

It was difficult to believe that it was only yesterday I lay on a stainless steel table, icy against my back and listened to the camera clicking over my belly as it photographed Joshua.

Sitting snugly against my shoulder on the sofa, Joshua's chubby fingers point to the photographs of him in my womb. His breath smells of peanut butter he had for lunch. "Mommy, why am I swimming in your stomach?"

"You never sat still, even inside, waiting to be born." I laugh.
"Now I know why I like to swim," he said.
He points out the glass doors toward our pool in the Hamptons. Outside, Joshua and I dive into the cool water. He's a shimmering tropical fish moving upstream. I follow in his wake. When he climbs out, I dry him off and his small frame melts into my own. His thick brown hair smells of chlorine as I kiss the top of his head. When he smiles, I see the space where his baby front tooth is missing. I want to keep him in my arms but he pulls away from me to march back into the house.

The image was so real that I jumped when the nurse said, "I'm done. You can change." When I quickly slipped on my maternity dress, I remembered my once small breasts and slim stomach. The changing room was drafty and goosebumps formed on my skin. In the doctor's office on the desk was a picture of his three sons. "Beautiful children," I said.

Abe, frowning, sits and waits for Dr. Ray to speak about our son.

"Thanks," Dr. Ray said with a half-smile.

"Is something wrong?" My stomach did a somersault.

"The baby's heart and organs have stopped developing," Dr. Ray said softly.

"How sick is Joshua?" I asked in a steely voice.

"He can't survive after he is born. Maybe he will live a few hours or a day. I'm afraid he has a rare genetic disorder called phenonkursia. I've consulted Dr. Chin at Children's Hospital in Boston and Dr. Schwartz at UCLA Medical Center. But unfortunately, they concur with my diagnosis. I'm so sorry," Dr. Ray said quietly.

Joshua is coming down the hallway of the hospital. I can hear him humming, "This Old Man." Any minute, he will come into the room and I will pull him onto my lap. He will search through the colored pencils on the desk and look for his favorite one, navy, and drew a picture of my father's sailboat. Since his chubby hands have trouble making a straight line, he draws my father with a crooked smile. "See, you were wrong," I say to Dr. Ray. Joshua is fine." Joshua looks up and says, "Feel my muscles." He pumps his arms and makes believe he is superman.

Abe was red-faced and banged his fist on the desk. "What the hell good are you if you can't save a baby?" He grasped my hand so tightly it hurt. When I looked outside the window, I was surprised that the buildings still stood and the sun glared.

On the way home in the taxi, Abe held me while I watched the white gulls swooping over the West Side Drive. Layers of dark clouds gathered over the skyline like a group of old men huddled together in prayer. I lowered my head to join them." Joshua is going to be fine."

"It's not your fault. It's nobody's fault," Abe whispered.

For a moment, his warm eyes comforted me. But inside I felt sick. I was defective. I couldn't make a healthy baby because my insides were charred. During the eight years we have been married, I've been trying to have a baby. I've had one miscarriage and one stillbirth, Leah.

My black Labrador had an easier time making puppies. Lying under the front porch, my sister Diane, my brother Dave and I, wide-eyed, watched her push out four babies, with slicked-back fur. It seemed so natural when she licked them clean as they searched for her teats. I didn't know enough to be awed.

That evening, I watch the boats sail up the East River from our apartment window. I climb aboard a sailboat to take Joshua away. He is wearing my father's white captain's hat while I steer the boat near the coast of Cape Cod. At eight years old, he is tall and thin like his father. Joshua yells with excitement as a whale frolics near us. The air smells salty. I turn the boat to follow the whales. Joshua says, "Hurry, we're losing the whale." He paces on the deck. His lip quivers. I salute him and make the boat go as fast as I can. Joshua claps his hands.

The phone rang and Abe gently nudged me to speak to my mother. She reminded me to bring a warm jacket for the weekend because Dad planned to build a bonfire on Saturday night for the grandchildren. I thought of saying "I don't give a damn," but I didn't because she'd only be hurt.

"Why didn't you tell your mother?" Abe asked when I hung up the phone.

"Maybe the doctor is wrong."

"The doctor checked with two experts."

"Well, I don't believe it."

"It's better if you face it."

"I don't want to worry my parents unnecessarily, especially my dad."

"Now is not the time to be concerned about your father."

"I can't help it."

"If we tell them, maybe they will understand, be helpful."

"Don't tell me what to do."

When he tried to kiss my lips, I turned my face and he lightly brushed my cheek. I went into my studio and closed the door. Stacked next to my easel sat a pile of old drawings. I stopped at one of a dark-haired boy pulling his wagon and a Labrador puppy squirming inside of it. The dog longed to sniff the lawn and romp through the park. The number of sleepless nights that I had stayed up to draw the soulful eyes of the puppy was hard to count. It was a puppy for Joshua. This book won a Caldecott award and I planned to read it to my son.

Joshua sits next to me as I read him the book. He pats the picture of the puppy. "Good doggy," he says. He makes a "ruff" noise to the picture.

"When you're a little bigger, we will get you a puppy," I say.

"I want one, now." He grabs my hand with his sticky one.

"Soon," I laugh.

Joshua was ours. No one could take him from us. I hurled the books to the floor. Abe opened the door to see what I was doing. "Stop it." He grabbed the book in my hand.

"I can't," I said.

"You've made a mess," he said.

"I don't give a damn," I said.

"Throwing things won't make it better." He shook his head and started to pick up the books. I felt guilty watching him work and started to help. He wouldn't look at me. I couldn't stand his disapproval. "I don't know what else to do."

"I know." He reached for my hand.

"I'm sorry," I said.

"Me, too," he said.

After we piled the books on the desk, I dragged my body into the kitchen where he made me a cup of mint tea. I sat across from him and tried to avoid his worried eyes. I watched the steam rise and wished that I, too, could evaporate.

That night I had a terrible nightmare. I woke up and my nightgown was drenched. After changing to a fresh one, I sat at my desk, hands in my lap, and bowed my head.

Joshua is drowning in the pool. He's kicking and screaming for me. By the time I jump in and try to wrap his thin arms around me, his body is limp. He feels heavy as I swim with him to the side of the pool. I scream for help, but no one comes. I drag him out and press my lips over his frigid ones. His skin is white, too pale. He coughs up water and makes a choking noise. He looks at me with frantic eyes. "What happened?"

"You're safe." I hold him close to me. I will never let him go. He's part of me, the best part.

The next day, I put on a crisp pink maternity dress instead of my faded one. I added blush to my cheeks and pulled my long black hair back into a bun. I managed to find a pair of high heel shoes that still fit. We drove to Vermont where the road stretched for miles, dotted by farmhouses and quaint villages. We stopped to have lunch in an old railway car with worn leather seats. A picture of the Three Stooges, one of Fred Flintstone hugging Dino and another of a puppet of Roy Rogers hung on the wall.

Joshua sprawls out on the floor beside me in front of the television as we munch on popcorn. "Look what Moe did to Curly. Did you catch it, Mom?" He laughs. I tickle the bottom of his smooth feet and say, "Of course." His face glows and his pale eyebrows are slightly bent. I admire how long like a beanpole he has become at nine years old but I do miss his chubby stomach and thick legs.

I took out my sketchbook and began to draw the Three Stooges and I placed Joshua on the page. He had long brown hair like Abe. He had bright brown eyes and was grinning. "It upsets me when you draw him," said Abe.

"I feel better, closer to him," I said.

"I don't understand." Abe lowered his head. When I placed my hand over his, I tried to think of something comforting to say, but nothing came to mind. There was an uneasiness between us I hadn't felt before. I knew he was angry with me for not being realistic but I couldn't help it. Joshua existed. I had to protect him. I refused to think about his sickness. The waitress brought our food but I only nibbled on my hamburger and fries. "Liz, I think if you tell your family, they will be supportive," said Abe.

"Not my dad," I said.

"Your dad will understand," said Abe.

"How can he when I don't? He wants a grandson as much as I need a son," I yelled.

"I want a son, too. But it's not going to happen. Your dad's a big boy. He'll have to deal with it. Otherwise, let's go home," Abe said. "It's going to be too much of a strain for you."

"It's not going to be too much of a strain on me. I'll handle it the best way I can. I'm not ready to give up on Joshua. Besides, I haven't seen Diane or the new baby. She flew in from California. I'm going to see her," I said.

"You're making this more difficult than it has to be," said Abe.

"No, you're right; it's not difficult; it's impossible," I wailed.

"You have to stop worrying about disappointing your family," he said.

"I can't help it." I crossed my arms to keep myself from crying. I rubbed my belly when Joshua kicked me. "Do you want to feel Joshua?" I said excitedly. But Abe's shoulders slumped. Instead, I kissed the inside of Abe's wrists. If Abe stayed close, maybe I would be okay.

After lunch, while driving, we passed the graveyard on the outskirts of town where Leah, my stillborn, was buried. On the day

155

of the burial, I could see my family, Rabbi Seymour and the bare trees, long skinny limbs reaching for the sky. I asked my parents not to invite all our relatives who lived in town. I didn't want a crowd. It was more than I could handle when Rabbi bowed his head to chant and our voices joined his in unison. "Yet Gadeal V'yettkadah Sh'may Raba...."

When Leah's wood casket was placed in the ground, next to my grandparents, my body felt numb. I wept. The tiny casket was bare, made of freshly cut wood from my father's factory. When I imagined Leah's small bluish lips, I knew I should be lying in the coffin with Leah burying me. I imagined her brown eyes like mine with a mop of dark hair as she stared down at me. Then my father handed me a smooth stone to place on the casket. I kept rubbing it in my hands unable to let go of it. How many Yom Kippurs had I sat through while I chanted the blessings to honor the dead? Up until now, I never questioned it, but that day I felt the stones were being placed on me. The weight of them was too much to bear and I couldn't breathe.

The sun was setting as Abe and I neared the house. Inside, all the lights were on, making it look bigger than I remembered. The red sky streaked with yellow outlined the top of it. My grandfather and my great uncle had hauled the timber from the family lumber mill to build it, a large Victorian with three stories encircled by porches. Wishing I were back in New York City, I sat in the car. When Abe stepped out, he lifted the presents for my nieces, but I trudged behind him and carried nothing.

My mother stood at the door. I had missed her welcoming eyes scooping me up and holding me. When she hugged me, her skin was soft and smelled like cinnamon bread. I thought about blurting out Joshua was sick but my mother stepped back to look at my belly. "You look wonderful in pink. How are you feeling?"

"I'm okay, Mom," I said quietly.

I used to listen to the owls when I couldn't sleep. Sometimes, I found their hooting comforting. But other times, I would run to my mother's side of the bed and cry until she gathered me in her arms.

She would stretch out with me on my bed until I fell asleep. Now I ached to lie down next to her. But my niece tugged on my mother's apron, "I want milk," she said. My mother patted my shoulder and returned to the kitchen. Once again, I was alone.

My father held court in the living room. He sat on a worn leather chair with one of his granddaughters on his lap. While my father read aloud, the four other granddaughters, mesmerized by his deep voice, sat cross-legged on the carpet and hardly moved. When he saw me, he placed my three-year-old niece on the floor and motioned for me to sit on his lap. "Dad, I'm too big for that," I laughed.

"You look wonderful," he said.

I kissed him on the cheek. His hair was grayer; his face was more lined and thinner. His complexion was darker. For a moment, I longed to put my arms around his bony neck and cry for him to make everything better the way he did when I was a kid. But instead I took a celery stick from the cocktail table.

Diane came into the room holding my new niece, Etta, sleeping in her arms. The baby's features were fine. I longed to raise my niece as my own, her plump body toddling toward me as she grew.

"You look fantastic," I said to Diane, who still wore a size four, always the thinnest of us.

"You'll take the weight off after the baby's born," said Diane. She handed Etta to me before I could object. She smelled like talcum powder and her skin was milky white. "She's perfect," I sighed.

"Isn't she beautiful?" My father chimed in.

Abe looked at me. I lowered my head to hide my tears. My father placed his arms around my shoulders. "You don't have to cry, only a few more months."

I looked into my father's proud eyes. "I'm just tired, Dad." Etta felt too heavy in my arms and I was afraid that I would drop her.

"Go take a rest. Later, I'll show you the surprise I built for Joshua." My father grasped my hand in his wrinkled one.

Abe took the baby from me. He kissed the top of her head. I whispered, "Thank-you." I climbed up to my old room. It still had pink floral wallpaper and the large canopy bed that I slept in as a child. From the bay windows, I saw the lake where my brother David would whip me around the pond with my skates sliding so fast that I begged him to stop. In the summer, I would slip on a swimsuit and wake Diane. We would head for the glistening water to swim to the raft in the middle. To catch my breath, I'd lie flat on the wood boards. Swimming was the only way to be comfortable because my father didn't believe in air conditioning. He said it was for "city slickers."

In my sketchpad, I drew the lake with the tall pine trees reflected onto the surface. Then I sketched Joshua skating with me on the ice.

His cheeks are rosy as he whips past me. At eleven years old, he is proud of his quickness. Then I draw a picture of him, at eight years old. He is selling lemonade with his cousins at the end of the long driveway. The sun is beating down on him and Joshua wipes his sweaty brow with his long thin fingers, like his father. His lips tighten as he carefully divides the coins between them. I design a picture of my father teaching him to ride a two-wheeler bike on the lawn just the way he taught me. My father claps as Joshua, age five, makes his first long turn by himself before he falls. Joshua doesn't cry but frowns "This is too hard," he says. He crosses his arms and refuses to budge.

"I'll help you," says my father. He goes over to him to examine his scraped knees. Then Joshua climbs back on the bike and my father leads him onto on the grass. My father runs with him. Then he lets go of the back of the bike and Joshua pedals across the lawn. My father turns to me and says, "Joshua is a natural athlete."

"I know," I say. My father hugs me. I'm safe within his embrace.

Joshua must see my childhood home. His place is here with my family. I gathered the sketches into my arms, hurried down the backstairs and stepped outside into the dark. When I turned around to look through the lit open window, I saw Etta sleeping in Abe's arms. He was admiring her heart-shaped face as he crooned "Hush Little Baby." His voice sounded light. Abe had perfect pitch. He sang in the men's choir of our temple and assisted with the children's choir. He said the young voices, "energized him."

I take the path to the lake where I float the drawings in the water.

Since they are drifting slowly, I poke them with a stick. Joshua is standing next to me as we skip stones. "I can't do it," he says. I find a smooth, flat stone and guide his hand. He skims the stone across the water. "Perfect," I say. He laughs and skims another. I notice his wrists are slender like mine. Maybe he will be an artist, too.

I hated nature for playing this trick on me. It must not take my son. If I had an ax, I would have cut down the pine trees that my grandfather planted many years ago. I would have pulled the daffodils out of the ground and plucked the wings off the most colorful butterflies. I would have sunk the float sitting in the middle of the lake. Then I noticed that the sky was filled with stars like candles leading me further into the woods. The pungent smell of pine engulfed me and the pale moon led me as I moved toward the old boxing ring.

When I was eight years old, my father and I had climbed into the newly built boxing ring while Diane and David clapped. He was tall and muscled. When he touched me lightly with his gloves, I fell to the ground and began to writhe. "Does anything hurt?" Dad asked.

"I can't move. Pick me up," I whispered.

"Lean into me," he said.

"Got you," I jumped up and pushed him to the ground.

Then Diane and David rushed into the ring and we sat on my dad until he begged for mercy.

Now in the star-lit darkness, someone called my name. I turned around to see Abe coming toward me. He wore my father's navy sweatshirt. He lifted the worn rope and climbed into the ring with me, "Are you okay, honey?"

"Joshua is here with us," I said.

"That would be wonderful," he said.

"There's no reason to tell my parents," I said.

"What are you talking about? They can help us through it."

"Not yet; Joshua is fine," I said.

"What?" He sounded impatient.

"You heard me," I whispered.

"Liz, honey, Joshua isn't fine." He wrapped his arms around me as we stood in the middle of the ring with its sagging ropes and rotting wood floor. I listened to the owls hooting and the crickets chirping. I wondered how nature could be so cruel. I didn't want to tell my parents that Joshua was sick. To speak about his illness was to speak about his death. My father would not have his grandson. As long as Joshua stayed inside me, he was alive. Once they removed him, he would die. The best plan was to keep him inside of me forever where he was safely soothed in warm water as he sucked his thumb.

On the way back to the house, on the lit porch, I saw my father pacing. He was smoking a cigar. "Your mother hates the smell of them," He ran his hand through his silver hair.

"She's been sending you outside to smoke as long as I can remember," I said.

"Want one?" He reaches into his pocket to give a cigar to Abe.

"You know I don't smoke," Abe laughed.

"I want to show you something in my workroom." Dad tramped down the steps.

"I don't think now is the time," said Abe.

"Of course it is." Dad took my hand into his callused one.

"Dad, later," I said softly.

"You have to see it. I've been working on it for months." When he grinned, I could see the space between his two front teeth.

Inside his workshop, pegboards lined with tools, he pointed to the center of the floor where an oak cradle sat. "Touch it. Feel how smooth the wood is. I used dark stain on the wood for my grandson," Dad ran his large hand lovingly along the rim.

He tugged me to the cradle. "It's beautiful." I was in the middle of our icy pond and it was cracking around me. I fled the workshop.

My dad asked Abe, "What's wrong with her?" I didn't hear Abe's reply. I climbed the stairs to my old room and closed the door.

Minutes later, Abe entered. "You told him?" I asked.

"Did you want me to?" He gave me a quizzical look.

"I guess he has a right to know." Then I reached for my nightgown and slipped it over my heavy body. Abe held me in bed until I fell asleep.

Joshua is lying in the cradle my father built. He is cooing, but then I see Leah's coffin with Joshua's tiny body inside of it. Joshua's body convulses. His thin lips are white. I pull him out of the coffin to wrap him in blankets but he doesn't warm up. He moans and writhes. When I can't stop his pain, I scream.

I woke up to a silent house. My heart was beating fast. Afraid to see Joshua's pained face staring at me, I crept out of bed. I wouldn't let anyone hurt my son. It was one-thirty. Since Abe was snoring, I didn't have the heart to wake him. I put on my robe and went downstairs where the full moon lit up every window. In the kitchen, my mother sat at the round oak table. She was drinking a cup of mint tea. I sat with her and placed my hands beneath the table because I didn't want her to see them shaking. When she offered me a cup, I moved my chair close to hers. I put my head on her soft shoulder while she stroked my hair. "What is it, my darling? Dad said you're upset."

I felt the words rushing out of my mouth like a dam being opened. I began. "Joshua is very sick."

"Oh no, Liz." As she pulled me closer, I smelled the mint on her breath. I told her everything. As I clung to her and wept, she wept, too. She cuddled me like I was a small child. She asked if she could accompany me to the hospital when I delivered Joshua but I said I would first talk to Abe. As we climbed the stairs to go back to bed, I said, "Please don't tell Daddy until I leave."

"Why not?" she asked.

"I'm afraid he will tell me to try again," I say.

"He will be upset," she whispered.

"He's waited so long for a grandson," I said.

"I know," she said.

My mother and I, arms entwined, climbed the rest of the stairs. I crawled into bed next to Abe, who didn't stir. I was envious of his peacefulness. I curled up next to him. As I fell asleep, I saw my father's puzzled face. I prayed my mother would keep her promise.

The next day, on the way home, I told Abe about my conversation with my mother. "I'm so relieved. Thank God," he said. But I hated God. I didn't feel better because I told my mother. Joshua's illness was more real.

Later, back at the same diner, I told him about my mother's offer. "I think it might be a good idea. More support for you," said Abe.

"My mother can't help me now," I said.

"She may be more helpful than I would be," Abe looked at his plate.

"You're enough." I knew at that moment how lucky I was to have Abe.

"Good." He caressed my cheek.

When we arrived home, there was a message on the answering machine from Dr. Ray for an appointment the next morning.

The next day, in Dr. Ray's office he said my blood pressure had skyrocketed and he was afraid for my health. He needed to induce my labor as soon as possible. "I'm not ready," I said.

"The baby is ready," said Dr. Ray.

I thought of yanking Dr. Ray and all the specialists into the old boxing ring with me and punching them, one at a time until their noses were bloody and they begged to climb down. I wouldn't let them leave until they handed me a healthy baby boy. I heard Dr. Ray making a plan with Abe to meet at the hospital in the afternoon but I couldn't listen.

I'm underwater swimming with Joshua in the ocean. He still enjoys playing tag and he won't let me catch him. He gives me a wide smile that shows off his straight teeth. Then I notice he has the same space between his two front teeth as my father. His body glides through the water. Even though I taught him to swim, he is more agile than me. His muscled body flashes above the waves from time to time. "Catch me if you can," he yells. At thirteen, he moves quickly like Abe. I swim toward him but I can't keep up with him. I'm breathless.

At home, I slowly packed a robe and a dressing gown. I didn't bother to brush my hair. I knew the drill. Then I dialed my parents' phone number and spoke with my mother. Her voice was sad but she didn't cry. She said my father was very upset and couldn't understand why I hadn't told him. I didn't tell her that I couldn't bear to imagine what he would do with the crib he built for Joshua. Any words of encouragement to try again would have made me furious. I didn't have any anger to spare. I had to conserve my strength for Joshua.

While I was on the phone, I heard Abe in Joshua's room. I moved to the door to watch him dismantling the crib. I clenched my teeth. For a moment, I imagined he was picking Joshua up from his nap. His cheeks would be pink and he'd smell like talcum powder. It took a moment for Abe to realize I was there but when he did, he stopped. "Why are you doing that now?" I crossed my arms.

"There's no point in leaving the crib," he said firmly.

"Leave it," I said.

"No, I don't want to see it." He shook his head.

"I wish there was a reason to keep it," I said.

"Me, too, but there isn't." He grasped the rail of the crib.

"I can't help you take it apart." My shoulders slumped.

"You don't have to help me. You're doing enough," he said.

I leaned against the frame of the door and sank to the floor. Abe sat down next to me and pulled me to him. "I love you," he said. He rocked me the way I once imagined rocking Joshua. He led me back into the bedroom where he packed my toothbrush. I had forgotten it. I was relieved he remembered such a small detail.

At the hospital, I changed into a gray gown. The dressing room smelled of ammonia. I stretched out on the gurney and tried to forget that I had done this before. I placed my hands over my stomach and told Joshua not to worry. After the nurse wheeled me into the delivery room, she stuck an IV into my vein and the pitocin dripped down the clear tube. Abe stood next to me and tightened his grip on my shoulder. "I'm right here."

I nodded my head but couldn't speak.

Dr. Ray entered the room and placed his hand on my arm. It felt too heavy and I shifted my body.

When I close my eyes, Joshua and I paddle a canoe down a river overhung with trees that form an arch. It's our last trip together. As we pass under the arch, the canoe is hauled rapidly downstream despite my best efforts to slow it down. I yell to Joshua to hold on,

"The current slows down up ahead." His eyes dance with excitement, another adventurer in the family. He tells me, "Don't worry, Mom." He looks at me for a minute. His face is solemn and he clenches his hands by his side. He stands up and he is taller than I am. After taking a deep breath, he jumps into the water. The current sweeps him away.

Dr. Ray asked me to bear down with all my strength. I grunted and pushed down. Abe placed an ice chip in my mouth and wiped my forehead with a cool cloth. "You can do this," he told me. My body felt tired and my head throbbed. But Joshua still needed me. I wanted more pain medicine. My body ached, but I bore down as hard as I could until I heard a wail. Joshua was born. The doctor placed him in Abe's outstretched arms. I didn't want to hold him. Yet, I never wanted to let him go. Abe cooed to Joshua whose legs were thin and his skin bluish. My eyes traveled to his face. He looked like me. He had black hair, an olive complexion and the same angled cheekbones. Joshua whimpered and I automatically reached for him. I cradled him to me. His heart fluttered against my own. I breathed in Joshua, my little blessing. I kissed his warm forehead and wiped the beads of sweat off his delicate skin. Joshua opened his brown eyes to gaze at me. Abe placed his finger in Joshua's hand and his son squeezed it. He had the tiniest, most perfectly round fingernails. I slowly kissed his fingertips. Grateful, at last, to be a family, I nuzzled Joshua's fuzzy hair, soft and silky.

Transactions

~

They are already fifteen minutes late for their appointment to show a Tudor home in Farmington. When Sheila's mother, Isabelle, yells from the top of the stairs, "I can't find my damn keys." Sheila rummages in the basket that holds keys and grabs the ones to her grandmother's Jaguar convertible. The two of them have been feuding over her mother's throwing out her father two weeks ago.

In stiletto sandals, walking carefully down the steps, her mother breathes laboriously, her bushy eyebrows moving up and down with every breath. She pats the red bow holding back her cascading brown hair. Her gold bracelets barely jangle on her thick wrists. Sheila has pleaded with her mother to lose weight but it's a lost cause. Sheila looks in the mirror to re-tie the bow of her ponytail and admires her recently tweezed eyebrows. Her mother relishes saying that when she was young, she looked like Sheila. At seventeen, Sheila jogs with her best friend, Jenny, to stay in shape like her father who works out with weights and her grandmother who takes yoga at the Jewish Center.

Sheila dangles the car keys, "Mom, take these. They delivered Grandma's car here after servicing. It must have been a mistake."

"Take your grandmother's car? I don't think so," says her mother.

"Mom, come on. What's the big deal?" Sheila asks.

"I guess I bought it for her, so I can use it when I want." She snatches the key.

"Mom, now you're being ridiculous," says Sheila.

"No, I'm not." Her mother flounces out of the house.

Her mother groans as she lowers herself into the midnight blue Jaguar. She has to move the seat forward since she is much shorter than Grandma Trudie. Sheila doesn't say anything about their height difference because her mother will be infuriated. Her mother hates that her own mother is tall. Her mother is also angry with Grandma Trudie about her father. Sheila doesn't want her mother to know she is on her grandmother's side. She agrees her mother made a mistake kicking out her father even if he was having an affair with the receptionist, Patty.

When Sheila and her mother pull up to the front of the Tudor, Mrs. Parson is pacing and speaking into a cell phone. She is in her late sixties with silver hair that looks like a lacquered bird's nest. Her lime green dress and white gloves date back to another era. She's wearing an outfit her grandmother wouldn't be caught dead in. She has to admit her grandmother is always more fashionably dressed than her mother. "Where have you been? I just called the office," asks Mrs. Parson.

"I couldn't help it. My car keys are lost," explained her mother.

"Well, I think it's rude to keep me waiting." Mrs. Parson glares at Isabelle.

"I told you, it wasn't my fault." The color rises on her mother's neck.

"We're really sorry. It's our entire fault." Sheila steps in front of her mother. They walk into the kitchen where Mrs. Parson opens every cupboard. "Why is everything dirty?"

"Is it? I didn't notice," her mother reassuringly answers.

Sheila and her mother look in the same places as Mrs. Parson. There are only a couple of dead flies that her mother flicks with her finger. "Everything looks perfect, now" Sheila takes a tissue to wipe up the insects and stuffs it into her pocket.

They walk into the bedroom where Mrs. Parson complains. "It's too far to the bathroom from the bed."

"If you want a roomy bedroom, it will be a walk," says her mother. Sheila watches the beat of her mother's fingers as they drum faster on the windowsill. Her mother is still wearing her wedding band.

"I know my mother will find a house for you," says Sheila.

"When you're less upset. I have one that would be terrific for you," says her mother, ignoring Sheila.

"I'm not upset," says Mrs. Parsons.

"My mother will call you later," says Sheila.

"I'll set up an appointment and we'll see it this afternoon," says her mother.

Before Mrs. Parson can protest, her mother leads her out the door. When she re-enters the foyer, her mother, hands on her hips, turns to Sheila. "What a pain! I'm sick of rich, bratty women."

"Mom, you and grandma have been telling me for years that women like Mrs. Parsons are our bread and butter."

"Listen, your grandmother and I have been handling women like Mrs. Parson for over twenty-five years. You have to whet their appetites, show them a few houses that may interest them. Finally, get them into a house they'd kill for. There's one on the other side of the golf course. It's renovated and lots of money, but I think she's ready to see it."

"What if it doesn't work?" Sheila asks.

"It always works. Worse comes to worst, I'll take her to lunch at the club or better yet bring along your grandmother. The two of them have played golf for years," says her mother.

They climb into the Jaguar. "We ought to call Grandma and tell her you have her car," says Sheila.

"My mother probably called the dealer and gave him an earful. She knows I have her car by now," says her mother.

"Why are you mad at Grandma because she likes Dad?" Sheila asks.

"She likes him because he sweet-talks her," said her mother.

"I know, but he's so good at it." Sheila tries to hide a smile.

"You don't know the half of it. When she retired, he tried to persuade her to give him half the business and it almost worked. The problem is that your father doesn't know a damn thing about selling real estate." Her mother lowers the roof of the jaguar.

"Mom, you've got to stop thinking about him," says Sheila.

At that moment, her mother's cell phone rings. Sheila realizes it must be her grandmother who needs to be picked up. Sheila leans back while the sun warms her face. She hates to admit it but part of her hopes her parents don't get back together because they fight constantly. She's mad at her dad for leaving because keeping her mother out of trouble is a full-time job. For the past two weeks, she has been baby-sitting her mom and hasn't been able to go out with her friends. Her best friend, Jenny, is probably lounging at the Hartford Golf Club right now. Jenny invited her to their beach house on Rhode Island for the weekend. Sheila plans to go even if her mother pitches a fit. The problem is that Sheila doesn't like to upset her mother. Also, she hasn't mentioned her plan to apply early decision to Emory University. She knows that her mother wants her to stay closer to home and attend Trinity College.

As they continue driving through West Hartford, Sheila waves to Mr. Jacob already setting out rakes for fall even though it is only July. The good part about working is that her mother has promised instead of a salary to buy her a Saab convertible. She imagines herself and Jenny driving down an open road, their hair blowing in the breeze and singing in unison "It's Been a Hard Day's Night."

Sheila reaches into the middle compartment for a brush. She reads out loud a receipt to replace the front fender from the mechanic shop. "I wonder what happened."

"I tell you what must have happened. Grandma tried driving the car after a few drinks. I told her that I'd take the car away if she got into another accident."

"You could be wrong." Sheila's sorry that she read the receipt.

Her mother parks the car at the top of the hill directly in front of the store window with the words "Solomon Real Estate Company." She marches down the hill and takes a tissue to wipe a smudge off the store window.

"I think we should at least ask her," Sheila says.

"I guess the best thing I ever did was have her to retire," says her mother.

"Grandma had enough. She told me it had become too ruthless. I wouldn't want to be in the real estate business, either," says Sheila.

"Are you saying I am ruthless? Don't forget that this business is going to pay for your college education," says her mother.

"I didn't say that I want to be a teacher."

"You'll never be rich on a teacher's salary." Her mother shakes her head.

"I don't need to be rich," says Sheila.

"Well, it certainly helps," says her mother.

"Does it?" Sheila sighs.

"You know the answer to that as well as I do." Her mother pats her on the head.

Sheila grits her teeth. She wishes she had the guts to tell her mother that she doesn't need any of her money. As soon as her mother knows she wants to go to Emory, her mother will try to make her feel guilty. She's working up the nerve to tell her.

Inside the office, Sheila stands in the doorway of the office while her mother holds a meeting with the agents. For a moment, her mother is all business and in charge the way she used to be before she found out about her dad. Her mother makes an appointment to show Mrs. Parson another house. Her mother writes the customers' names with a marker on a large white board alongside the name of their agents as she speaks to them. When the meeting is over, her mother stops at an agent's desk to help her on an impending contract.

Walking over to her father's bare desk, Sheila notices that he left the clay pencil holder she made one Father's Day. She fingers the picture of the three of them. They hold fishing poles in front of a boat on the island of St. Thomas. She wishes they were back on the island and lying on the white sand where the only sound was the lapping of the waves. Her dad won't be upset about her going to Emory since he moved out. Her thoughts are interrupted when her mother tells her they have to pick up her grandmother.

At the doctor's office, they wait until Grandma Trudie steps out of the building. Her white linen dress accentuates both her height and thinness. Her silver hair is carefully pulled back in a bun. She doesn't look sixty-five. Her grandmother caresses the side of the car. "Here's my baby as good as new."

"What happened to your baby?" her mother asks.

"Grandma, get in the car so we can go to lunch," says Sheila.

"She needed some work," says her grandmother. Sheila pushes her seat forward and her grandmother steps into the back seat of the car.

"What kind of work?" her mother asks.

"What does it matter?" Sheila says.

"Routine maintenance. Why the twenty questions?" her grandmother asks.

"There was a bill in the car for body work. I wouldn't call that routine," says her mother. She jerks the car to a halt at the red light.

"I was parked at the bank's cash machine and an old guy ran into me. What's the big deal?" her grandmother says.

"That's difficult to believe. The car needed a new front fender. Are you sure you didn't crash into him?" her mother asks.

"Are you accusing me of lying? Do you hear that, Sheila? Your mother is calling me a liar!" her grandmother yells.

"I'm sure she doesn't mean it," says Sheila.

"She means it. She doesn't know how to be nice like Steven. He would never yell at me." Her grandmother pouts.

"What are you talking about? I supported Steven for twenty-five years. I sold real estate while he went to the gym, the tailor and flirted with customers. I think he had a good deal. I'd say he was hard on me. I deserved to be treated better," says her mother.

"Well, she didn't need to kick him out. Did she Sheila?" her grandmother asks.

"I guess not," says Sheila.

"Now you're both ganging up on me? Where's the justice? You two should be on my side. I'm taking care of both of you," said her mother.

"You're going to give me a heart attack with your rudeness. Take me back to the doctor." Her grandmother hugs her chest.

"Did the doctor say you have a weak heart?" Sheila's forehead pounds.

"No, he said I weighed one hundred and twenty-one pounds. I told him I hadn't gained a pound in five years. He needs to check his scale." Her grandmother smooths back her hair.

"He must have enjoyed hearing that." Her mother shakes her head.

"Grandma didn't mean to offend the doctor," says Sheila.

"Sheila's right. Why are you picking on an old lady with a heart condition?" Her grandmother puts her hand on her forehead.

"What heart condition? All I was trying to say was that you never take my side against Steven. You should apologize," says her mother.

"She didn't mean to upset you," said Sheila. "Right, Grandma?"

"I'm the one that is upset. First, you steal my car. Second, you accuse me of lying and now you want me to tell you that you did the right thing by throwing out Steven?

"Men will be men. Your father was the same way." Her grandmother purses her lips.

"Why don't you both calm down. Let's go to lunch." Sheila turns toward them.

"I want to go home. I've lost my appetite." Her grandmother crosses her arms.

"Please, stop fighting," pleads Sheila.

"Sheila's right. Let's go to lunch," says her mother.

"I don't want to eat. I can skip a meal without a problem," says her grandmother.

"Are you talking about my weight, again?" her mother asks.

"It's not like you watch what you eat. You've no discipline." Her grandmother reapplies her red lipstick.

"Stop it. You're not being fair. Mom is disciplined. She works hard."

"She works hard ruining the company that I built with her father," says her grandmother.

"Grandma, please, stop fighting," says Sheila.

"I've had enough. Don't say another word," says her mother.

"They say silence is golden." Her grandmother powders her nose.

They ride in silence. Sheila doesn't know what to do because if she talks to either one of them, the other one will be angry with her. She feels like her head is in a vise. It's the same way she feels when her parents fight over nothing. They like to argue just to hear their own voices. She imagines jumping out of the car. She will grab her clothes and take the next plane to Atlanta.

Her mother halts the car several blocks from her grandmother's condominium, the one her mother bought for her. Her mother says,

"You can walk the rest of the way."

"Mom, just drop her off at the door." Sheila doesn't understand how her mother could leave her on the street.

"I can't believe you're my daughter. No wonder Steven left you," says her grandmother.

"What a terrible thing to say about Mom." Sheila's eyes widen. The two of them are well matched. In a boxing ring, she doesn't know who would go down first.

"Now you know why I'm not driving her home," says her mother to Sheila. Her mother turns up the radio to hear the weather report. Sheila imagines smashing the radio.

"Do you want to come in for a cool drink?" her grandmother yells to Sheila.

"No, I don't want to drink with either of you. You're both screwed up. I can't wait to leave the two of you," Sheila cries out.

"Don't get upset. Grandma will be fine after a whiskey sour and her show, *Guiding Light*," says her mother.

"What's wrong with both of you? Can't you get along?" Sheila asks.

"We get along just fine." Her mother starts to drive again. She turns into a Dunkin' Donut's parking lot.

"Take me home, right now. Give me back my car and you can walk," says her grandmother. "I'll drive you home," says her grandmother to Sheila.

"When I'm good and ready, I'll take you back." Her mother slams the car door and enters the doughnut shop. Sheila doesn't want to get out of the car but she's afraid her mother is going to make a fool of herself. She follows her inside the store where a girl with a nose ring and pink hair serves them. Sheila gives the girl a half-smile and moves to the end of the counter. The last thing she wants is for the girl to question her. Her mother orders one of each kind of doughnut, sixteen in total. Since she was a small child, her mother has had this ritual of buying every flavor of doughnut. Sheila thinks about going back to the car to wait but her mother is breathing heavily. She's afraid her mother will have a heart attack.

For a moment, she imagines an ambulance racing to her mother. At the hospital, her grandmother and father are contrite. Her grandmother holds her mother's hand. They make a pact not to fight. In the meantime, Sheila worries if inherited genes cause such nasty behavior. Sheila looks out the window and watches her grandmother in the back seat of the car. She's smoking a cigarette, flicking the ashes out onto the ground.

When they return to the car, her mother says to her grandmother, "Your insides are tar."

"We all have our vices." Her grandmother looks her mother up and down.

"Haven't I told you that cigarette smoking makes me nauseous," says her mother.

"The top is down. You're not inhaling the smoke." Her grandmother flicks the cigarette near her mother's feet.

"I'll drive you home as soon as you put out the cigarette," says her mother.

"Please, put it out. Don't you want to go home?" Sheila asks.

Her grandmother hands Sheila the cigarette to stub on the ground. "I don't want to be here one extra minute." Sheila wishes she were already at college. She wouldn't have to deal with either of them. Her life would be normal.

"I'm glad you're willing to listen to your granddaughter because I've had enough," her mother says to her grandmother.

"At least she has some sense," says her grandmother.

"You're being ridiculous. I refuse to fight with you any longer." Her mother tightens her lips. When her grandmother steps out of the car, she kisses Sheila, "Bye, love." Then she glares at her mother. "Enjoy your doughnuts."

"I will. Every last one of them," shouts her mother.

Her grandmother slams the car door.

"I can't stand when you fight," says Sheila to her mother.

"I'm sorry, honey. Your grandmother gets me going." She turns to Sheila. "Your face is red. Are you okay?" She places her hand on Sheila's forehead and for a moment, it feels cool, comforting. Sheila leans toward her mother, who pats her cheeks and says, "Don't worry, Grandma and I will work it out. We always do."

"They have your favorite flavor, blueberry." Her mother hands her a doughnut.

When Sheila takes a bite, the doughnut sticks to the roof of her mouth, dissolving slowly. The taste of the sweet doughnut reminds her of old times when she and her mother would travel to different shops to find ones they hadn't tasted before. One time they drove to the Connecticut shore, Old Lyme, because a new shop was written up in the *Hartford Courant* as having the best blueberry doughnuts. They sat on the beach while they ate, stirring the sand with their toes and watching the children wade in the water.

Sheila watches her mother chewing on her doughnut with a beatific smile on her face. It doesn't take much to make her mother feel better, just like her grandmother who enjoys her whiskey sours. After a few drinks, she's a different person, mellow, fun to be around. For a moment, she feels sorry for them. She wonders how they are going to survive when she goes away to school. She envisions her mother lying immobilized in bed. Her grandmother watching one television show after another. Munching on a second doughnut, Sheila's mouth feels dry. She can't swallow the doughnut. Realizing she hates doughnuts, that she has disliked them for a long time, she spits it into a tissue.

"Is the doughnut bad? Take another," her mother says.

"I don't want anymore." Sheila can hear her stomach churning.

"But it's so good. They're our family tradition," chides her mother.

"I don't care," says Sheila.

"You don't know what you're missing." Her mother places a doughnut by Sheila's mouth.

"Stop it. Just stop it. I don't want a damn doughnut. I don't want anything from you. I want to get the hell out of here. I want to go as far away as possible." Sheila shoves the donut away and it crumbles.

"What's the matter with you?" Her mother starts to pick up the pieces.

"How can you ask me that? I don't want to stay here. I can't live at home and go to school. The fighting is killing me. I want to go to Emory." Sheila reaches into her pocket for a tissue. She finds the one with the squished bug and tosses it.

"You can't be serious. Why would you want to live in the South? It's too hot. You've all your creature comforts at home. I won't bother you. It will be like having your own apartment. You don't have to help me with the business. Didn't I have your bathroom redone last year? I told you I would buy you a new television and computer. Trinity's an excellent school. It has a terrific campus." Her mother looks contrite.

"The campus is in the middle of Hartford. It's a slum. I want to go to a school that has sunshine all year long," says Sheila.

"You won't have the four seasons. I'm sure you will miss it," says her mother.

"I need a change. I can't live with you. I have to go to Emory!" Sheila yells.

"What about your grandmother? She adores you," says her mother.

"She can adore me when I'm living in Atlanta," says Sheila.

"It's out of the question." Her mother speeds out of the parking lot, tossing the box of doughnuts out the window. A doughnut slaps against a tree, crumbs flying. The quick turns of the car give Sheila a stomachache.

There is no good time to discuss Emory with her mother. Her mother has stayed around to care for her grandmother and she expects Sheila to do the same for her. She knows that her mother does things for her grandmother because she feels she has no choice. Sheila doesn't want a life of obligation. She wants to make her own decisions. She doesn't give a damn about the family business. Her family needs to mind their own business. They are constantly harping at her "to bring home a boyfriend." She rarely dates because she won't allow any boy to be scrutinized by the two of them. How many times has her grandmother said, "Did you know your mother married Steven because of me? I told her to not let Steven get away."

Sheila's throat tightens when tears run down her mother's cheeks. She feels like someone is holding a plastic bag over her head. She can't stand when her mother cries. Her mother tries to hide her sadness, but she can be overly sensitive. Sheila places her hand on her mother's shoulder. "It's going to be okay."

"I don't think so," whispers her mother.

"Don't worry." Sheila looks out at a barren pasture.

Her mother's makeup is smeared and gunk drips from her nose. She's a wreck. Her dress is soaked with perspiration; it clings to her body, making her look heavier. Sheila suggests that they drive home so that her mother can change.

In the house, Sheila guides her mother upstairs. Leaving her mother for a moment, she goes into her room to call Jenny's answering machine. "My family is at it again. I'll call you later."

Sheila walks over to the dresses lying on the floor of her mother's room. Her mother sits on the bed while Sheila searches the closet. Taking out a navy dress, Sheila says, "Put this on. You'll feel better."

"I don't want to do anything. I just want to crawl into bed," says her mother.

"You can't do that. Mrs. Parson is expecting to hear from us." Sheila unzips the dress to help her mother step into it, a big rag doll with limp arms. Wringing her hands, her mother gazes into the mirror. "I look awful."

"You look fine." Sheila squeezes her mother's shoulder.

"You're a good girl. I don't know what I would do without you," says her mother.

"You'd manage," says Sheila quietly.

"I wouldn't." Her mother smiles weakly.

"Let's not discuss it now." Sheila looks in the mirror while embracing her mother. They both look pitiful.

When they get back into the car, her mother pulls down the flap of the windshield and uses the mirror as she reapplies her red lipstick.

"It's a little bright. Why don't you blot your lips?" Sheila suggests.

"I feel like wearing bright lipstick." Her mother throws the tissue out of the car.

"Okay, suit you," says Sheila.

"I will," says her mother.

Sheila doesn't bother to answer because she's tired of her games. She looks at her watch and realizes she has one hour to get to Jenny's house before she leaves for the beach. She imagines lying on Jenny's deck while the only noise is the roar of the ocean.

At the office, her mother slams the car door and walks briskly down the hill. She forgets to take the key to the car. Sheila slips it into her pocket. Sheila watches her mother talking to the new receptionist, Glena, who has a pointed chin and a lumpy body. Leave it to her mother not to make the same mistake by hiring someone with Patty's voluptuous figure. Behind her car, Sheila sees a taxi stop and her grandmother steps out. She's changed into a white blouse and tight pedal pushers. "What are you doing here?" Sheila asks.

"I want my car back." Her grandmother leans into her car.

"Please, don't upset Mom." Sheila can smell alcohol on her breath.

They both turn to watch her mother climbing up the hill toward them. "I just got off the phone with the West Hartford police. They want to speak with you about an accident in the Bishop's corner parking lot. A man filed a report that you hit his Volvo."

"The old geezer hit me," says her grandmother.

"Not according to the police," says her mother.

"You're going to take their side against me?" her grandmother asks.

"That's funny. After the last accident, you need to ask?" her mother says.

"What is wrong with the two of you?" Sheila screams.

"Come into my office," says her mother to her grandmother.

"Your office, my old office!" Her grandmother wobbles behind her mother.

Sheila watches the two of them go inside. She wonders how much her grandmother has had to drink. She wipes the sweat from her forehead. They are standing at Glena's desk and yelling at one another. Glena keeps her head down. Her grandmother slaps her mother across the face. Her mother starts to shake her grandmother. Sheila holds her stomach. She leans out of the car to throw up. Mashed doughnuts splatter everywhere. She takes a tissue from her pocket to wipe her face. She can't stand either of them. She needs to get the hell out of here before she cracks up. They have to see she is not a good girl.

Sheila climbs out of the car. She holds onto it as she walks around to the driver's side. She climbs back into the Jaguar. She leans her head against the seat. Her mind is racing. She fingers the leather seats, silky smooth. The car is in mint condition with a new car smell, recently waxed. She slips the key in the ignition and turns on the engine. She takes deep breaths to calm herself. Leaving the car door open, she focuses her eyes on both of them. Her mother has her hands on her hips. Her grandmother wags her finger in her face. They are still screaming at one another. Sheila squeezes the steering wheel. Her knuckles whiten. She places her foot on the gas pedal. Glena bursts into tears. Sheila aims the wheels of the car toward her mother and grandmother. She pushes her foot down on the gas pedal. As soon as the car moves down the hill, she jumps out. When she lands on the pavement, her knees are cut; blood trickles down her leg. The Jaguar smashes into the window of the office and hits Glena's desk, shards everywhere. Glena shrieks. Papers from her desk settle on the nose of the car. The horn beeps. Sheila sees her mother and grandmother, wide-eyed, staring through the broken window. Sheila carefully lifts herself off the ground.

Time of Her Life

~

On the weekend after Dolores didn't return to Yale, her family had breakfast together. While her father cooked chocolate chip pancakes, her mother said, "Chocolate is bad for your diabetes. What are you trying to do, kill yourself?" Her father continued cooking and sneaking chocolate bits to both of them. He winked at Dolores when her mother wasn't looking. Her mother finished her black coffee and shook her head. Dolores tried not to make direct eye contact with her father because she knew they would both laugh. Since her father enjoyed watching her eat, she ate as many pancakes as she could. It seemed like a small gesture for not giving her a difficult time about staying home.

The next day, while she was watching Hollywood Squares, her father eased himself down into his brown chair. His bushy eyebrows slanted inwards. He asked, for the second time, "What happened at Yale?" Then he added, "The psychologist said the coach found you banging your head on the floor of the locker room. They said you wouldn't sign a release form to give us more information. Why not?" he asked.

"Mom says I should see a shrink."

"You should see one. Don't you eventually want to go back to school and become an English professor?"

"I don't want to do anything." She turned the television sound back on.

He heaved himself off the chair and muttered, "Poor Dolores."

"That's me, all right," she whispered.

She muted the sound to listen to her parents' arguing in the kitchen because they knew only that she had stopped going to class, but not why. Her father told her mother. "Let the kid breathe."

Her mother said, "What do you know about goals?" Then she heard the back door slam and her father's heavy tread on the outdoor steps. Her mother immediately telephoned her sister. "When I went

to college, I had the time of my life. I wanted the same for her."
Dolores tried to concentrate on the television but she kept hearing
her mother's shrill voice. She walked into the kitchen. "I was just
chatting with your aunt." Her mother covered the mouthpiece.

"I'm sick of your talking about me." Dolores went to her room

During the next seven months, she didn't go anywhere. It was
comforting to be home alone when her parents were at work. Every
morning, her father left to open the hardware store by eight o' clock.
Her mother woke at six and showered first. When Dolores was little,
she'd stand at the bathroom door to watch her mother brush her long
black hair into a tightly coiled bun. She never wore makeup because
she thought it "cheapened" her appearance. Then she dressed in one
of her dark polyester pants suits. She took her work seriously as the
head librarian. She was always reading or bringing home a good
book for Dolores because she didn't like to go into the library. On
more than one occasion, Dolores had ducked behind a row of books
while her mother escorted one of her classmates to the door for talking
too loudly.

Today, after her mother left, Dolores took a long shower. She
wrapped herself quickly in a towel when she stepped out of the stall
because she didn't want to see her body that had thickened since she
had come home. Her blue eyes clouded over with a thin film. She
imagined she was back sitting in the Yale bookstore café as she drank
coffee. The lecture halls were filled with rows of students talking to
one another. She remembered curly, black-haired Joe who sat in front
of her in biology.

He had talked to her at his fraternity's party. She had noticed how
much taller he was than she was. He had worn a buttoned down shirt
and khaki pants. He had given her a beer, but she didn't tell him she
hated to drink. His eyes were deep blue like a cloudless sky. Flattered
that he was paying attention to her, she went with him into his
bedroom. He had handed her a joint. First she had shaken her head
"no," but he pressed her. They had smoked dope and lay on the single
bed while listening to the Moody Blues. Then he had pulled her
toward him and they kissed.

The following week, Joe had invited her to another fraternity party. When she mentioned on the phone that she had met a pre-medical student, her mother was impressed.

In her bedroom, Dolores slipped into the same gray sweatshirt and pants. She had to buy new outfits but she didn't want to leave the house. In high school, she couldn't wait to go to the mall with her best friend, Sherry. She would pick her up to be at the Hempstead Mall the minute it opened. Dolores missed those days. Sherry visited her when she first came home. She looked terrific in her fitted tee shirt. The two of them had been varsity soccer players in high school and every afternoon had run three miles around the reservoir. Dolores' parents had attended all of her games. Her mother had embarrassed her by shouting. "Dolores, faster, you go, girl." If Dolores had looked over, she would have seen her father trying to pull her mother back into her seat. In the locker room, her teammates teased her by saying, "You go, Dolores."

Now at home, during a visit, Dolores told Sherry she wasn't returning to Yale. "What are you talking about?" Sherry asked.

"I don't want to go back," said Dolores.

"You're kidding, right?" Sherry's eyes widened.

"No, I'm better off at home," said Dolores.

"Did something happen to you? You're not acting like yourself," said Sherry.

Dolores steadied herself and changed the topic. She hadn't talked to Sherry since that conversation. She didn't want to see anyone from high school. How many times had she heard her mother bragging to her friends about Dolores' grades or her goals at soccer? Her mother said, "Dolores needs a rest." Dolores felt sorry for her mother's inability to accept her failure.

These days, Dolores spent her mornings washing the breakfast dishes and throwing a load of laundry into the washing machine. In the living room, she plumbed the pillows and returned them to the exact place on the couch where her mother kept them. The red couches and two matching green chairs with ottomans that faced the large television had been in the room for as long as Dolores remembered.

When she was a child, she had crept into the room and moved the coasters or vases to different locations. But her mother would catch her. "Don't be a nuisance. Leave my things." Her mother had to have everything in their proper place.

Since Dolores didn't have much to do with her afternoons, she blended milk shakes and watched soap operas. If her mother came home early from work, she'd complain, "Can't you watch something educational?" Then Dolores would turn on the food channel to watch Chef Pierre prepare chicken stir-fry, beef with broccoli or spinach lasagna. She was sick of her mother's tasteless broiled chicken and peas from a can. At dinner, her mother complained to her father, "She has to do something besides watch television."

"I'm sitting right here, Mom. Why don't you talk to me?" Dolores asked.

"Dolores will do something if you give her a chance," her father said.

"I hate when she talks about me as if I'm not here," Dolores said to her father.

"You never give me a straight answer," said her mother.

"What do you want to know?" Dolores asked.

"What happened to the girl I sent to Yale?" asked her mother.

"If she wanted us to know, she would tell us," said her father.

"The girl that went to Yale is going to Elysium Fields Foods tomorrow and cook dinner tomorrow night." Dolores said. Then she wondered why she said it. Before she could undo it, her father patted her shoulder. "See, I told you she'd find something." Dolores frowned at her mother but kept her mouth shut.

The next morning when she finally left the house, she walked to town. She passed the Food Emporium with its new striped awning, the post office and The Stride Rite Shoe Store where her mother had bought her shoes when she was little. Near her dad's hardware store, she stayed on the other side of the street. She didn't want to have her Uncle Ed pinch her cheek and ask if she would help in the stock room. Inside Baskin Robbins, she ordered a triple fudge brownie ice cream cone and licked it while standing in front of the Toy Chest where an electric train rode on a track with tunnels, bridges and trainmen. She pretended climbing aboard.

At Elysium Fields Foods where the fluorescent lights were bright and the shelves stocked with different colored pastas, she passed canisters of aromatic coffee beans. She stopped to touch the red leaf lettuce covered with a fine mist. She squeezed the ripe green melons the way her mother taught her. She snapped a carrot in half and took a bite.

A boy with curly brown hair down to his shoulders, a broad nose and pocked skin was offering customers samples of a soufflé warming on a burner plate. He wore a tight black sweatshirt and jeans with black sneakers. As she was about to walk past him, their eyes met. His eyes were true green with amber sparks radiating from his pupils. "You look like you could use a treat," he said to Dolores.

"What do you mean?" Dolores feared he was referring to her weight.

"Would you like to try my soufflé?" He smiled.

"What kind is it?" She realized he was trying to be nice.

"Carrot and made with all natural ingredients. Here's a copy of the recipe." When he gave her the paper, his hand was warm. "Come back, anytime."

"Maybe tomorrow," she said.

"Great," he said.

That night, when she made the carrot soufflé, her dad helped her. The only sound was the hum of the refrigerator as she pureed the carrots but it reminded her of when she was little and he had baked her chocolate birthday cupcakes. He hadn't cared how much frosting she smeared on the cupcakes. At dinner, her father said, "We had fun."

"Just like old times," Dolores sighed.

"The dish is terrific." Her mother patted her hand.

"Really?" asked Dolores.

"You're good at anything you put your mind to." Her mother nodded and took another mouthful. Her father served himself a second helping. Dolores beamed.

Every day for the next month, she walked to Elysian Fields Foods and talked to Danny. He spoke to her in a kind voice. When she told him she didn't want to go back to school, he said, "It doesn't matter. Just enjoy now."

"I wish I could," she sighed.

"I promise it will get easier," he said.

She learned he lived with his grandmother, a retired postal clerk. "She's great, my grandmother. Would you like to meet her?"

"What do you mean?" Dolores asked.

"Come to dinner on Friday night," he asked.

"Are you sure?" Dolores asked.

· "Absolutely, it will be fun," he said.

"Okay." She figured it wasn't a real date if his grandmother was there. Nothing bad could happen.

But once she left Elysium Fields Foods, she realized she had nothing decent to wear. What would Danny's grandmother think of her? She could hear her mother's words, "How can you walk around in torn sweats?" She had an image of herself as a fat girl in smelly rags picking through garbage containers. By the time she arrived home, she was ready to crawl into bed. She couldn't believe she had ventured out. She was afraid Danny could turn out to be like Joe. What possessed her to speak to Danny in the first place? It was because she was tired of being alone. Dolores rolled onto her side and fell asleep.

When her mother came home from work, she shook Dolores' shoulder, "What's the matter, honey? Are you sick?" Her mother's worried eyes peered into her face. "Norman, come in here. Dolores looks green."

"Do you have a stomachache?" her dad asked.

"Did she eat something strange at Elysium Fields Foods?" her mother asked.

"What could she have eaten?" her father answered.

"I don't know but they have so many weird-looking vegetables and grains. Have you noticed how peculiar the kids are? They wear turbans and don't shave."

"Get out of my room." Dolores pulled the cover over her head.

That evening, she told her mother that she had met an old classmate who attended a local college, "Well, at least, he's a college boy," her mother said.

Dolores didn't bother to tell her mother Danny's aspirations were to run the vegetable section of Elysium Fields Foods and that was fine with her.

As she tried on jeans the next day in the changing room of The Gap. She had moved from a size ten to a size fourteen in only seven short months. When she felt her sides, she touched love handles. Her body had taken control to inflate itself like a balloon. She jammed herself into a pair of jeans. She had no choice, but to buy them. She had agreed to go to Danny's house because she needed to get out of her own.

When she came home with several packages, her mother came out of the kitchen.

"Let's see all the goodies you brought."

"Not right now. I'm tired." Dolores plopped on the couch. Her mother reminded her of the perky woman advertising Betty Crocker mixes on the television.

"Is this the girl who once couldn't wait to show me all her pretty outfits?" Her mother clapped her hands like a tiny child.

"I'm not that girl, anymore. She's gone."

"Of course you are, honey."

"Mom, are you blind? Don't you get it?"

"Whatever happened at Yale is over. I don't know much, but the psychologist said you suffered some kind of trauma. Can't you tell me?"

"I don't want to talk about it," Dolores looked out the window.

"You're safe here. I'm trying to reassure you."

"Well, I don't feel reassured."

Her mother left the room. She hated the way her mother tried to force her to open up. It reminded her of Joe who forced her do things she didn't want to do.

Later her father approached her, "I know you have had a difficult time. I wish you'd let us help you. Try to give your mother a little slack," he said.

"Right, just like she always gives me," she said.

"She's concerned. I'm worried about you and Danny, too," he said.

"Don't worry about Danny," Dolores said.

"I hope you're right." He shook his head.

On the evening of her date, she heard the roar of a motorcycle before Danny pulled up in front of her house. Her eyes widened. She couldn't believe she was going to ride on the back of his bike. It was a reckless thing to do, but she trusted Danny. Her mother watched Danny walk up the brick path. "Don't tell me he's your date? He works at Elysium Food Store and bags my groceries. He's not a college boy." Her mother crossed her arms. "Norman, see what your daughter is doing?"

"Is that a motorcycle?" her father asked.

"Your daughter has lost her mind." She turned to her father.

But before he said anything else, the bell rang and Dolores hurried to answer it. Danny wore a yellow T-shirt, black leather pants and boots. He looked like one of the sexy gang members she saw in the motorcycle magazine that she picked up while waiting at the checkout line. She invited Danny in to meet her parents. Her mother, blanched complexion, barely shook his hand. Her father grasped his shoulder. "You'll be careful with my daughter, right?"

"I promise, sir. I'll drive slowly," Danny said.

She could hear her parents arguing as she closed the front door behind her. When Danny helped her on the bike, she placed her arms around his torso. As she leaned into him, his scented cologne smelled like a bed of autumn leaves. She pressed against his shoulders and wondered how his arms would feel wrapped around her. She contracted her stomach muscles and wished she were thinner. She wondered if Danny found her body repulsive. "What's the matter? You stopped leaning against me. It felt good," he said.

Dolores hugged him and riding through town, she felt free. No longer weighed down by her worries, she and Danny became one body flying down the road.

Brown lawns and broken cement sidewalks were in the section of town where Danny lived. Dolores faced a small home painted gray that looked like a bungalow. The smell of tomatoes filled the air in the living room. Dolores adjusted her eyes to the darkly lit room. She saw a worn sofa and a chipped coffee table. Bright crochet doilies covered the furniture and on the rocking chair sat his grandmother who wore a sky blue dress with a matching shawl. Dolores noticed she had the same green eyes with amber streaks as Danny. His grandmother smoothed back her gray hair. Dolores smiled. She felt they had met before.

In the kitchen, Danny stirred the freshly made spaghetti sauce. As she helped his grandmother set the table, she told Dolores she had arthritis. She said it was difficult for her to get out of bed because her legs were stiff. "I couldn't manage without Danny. He's such a good boy."

"Don't embarrass me. I'm not always a good boy." He winked at Dolores.

"Everyone gets cranky. I would if I had to care for an old lady like me," she said.

"Neither of you seem cranky to me," Dolores said.

Dolores dried the dishes after Danny's grandmother washed them. She even kissed Dolores on the cheek before she retired to her bedroom. Dolores noticed on the mantle a picture of Danny standing between a man and a woman. "Those are my parents. They died." She realized Danny, like her, had been through hard times. But before she could say anything, Danny brought out a six-pack of Budweiser from the kitchen and offered her one. "Sure," Dolores said even though she still hated the taste of beer. "You're so nice to each other," said Dolores.

"We stick together," he grinned.

"Not my family," mumbled Dolores. She wished she had a grandmother like Danny's. She was about to question him more about his family, but he turned on the television to a football game. She didn't say anything even though the players reminded her of gladiators. Danny placed his arm around her. Her body stiffened. For a moment, she felt Joe's arm around her.

"What's the matter," Danny asked.

"I'm not used to hanging out with a boy," she said.

"I promise never to hurt you," he whispered.

"Are you sure?" she asked tentatively.

"Yes." He pulled her closer. She put her head on his shoulder. Her body relaxed.

The next day, she went to Elysium Fields Foods and watched Danny from the organic cookie aisle. He chopped the zucchini. He talked to a small group of women who gathered around him. It seemed to Dolores that everyone liked him. He was a person who wouldn't take advantage of her. Danny called her over. "What are you doing?"

"Just looking," she said.

"Watching what?" He laughed.

"How nice you are," she said.

He leaned over to kiss her and her eye twitched. "Do I make you nervous?

"No, you make me happy," she said.

"That's funny. My grandmother says the same thing about me," he said.

"I guess your grandmother is right." Dolores laughed.

When Dolores was with Danny, her college days were far away. Danny wasn't at all like Joe. He taught her how to drive his motorcycle. They drove to Ben's Apple Orchard late at night to steal apples while trying to elude Ben's two black shepherds.

Dolores and his grandmother helped Danny prepare his recipes. One morning, they were making banana bread. The kitchen was sunny and warm from the oven.

"Please, hand me a cup of sugar," said Danny.

"I'll do it." His grandmother patting Dolores on the shoulder.

"Here's a cup of flour while Grandma gets the sugar," said Dolores.

She took the cup of sugar from his grandmother because her hand was shaking.

"I'm so clumsy," said the grandmother.

The sugar had spilled on the table and Dolores quickly wiped it with a sponge, "No, you're not."

"Stop gabbing and help me," Danny said playfully.

When the cake came out of the oven and they tasted it, Danny said, "That wasn't sugar. You two girls handed me salt. The cake is disgusting." The three of them laughed.

"We'll do better next time." His grandmother winked at Dolores and hugged her.

For a moment, Dolores imagined she was her granddaughter.

While Danny was at work, Dolores went to his home to help his grandmother clean the house. They played cards and scrabble, activities for which her mother had no patience. As a child, her mother told her board games were "stupid." Some afternoons, they watched soap operas and ate peanut butter sandwiches. One day, while the two of them played gin rummy, Danny's grandmother said, "I'm so happy Danny found you."

"Are you? He's my first real boyfriend," Dolores said shyly.

"He told me you were at college for a while. I figured you had a beau."

"There was one boy, Joe," she said hesitantly.

"Did he break your heart?" She put her wrinkled hand over hers.

"He hurt me badly," Dolores lips trembled.

"Do you want to tell me about it?" His grandmother squeezed her hand.

"He wouldn't take "no" for an answer." Dolores wept.

"He forced you?" His grandmother held her.

"Yes." Dolores wrapped her arms around his grandmother.

"Oh my God, you poor thing." His grandmother rocked her.

"It was awful," whispered Dolores.

"I can't believe anyone could hurt a gentle girl like you."

"Please don't tell Danny."

"Your secret is safe with me." His grandmother hugged her.

"I wouldn't want to upset him," said Dolores.

"You're right. I won't tell him. I'm not sure he could handle it."

"What do you mean?" Dolores looked into his grandmother's concerned eyes.

"He hasn't had many girlfriends" His grandmother kissed her forehead. "We'll keep it between us."

"You promise?" Dolores implored.

"Absolutely." His grandmother held Dolores until the room grew dark. Then the two of them stood up to make supper.

After dinner, while Dolores and Danny cuddled on the couch, she wondered if she should tell Danny about her conversation with his grandmother. But she sensed from what his grandmother said that he might not be able to handle it. Her mother said boys matured more slowly than girls do. Maybe, that was what his grandmother meant. She couldn't stand telling Danny and being rejected. Instead, she turned to watch Danny intensely watched the two wrestlers thumping each other to the ground. She teased him about his room covered with posters of wrestlers. Danny asked, "Do you want to meet my friends?"

"I don't know if they would like me," said Dolores.

"I know they will," said Danny.

The next day when the phone rang, her mother handed it to her. "It's that boy from the food store," she said. Danny invited her to go to a friend's party and she agreed. When she hung up, she thought about asking her mother why she disliked Danny but she already knew. Danny was not her mother's idea of a "catch." Her mother still expected her to go back to Yale, meet a doctor and live in the suburbs. She went into the living room to tell her father she was going out with Danny. "Why doesn't he ever come over here?" He frowned.

"We're going to a party tonight. Maybe another time."

"I'd like to know Danny better."

"He's kind and his grandmother is terrific."

"But is he your type?"

"I don't have a type. Danny is good to me," said Dolores.

"I hope he is, but I'd still like to see more of him and you."

Back in her bedroom, she looked through her closet for something to wear. Couldn't her dad tell how much Danny meant to her? He wasn't taking her to a fraternity party where everyone drank until they threw up. As she sat on the bed, she decided she was sick of the color pink. The bedspread with pink daisies had to go, as well as the lamp with pink pompoms. Tomorrow she was going to throw out every pink thing.

After putting on a tight black sleeveless tee shirt and jeans, she outlined her eyes with mascara and spread lipstick on her thin lips. It was a deep shade of red that her mother would never wear. She wanted to look pretty for Danny. In the living room, her mother nudged her father. "Isn't it a little chilly for a sleeveless shirt?"

"I think it's a perfect night for one," said Dolores.

"Maybe you want to take your sweater just in case," said her father.

"I'm going to wait outside." She took a sweater from the closet.

"Bring Danny in to say hello," said her father.

"Right, Dad." She slammed the door behind her.

On the porch, the air was filled with the scent of her father's white roses she helped him to plant when she was little. She walked down the steps to smell them. At that moment, Danny pulled up on his bike and screeched to a halt. "Why are you out here?"

"I smelled the roses."

"Now you look exotic," he placed a rose in her hair.

"Do you think so?" She kissed his cheek.

"I know it," he nibbled her ear.

While she held him tightly, they sped down the street. The rose fell on the ground. They traveled into the countryside with farmhouses scattered along the road. The stars lit up the sky like sprinkles. The salty smell of the ocean was invigorating. She thought about asking Danny where they were headed but she didn't care.

At the end of a long, dirt road stood an enormous beach house with brightly-lit lights like a lighthouse beckoning them. Through the large picture window in the living room, Dolores watched bodies swaying in unison. Motorbikes were scattered the lawn. When Danny opened the door for her, she was deafened by the music. She wanted to place her hands over her ears but she didn't want Danny to think she was uptight. She smoothed down her shirt as they passed a group of girls in scanty bathing suits. She felt overdressed. She looked over at Danny to see if he was eyeing the girls but he took her hand to walk through the living room. Abstract paintings hung on the walls. In the center of the kitchen table sat a large keg of beer. While Danny filled two cups, Dolores noticed a group of boys looking at her. One of them was quite handsome with dark curly hair, but he reminded her of Joe towering over her. She felt Joe tugging at her underwear. She tried to break free but Joe was too strong. She was too drunk. He pushed her legs apart. She tried to hold her thighs together, but she couldn't. Joe snickered. She pleaded with him to stop.

She closed her eyes. Her stomach ached. She wished they were at home with Danny's grandmother. She turned quickly away from the boy to face a girl wearing a red bikini. The girl, a cashier at Elysium Fields Food, sat on the lap of a boy who bagged groceries. She asked Danny, "Who's your date?"

"It doesn't matter." Danny put his arm around Dolores and led her toward the living room. "What was that about?" Dolores asked.

"Just a girl from work," said Danny. But Dolores felt the girl's eyes on her as they left the room. She had the sneaking suspicion that Danny knew her better than he was saying. Maybe, Danny had dated her. She unfolded her sweater from around her waist to place on her shoulders. She couldn't think with all the noise in the room.

Then Danny squeezed her hand. He led her over to a couch. Danny tapped the beat of the music on her knee. The song began to vibrate through her body. She hummed to herself while they finished their beer. After they drank a third beer, Danny asked her to dance. When she protested, Danny pulled her onto the dance floor. At first, Dolores moved awkwardly but Danny twirled her around the room. He held her close and told her to follow his lead. She moved with him. She felt a pull toward him she had never had before. They had a connection that couldn't be broken. They kept dancing until her shirt was soaked. She pointed to the couch and sat down. Danny continued to caress his own body as he gyrated by himself in front of her. She was fascinated by how boldly he touched himself. She had the urge to lie on the beach with their bodies intertwined.

The boy with black curly hair who reminded her of Joe entered the room. He danced by Danny. He was taller than Danny was but not as muscular. When he grinned at Danny, she saw he was very handsome with a fine chiseled nose and full lips. She told herself she didn't need to worry about him because she had Danny. But both of them began to move together. She wasn't sure what to make of them. It seemed weird that Danny would dance with him, especially close together. She wanted to grab Danny's hand and run away. But Danny pulled her up. The boy watched for a moment and then began to move with them. Danny told her, "It's okay. Relax, I'm here." She didn't want to disappoint him. She glided between the boys while Danny gently touched her on the breasts and buttocks. Dolores felt electrified. The boys put their hands above their heads and clapped as they circled her. She grabbed both their hands as they continued to dance together. Now she knew what her mother meant about "the time of her life."

A girl in a yellow bikini offered Danny a joint that he passed to Dolores and the boy.

When she felt light-headed, she suggested they go outside for fresh air. While the three of them sat on a porch swing, her head ached and she closed her eyes. The breeze felt cool on her sticky body. She leaned against Danny. The two boys began to whisper but Dolores couldn't hear what they were saying, only that the boy's name was Rick. The air smelled sweet and another boy offered them a joint. The three of them smoked while she rested her head against the back of the swing. The boys pushed it lightly with their feet and placed their arms around her. She began to feel dizzy. "Stop swinging," she said. She elbowed the strange boy who wore the same pungent cologne as Joe. She moved closer to Danny who kissed her forehead. Dolores wanted to be alone with Danny to walk on the beach. On the other hand, by the intense look on Danny's face, she could see that he didn't want to exclude the boy. Then Danny pointed to the seashore. She stood reluctantly when she realized Rick planned to go with them. She glared at Danny but he grabbed her hand. When they left their shoes on the porch, the sand felt cold on her bare feet.

Near the ocean, the air was chilly. The sky was pitch-black and the waves sounded like thunder. Lightning lit up the night sky and Dolores covered her head. As a child she always was so afraid of thunder that she would wake her father to hold her. "Don't be afraid," Danny said.

"We will both take care of you," Rick took her free hand and the three of them ran down the beach until they dropped to the ground. Lying next to one another, Danny in the middle, he lifted her shirt and kissed her breast. His lips felt soft against her body. She tried to block out Rick's silhouette. She concentrated on Danny's warm touch. But then she realized Rick was kissing Danny's shoulders. Danny arched his body toward Rick even though he continued caressing her. When the two boys moaned, Dolores couldn't catch her breath. She moved her body slightly away from Danny. "What's the matter?"

"I can't do this," she blurted out.

"It's no big deal," said Rick.

"It's a big deal to me," she looked at Danny.

"Just relax." She felt Danny's breath on her face. It was sweet and familiar.

"Let's leave, Danny," she pleaded. When she struggled to her feet, she saw the two boys lying with clasped hands. They giggled. She wrapped her arms around herself. "I have to go," she cried.

Dolores ran up the beach towards the lights but not as fast as she wanted because her feet kept sinking in the sand.

Red Dress

~

With her mother's eyebrow pencil, Mariana circled on the calendar each of the seven days her mother had been gone. At breakfast, she asked her father when her mother was coming home. "I hope tomorrow." He sighed while he stared out the window. But when Mariana looked, she saw only the open field. She rinsed her dish as she watched her grandmother drive up in her car from town. Her grandmother, hair smoothed back in a bun, entered the house and patted Marina on the head. Her grandmother's ragged nails were different from her mother's rounded painted ones. Her father nodded and left to work in the field with Luke, the hired hand. Marina helped to shell the peas. Her grandmother smelled of ammonia, not her mother's apricot perfume. She reached for her grandmother to sit on her lap but it felt hard, her arms were thin and her legs were bony.

In the afternoon, Mariana lay flat on the grass near the ocean, while her grandmother fanned herself with a straw hat under a shady tree. The sand near the edge of the property was covered with small stones making it difficult to lie down, but she was reminded of the last time her family went to the public beach.

After her father and her mother had dug a big hole, Mariana slid into it and they covered her body with sand, rough against her brown skin. Her mother held a bottle of lemonade with a straw to Mariana's lips. She wiped the sand from Mariana's forehead and her touch was gentle. Her mother leaned to kiss her father. Then she licked her full lips, "too gritty." She shook her head causing her dangling earrings to shimmer. Her father grinned, a wide smile. He continued to pat the sides of the mound of sand just the way he did when he made hamburger patties. Mariana closed her eyes trying to take a snapshot of the three of them on their special Sunday outing to the public beach on her island, St. Thomas, to keep forever. After sitting for sometime, she asked her parents to help her wriggle free. Her father turned to her mother, "Do you hear someone calling us?"

"I don't know," said her mother.

"I can't move," squealed Mariana.

Her father scanned the beach while her mother covered her squinting eyes to look out at the sea. "I wonder what happened to our beautiful daughter?" her mother asked.

"She must have gone for a swim," said her father.

"Here I am. Hurry, I can't breathe." The sand felt like a basket of corn weighing her down. Her mother and her father scooped away the sand as quickly as they could. Her father and her mother pulled her up. Mariana's body felt stiff. "You're okay now, baby," said her mother.

"I thought I'd die." She stretched her thin arms and legs.

"Do you think I would let you be hurt?" her mother asked.

"I hope not." Mariana curled her feet in the sand.

"Don't worry." Her mother hugged her.

Mariana scampered down to the blue-green water where she stood still to see the fat golden fish swim by her toes, tickling her. She spread her legs apart making a bridge for them to pass through. She motioned her parents. Her mother walked into the water and allowed a large red fish to swim between her long legs. "They are beautiful." She kissed the top of Mariana's head. Then she splashed Mariana until the sand washed off her. Mariana squealed and shook her skinny ten-year-old body. She wanted to grow up and fill out her bathing suit like her mother and have her father called her "a peach." Instead, he told Mariana, "You're all arms and legs, a baby octopus."

"I'm not." Mariana reminded her father about the scary creature, dull gray with black spots, she saw when they fished on his boat. The monster glared at her and she screamed for her father to hold her until they reached the shore. "I don't want to be ugly and scare people." She crossed her arms.

"You're frightening her," said her mother.

"I'm just kidding," said her father.

"You're beautiful, not ugly like an octopus." Her mother tugged her down to the water's edge where she placed her wide brim hat on Mariana's head. They splashed their feet in the cool water. Then her mother took her hand. "Let's help Daddy." She pointed to her father who had already put on his white tee shirt. He folded the gray blanket into squares. Her mother pulled her own long hair back into a ponytail and slipped on a pair of shorts over her bikini. Mariana turned to her father as she sifted the sand through her toes. "Can't we play a little longer?"

"No, it's time to go. I have to care for the animals, even on Sunday." He snapped the folding chair shut.

"It's so beautiful here. How about one more swim?" Her mother tilted her head.

"The cows can't wait to be milked." Her father picked up the cooler.

"Please, Daddy," said Mariana.

"We have to go, now." Her father marched up the beach.

"Those cows are too much trouble," whispered her mother to Mariana.

But before Mariana could answer, her mother ran to her father and grabbed one handle of the cooler while Mariana placed her feet in her father's footsteps. In their silence, the ocean's roar sounded louder then ever. She looked back at the water to wave goodbye. Jumping from her mother's to her father's footsteps, she pretended she was a slippery frog going from one lily pad to the next.

If her mother were home, she would ask her parents to go back to the public beach. They would bury her in the fine sand. She imagined her parents swinging her in the water, strong hands tightly holding her while she kicked her feet. She could see her mother's wide smile and hear her father's deep laugh.

But her grandmother couldn't swim and refused to let her go into the water any further than her knees. Her grandmother, a red kerchief wrapped around her head, sat under a tree with a towel covering her thin legs. Mariana stood next to her. "My mother and I swim all the way out."

"Well, your mother isn't here," said her grandmother.

"Where is she?" Mariana crossed her arms.

"I wish I knew." Her grandmother picked up her Bible.

She recalled her mother calling her grandmother, "a good, Christian woman."

"Aren't you one, too?" Mariana asked her mother.

"Not me. I never went to church until your daddy insisted," she said.

Mariana walked carefully on the sharp rocks down to the water. She started to wade out into the ocean while her grandmother read. But her grandmother started waving her arms. "Come back here right now. I'll tell your father!"

Mariana stomped through the water back to the beach because she didn't want her father to be mad. The bottom of her feet stung from quickly crossing the pointed stones. Her grandmother tried to wrap her in a towel. "I don't want help," said Mariana.

"You don't have to be rude," said her grandmother.

"Sorry." She looked at the ground. Her grandmother couldn't see her angry eyes.

When Mariana and her grandmother walked up to the house, they passed Luke who waved from the tractor. When they reached the backyard, she looked for her mother. She imagined saying, "Why did you leave me with grandma? She's too bossy."

She felt her mother tightly squeezing her, but her mother wasn't there; only the clothes hung on the laundry line-jeans and underwear. Her horse, Charlie, lifted his head and she waved to him. The chickens clucked. She went over to the fence to watch Luke in the field. He wasn't wearing a shirt. He had bigger muscles than her father did. "Hey, Luke," she yelled. He came over and he wiped his brow with a fine linen handkerchief. "How are you, today?"

"Okay." She stared at the handkerchief. "Is that my mother's?"

"No, why would you think that?" He stood up straighter.

"She had one just like it," she said.

"What did you want?" He frowned.

"Nothing, I wanted to say hi," she said.

"I have to finish my work." He walked back to the tractor. Charlie came over and Mariana nuzzled against his warm fur. She didn't understand why Luke was mad at her because he always lingered when she was with her mother. She wished the handkerchief had been her mother's because she would have asked him to give it back to keep in her pocket. Mariana wondered if it smelled of her mother's apricot perfume.

She went onto the porch where her kitten, Calico, too lazy to greet her, sprawled out as he baked in the sun on the porch. She patted his fur. Her father dressed in muddy overalls walked onto the porch. "Go in and help your grandmother."

"I'm saying hello to Calico," she said.

Her father scowled at her the way he had at her mother when she asked about Carmine's Bar. "That's no place for a woman, only on Saturday, Ladies' night."

"Let's pretend it's ladies' night." Her mother had grabbed his hand.

"I don't know what has got into you, lately!" He had shaken his hand loose.

On the porch, Mariana realized her father was talking to her. She looked up at him. "What is it, Daddy?" she asked sadly.

He kissed the top of her head. "Come in when you're done petting the cat." She was surprised that he didn't scold her.

Since Mariana had no school on Saturday, she lay in bed. She could hear her father on the tractor as he mowed the fields and the cows mooed. He would not come in until lunchtime. She wished he didn't spend so much time in the fields. She was supposed to pick the tomatoes without her mother, but she didn't want to. She didn't care if they rotted. She kicked off the pink comforter her mother had sewn. She pulled on a pair of shorts and tee shirt. She circled the date on the calendar with eyebrow pencil. Her mother had been away eight days.

She went into her parents' room where the sunlight streaming through the white lace curtains made diamond patterns on the bed. Mariana sat at her mother's dressing table. She remembered when her mother had been here, the surface of the table was crowded with pots of rouge, lipsticks and a pink crystal perfume bottle that her aunt living in San Juan had sent for her mother's birthday. The pictures of Mariana, on each of her birthdays, were gone. She wondered why her mother had taken them, but was happy that her mother wanted her near. She pulled out the drawer of the vanity and found a tiny sample of perfume that smelled like apricots. She dabbed some behind her ears.

A few days before her mother left, Mariana remembered watching her apply eyebrow pencil, drawing on lines as thin as matchsticks. Her mother rubbed rouge into her light brown cheeks until they turned pink, then took green shadow, mixed it with her beige and spread it evenly over each eyelid. Her open eyes looked dark brown like the sea before a storm. Mariana leaned her head against her mother's to stare at their reflection. "Can't you put makeup on me? Daddy will call me his peach, too."

"You're much lovelier than me," her mother exclaimed.

"How can I be as pretty as you without lipstick?" asked Mariana.

"Sit on the stool and I'll see what I can do," said her mother.

"Really?" Mariana sat at the vanity table with her back to the mirror. Her mother used a q-tip to apply blue eye shadow and rubbed pink rouge on her cheeks.

"Close your eyes." Her mother turned her around, "Now open them and look in the mirror."

When Mariana opened her eyes, she looked like a princess, too. Her brown eyes were deeper and her full lips pink like her mother's. "Please don't make me wash it off."

"Daddy says you're too young for makeup. Wash it off before he comes home."

"Why?" Mariana continued to stare at herself in the mirror.

"When I met your father, he made me promise not to wear so much makeup."

"I don't understand," said Mariana.

"It's too hard to explain. We have to do our chores," her mother said abruptly.

Mariana took one last look at her pretty face in the mirror. She didn't understand how her father could be angry. She followed her mother into the kitchen." I think you are beautiful," said Mariana.

"Your daddy used to think I was, too," she sighed.

"Doesn't he now?" Marian asked.

"If he does, he hasn't told me," said her mother.

"I'll tell him to tell you," said Mariana.

"Don't say anything to Daddy. It's between him and me." Her mother took two large straw baskets to carry to the garden, where they picked peppers and tomatoes. Mariana inspected them for ants, which she flicked with her fingers. It wasn't fair to squish the poor creatures since the minister at their church said all animals were put on this earth for a reason. Every Sunday, they took their extra vegetables to church where they distributed them to the families who didn't have gardens. The sun felt hot on her back. Mariana looked down the hill where the grass ended, the beach began and the water crashed against the rocks. She imagined running straight into the water to cool off.

Her mother talked to Luke who leaned on the fence. Mariana wondered if Luke thought her mother was pretty. Mariana overhead her say, "why not?"

"I can't, but I wish I could." He placed his large hands over hers.

In the distance, her father stopped the tractor to watch them. When her mother noticed her father, she moved away from the railing and raised her hand to him but he didn't wave back. "I have to go," said Luke.

"You're right," her mother sighed.

Mariana wondered why she spoke to Luke when her father needed him in the field, but her mother didn't like to be questioned. She knew because the day before they had gone to the post office and bumped into Luke who said, "Fancy meeting you here." Her mother smoothed back her hair.

"I heard your husband say you were going to town," said Luke.

"Well, aren't you a smart one?" said her mother.

"Could I have a root beer?" Mariana asked.

"You don't need a soda," said her mother.

"I don't mind. "Luke smiled at her mother.

"Are you sure?" Her mother placed her hand on Luke's arm.

"I'm thirsty," whined Mariana.

"Hush up, Luke is going to buy you a soda." Her mother frowned.

"Can I have anything I want?" Mariana looked at Luke.

"Sure," Luke laughed.

"You're too kind." Her mother laughed.

Then the three of them walked over to Carmine's Bar. Mariana drank her soda on the hard porch bench while her mother and Luke went inside. In the truck, she told her mother, "I didn't like sitting outside. It was too hot."

"I'm sorry, but I couldn't bring you inside," said her mother.

"Why not?" she asked.

"You would've been bored. We were just gossiping."

"You mean like when you and Daddy talk after I go to bed?" she asked.

"No, Daddy doesn't like to chit chat," she said.

"What do you and Daddy talk about?" she asked.

"Grown-up things!" She laughed.

"What about you and Luke?" Mariana asked.

"I told you nothing important," her mother said in a cold voice she rarely heard except when Mariana did something really bad.

In the garden, Mariana continued to pick tomatoes that were big and plump and when she bit into one, the juice dribbled down her chin. Her mother laughed and took a bite of one, too. "Delicious," she said. Marina wiped her sticky face on her shirt. Then her mother told her to bring in the basket. "Go wash off your makeup," said her mother.

"Do I have to?" she asked.

"Right now, I told you Daddy won't like it."

Mariana trudged to the bathroom but stopped to rock her Betsy Wetsy doll. Then she heard her father talking with Luke on the porch. They spoke in low angry voices. She couldn't hear their conversation. The screen door opened and her father came into the living room. But instead of hugging her, he gave Mariana a cold hard stare that made her drop the doll. Before she could figure out why he was mad, he marched into the kitchen.

"Why is Mariana wearing make up?"

"Girls like to pretend," said her mother.

"I don't want her to be fancy," said her father.

"Is that what you think?" her mother asked.

"If she's too fancy, she might get big ideas," he said.

"What does that mean? she asked.

"I've got eyes." He went past Mariana as though she was invisible and she grabbed his arm, "I asked for the lipstick." He left slamming the screen door.

In the kitchen, her mother stared out the window as her father marched toward the fields. "I'm sorry I wanted to look prettier," said Mariana.

"You're a good girl." They went into the bathroom where her mother gently washed Marina's face. Her mother's soft lips were drawn tight as though she had forgotten how to smile. Mariana asked, "Are you mad at me, too?

"Tu. eres la mejor hija que tengo," said her mother.

Still upset by the somberness of her mother's face, Mariana clung to her mother who smelled familiar, like fresh earth. Her body relaxed.

In the middle of the night, through the walls, she woke to her mother's crying and her father's deep voice but she couldn't hear exactly what they were saying. But she knew her dad was angry that her mother had talked to Luke. She wasn't sure why because Luke was always nice to them. When they met him in town, he always carried their grocery bags. He had big muscles that her mother said he liked to show off. He always gave her a piece of Wrigley's gum while he spoke quietly to her mother. They never yelled like her parents did. Mariana curled up with Calico and hummed her mother's favorite tune, "Moon River" while pretending she lay beside her, the two of them having good dreams.

At her mother's vanity, Mariana looked at her face in the mirror. She had circled the fourteenth day on the calendar that her mother was gone. If her mother were standing behind her, she would have taken her hand and led her into the kitchen where her father had set a box of corn flakes on the table. They would eat together. Her mother would chat about the laundry to be washed or vegetables to be picked. The house felt too quiet. Her grandmother had not visited for five days because she had bronchitis. In the kitchen she poured more sugar than her mother would allow over the cereal. After she ate, she left her bowl in the sink and didn't wash it the way her mother had taught her to do. The house was a mess with dirty clothes on the floor, drooping plants to be watered and a ring of dirt in the bathtub. She felt bad her mother would have to clean as soon as she arrived home. She went back to the sink and washed her bowl and spoon. Then she stepped onto the porch to draw a picture for her. Finally, she heard the tractor stop and saw her father climb off. He said a few words to Luke who kept shaking his head. Luke put his hands in his pockets. Her father turned abruptly away from him.

On the porch, her father wiped the sweat from his brow with a handkerchief and stuffed it back into the pocket of his dusty overalls. He went into the house and came out two tall glasses of lemonade. While he sat quietly, Mariana kneeled at a low table and continued to draw. Her father smelled like mud and hay, a familiar scent. Using her brightest yellow crayon, she drew herself and parents at the beach with the hot sun above them, crayoning her mother in her pink bathing suit, herself wearing her mother's hat and her father in navy trunks. She stared at the picture and touched the outlines of the bodies while her father studied it. "We had a special day, didn't we?

"I wish we could go, again." Mariana stared at the picture.

"When mother comes home from her trip, we'll go," said her father.

"When is that?" Mariana asked.

"Let's just enjoy our time together." Her father kneeled down next to her and began to draw a picture of them digging a castle; the three figures pressed close together. His hands were coarser than her mother's was but he drew delicate strokes on the paper. As Mariana intently watched, her father was a good artist sketching her face to look so pretty. He went out to the shed and came back with a box of pastels, carefully wrapped in tissue paper. Mixing the colors, he told her how to make her mother's hair look textured. "You've beautiful hair just like your mother."

"I do?" Mariana leaned against his warm knee and continued drawing. But she pressed too hard on the pastel, breaking it into pieces. "I'm sorry."

"The pastels are soft." Then he placed his hands over hers. They became one form, smooth and rough mixed together, building something important. When she asked him how he learned to draw, he said, "My mother taught me when I was little." Mariana cocked her head trying to imagine him as a small boy sketching with grandmother. It was difficult to see her grandmother sitting quietly since she was always busy in the kitchen. He hugged her. "What a lovely picture." She felt a special connection that they were both artists. When they finished, they hung the drawing in her bedroom; her father's arm draped around her while they admired it. Standing at the foot of the bed, Mariana realized she liked being alone with her father. He was fun, but she sensed she shouldn't ever tell her father about her mother and the red dress.

The day before her mother left, they had shared a secret. Mariana had come home from school to find her in a sequined red dress that showed off her full breasts and thin shoulders as she danced gracefully across the bedroom. The dress, with many layers, rustled. The radio played "Moon River," the tune played on her wedding day, she said. The sun streamed into the room like a spotlight and made the dress sparkle. Mariana stood by the doorway to admire how well her mother danced. Her forehead was covered with tiny beads of sweat like the pearls on her necklace, the one her grandmother had given her mother when she married. Her mother's eyes widened when she noticed Mariana and she hurriedly tried to step out of the red dress. Mariana said, "I've never seen such a beautiful dress."

"I wore it a long time ago. Before I met your father," she said.

"Can you dance for me?" Mariana asked.

"If you don't tell Daddy." Her mother put her fingers to her lips.

Mariana climbed on the bed, where she flopped over on her stomach and propped her hands under her chin. Her mother turned up the radio and with her eyes half closed, her hands moved above her head like shadow puppets to "Good Golly Miss Molly." Her mother hips sloped to the right and then to the left. Her bare feet with painted pink toenails squeaked on the wooden floor. She pulled Mariana up. "I'll show you the steps."

Her mother guided her effortlessly across the floor. "You're a natural." Then she squished her mother's foot and they both laughed. Mariana draped her arms around her mother who smelled like ripe peaches from the garden. "I want to grow up and dance like you," said Mariana.

"Your life is better. It's more settled," said her mother.

"What do you mean?" Mariana asked.

"We didn't have much food. No pretty clothes," said her mother.

"You had this dress," said Mariana.

"Not when I was little," said her mother.

"Tell me more about when you wore the red dress," pleaded Mariana.

"I was a dancer. I wore pretty clothes with high heels. Men would clap. It was exciting," she laughed.

"Can I put on the dress?" Mariana asked.

"No. Dad will be mad," she said.

"Why? You're beautiful." Mariana rubbed the dress's material between her fingers.

"Someday you'll understand." Her mother slipped off the dress and placed it in her hope chest at the foot of the bed.

Putting her arms around Mariana, she looked out the window at the ocean where the waves crashed against the rocks and in the distance fishing boats swayed. Mariana imagined taking a boat to San Juan where her mother had lived as a girl. She would wear her mother's red dress. Her father would dance with her in the music hall. When the sun turned from yellow squash to pumpkin orange over the water, Mariana trailed behind her mother into the kitchen.

Lying on her bed, after admiring the picture she and her father drew, Mariana wondered if the red dress had something to do with her mother's leaving. It didn't make sense that her mother wouldn't want her father to know about it. She wished her mother had talked more about her life in Puerto Rico before she married her father. She could see her mother twirling and the audience clapping. Her mother could have been a famous dancer before she met her father. Maybe her mother talked to Luke about being a dancer. One time, he brought them both heart necklaces, but her mother didn't wear it. Mariana had lost her necklace jumping in a haystack.

In the kitchen, she was happy to find her grandmother wearing an apron and banging pans, "I don't know where your mother keeps her skillet."

"Look on top of the refrigerator," said Mariana.

"Well, aren't you smart," said her grandmother.

"Can I help you?" Mariana asked.

"Sure can," said her grandmother.

Mariana peeled potatoes and her grandmother diced them. She decided to ask about her mother, again. "Why did my mother go away?"

"She missed her life in San Juan, especially the night life." Her grandmother furiously chopped onions.

"She was a dancer. She wore pretty dresses." Mariana whispered.

"Who told you that?" her grandmother asked.

"My mother," she said.

"What else did she say?" Her grandmother frowned.

"Nothing, Is there more?" Mariana asked.

"Did she say when she would be back?" her grandmother asked.

"You don't know?" Mariana wrapped her arms around herself.

"I have no idea." Her grandmother's lips tightened.

Mariana sighed. Her grandmother was of no help.

Later in the afternoon, still upset about her mother, Mariana slowly climbed into the rusty pickup truck with her father. They drove into town. As they followed the dirt road that hugged the ocean, she saw on the hillside the grass had turned brown and the cows were barely moving. She squinted in the hope of seeing San Juan, but all she saw was endless ocean. She wiped her sweaty face with a handkerchief her mother had embroidered with flowers along the edge of it. "Didn't Mom do a good job on my handkerchief?"

"Her stitches are so fine," said her father.

"Why did she leave?" Mariana heart beat fast as she stared at her father.

"It's hard to say." Her father tightened his grip on the wheel.

"When will she be back?" Mariana asked.

"I wish I knew." He shook his head.

Her mind raced with questions to ask him, but he looked straight ahead; his lips curved downward as he fiddled with the radio. She looked at her chipped pink nails needing to be polished but it was her mother's job. She wondered if her father would be any good at painting her nails. "Have you ever painted fingernails?"

"No, but I could try when we get home," he laughed.

"Good, won't mother be surprised?" Mariana said.

"Yes." Her father bit his lip. She slipped the handkerchief into her pocket.

Her father stopped at the post office to mail a large pink envelope. She offered to drop it into the mail slot, but her father said, "I'll do it."

"Please, pretty please," she said in a singsong voice.

"No, wait right here," he said firmly.

"Who did you write to?" she asked.

"No one special," her father smiled.

She folded her arms. She didn't understand why writing to her mother was a secret. For a moment she wished she had sent a letter to her mother and had included the picture that they had drawn of the beach. She would tell her mother to "hurry home."

While she waited for her father, she watched two goats grazing on the hill, searching the dirt for a few blades of grass. By the side of a white stucco house, two children jumped rope. Their mother, on her knees, planted in the garden. Two fat pigs lay in the mud. Her father climbed back into the truck and they drove to the grocery, on the corner of two dirt roads. It was a plain wood building with white paint and a newly mended screen door.

Inside, it was cool and dark with the smell of freshly baked bread. Looking at the food list grandmother had written, her father asked

Mr. Gregory, wearing a white apron, for help. "How are the two of you doing?" he asked.

"Okay, I guess." Her father sighed.

"Well, tell me what you need," said Mr. Gregory.

"I know where everything is on the shelves," said Mariana.

"My little helper," Her father patted her head.

"I'll holler if we can't find something." Her father abruptly turned his back on Mr. Gregory and read Mariana the list. She handed him the flour, sugar and a loaf of bread to place in the cart as they walked down each aisle. While her father stood at the register, Mariana lingered in front of the bakery counter where her mother always allowed her to pick out a large chocolate chip cookie for the ride home; she held the sweet chocolate bits in her mouth as long as she could. She eyed her father to see if he noticed her, but he didn't. "Dad, could I have a cookie?" asked Mariana.

"Why?" He turned toward her.

"Mom always let me have a cookie," she said softly.

"You don't want to get fat, do you?" her father smiled.

"Just one cookie, please," said Mariana.

"I guess you're going to keep asking. You can have one," said her father.

Mr. Gregory walked over to the case, "A cookie for a sweet girl."

"Thank you," she said.

"Just as polite and pretty as your mother," said Mr. Gregory.

"Prettier," said her father.

The three of them laughed. But her father's shoulders sagged as he climbed into the truck. He fiddled with the radio but when the only station that came on without static was the "oldies station," he switched it off. She thought of telling him that was her favorite channel but she didn't want to make him sadder. She nibbled on her cookie but it had tasted better when she shared it with her mother. Turning to her father, she hesitated, "do you want some?"

"No," he said.

"Are you sure? Mom always shared with me." She looked at the floorboard.

He glanced over at her. "You don't mind?"

Mariana broke off a piece and her father ate it. "Delicious," he said. Mariana kicked off her shoes and wiggled her feet.

After she helped her father put away the groceries, she went into the living room to play with her Betsy Wetsy doll. She spread her doll clothes on the worn green couch that her mother always asked her father to replace. Her father stayed in the kitchen with the door shut but she heard him on the phone. For a moment, she thought he was crying. She tightly hugged her doll. She wondered if he were talking to her mother about coming home. She thought of bursting into the kitchen, but he would yell.

Instead she tiptoed into her parents' bedroom where the bed's blankets were rumpled. Her father's tee shirts hung out of the open dresser drawer. She stood in front of the hope chest; the sun had bleached the wood. Very gently she lifted the lid to search for the red dress. Inside, she found a photo album filled with pictures of her mother. In one picture, her mother hugged a tall man who wasn't her father. Her eyes were smiling. The man was broad like Luke. He had cocoa skin and wore a white suit. He was the handsomest man she had ever seen. Underneath the album was a wide brimmed hat with frayed edges. She lifted a pink satin dress, a stuffed panda bear missing one ear and a set of keys on a black rabbit's foot key chain. She wondered what had happened to the red dress. Could her mother have taken it with her or did her father throw it out after she left? She replaced everything except the keys on the rabbit's foot; she slipped them into her pocket and returned to the living room.

When her father came out of the kitchen, he looked tired like after a day of planting. Looking out the window, he said, "I have to go tend the animals."

"Can't you stay?" She took his hand.

"They're hungry," he said.

"Who was on the phone?" she asked.

"Grandma," He dropped her hand.

"You're upset with grandma?" she asked.

"Don't listen to my calls. Go crayon." He gave her a playful slap on her bottom.

Mariana glared. But she went into her room and turned on her radio, a present for her birthday, to her mother's station while she petted the rabbit's foot in her pocket. She was mad at her mother for staying away such a long time. She didn't understand why she hadn't even written to her. She felt sad for herself and her father. He had a right to know when she was coming back. When her mother came home, she would yell at her and give her the silent treatment the way her father did when he was angry.

On Sunday, Mariana circled the fifteenth day on her mother's calendar with the eyebrow pencil. Mariana picked out a blue dress with ivory buttons to go to church; it was the one her mother had sewed for her out of silky material. Even after she brushed her long brown hair, it was knotty and she called her father to help. He wore dress up, a white shirt, red tie and blue pants. She handed him the brush and was surprised how gently he combed her hair. But he fumbled with the rubber band as he tried to make a ponytail. "I'm too clumsy. Your mother does a better job."

"I wish she were home, now," said Mariana.

"Me, too," said her father.

"Make her come home." She crossed her arms.

"I spoke to your mother and she's not ready," her father said quietly.

She thought of asking why he couldn't make her, but he had a pained look on his face and she thought he would cry. She wanted to know more about his talk with her mother, but she was afraid that he might say her mother was never coming home. She slipped her hand into his callused one. He kissed the top of her head and called her a "sweet girl." As they walked out of the room, Mariana avoided looking in the mirror at her sloppy ponytail because she didn't want to make her father feel bad.

The white wooden church stood on the outskirts of town. Her father edged his pick-up truck next to her grandmother's white Chevy. He shook hands with the preacher, his wife, Mr. Gregory and several other members of their church. The sun was so blisteringly hot that

Mariana skipped ahead of her father into the church to get away from the heat. Inside the coolness of the room tickled her skin. Grandmother waved her white-gloved hand and Mariana slipped into the pew next to her grandmother but turned to watch for her father. Mariana noticed Luke, in a white shirt, sitting several rows behind her. He winked and she smiled back. Later, she would ask him if he had heard from her mother. When grandmother told her to face the pulpit, she pretended she didn't hear her but kept her eyes fastened on the door. As her father walked up the aisle, the organ began to play and she looked toward the front. Her father slid in next to her and placed his arm around her shoulders. She tried to listen to the sermon, but the preacher kept repeating the word "forgiveness." Mariana shifted her eyes to the left, towards her father's bowed head; then she looked to the right, her grandmother, mouthing the preacher's words. Mariana stared at the red and yellow stained glass figure of Mary and lowered her head to pray for her father and grandmother. Then she prayed that her mother would telephone her from San Juan. She hoped her mother was dancing, again.

After the service, she ran to snatch three chocolate chip cookies from the refreshment table and joined the other girls in party dresses on the side of the church. She nibbled her cookies while her father and grandmother talked with neighbors. She looked for Luke, but his truck was gone. Her father lifted out a basket of vegetables from the back of the truck and placed them on a table by the side of the church. When he called to her, she hurried over and he hugged her. Grandmother kissed her good-bye. I'm feeling much better. "I'll be by later to make dinner."

In the truck, Mariana flipped off her party shoes and looked out the window as they drove through town. Mr. James was sitting on a bench in front of his closed hardware store. When she waved to him, he raised his hand. Carmine was sweeping the porch of his bar while his wife dusted the chairs. "Hello, Carmine." her father drove slowly.

"Come have a drink later. Bring Mariana if you want to," Carmine shouted back.

Mariana clapped her hands with excitement at the thought of going into the bar.

They passed a group of homes set close together with wash lines filled with shirts, dresses and underwear strung like banners. Farmhouses further from town were set apart–horses grazed, cow tails swished and dogs barked. Finally, the cement road turned into the dirt one hugging the ocean. The bumpy road felt familiar. The coolness of the sea felt good on her warm skin. She never wanted to live anywhere else. She wanted to wake every morning and smell the ocean. She was a country girl, but she understood her mother wasn't. She turned to her father and she said, "Let's go to the beach after lunch."

"I haven't gone to the beach without your mother since I was married," he said.

"We'll jump in the waves," she said.

"You won't mind?" he asked.

"We have to do fun things on our own now," she said.

"How'd you get so smart?" He looked at her out of the corner of his eye.

"I don't know. I must take after you," she said.

"You're the best of your mother and me," he said softly.

"Of course." They clasped hands as they continued down the unpaved road.

Printed in the United States
21567LVS00002B/109

9 781413 727722